SAD FACE, HAPPY FACE, BRAVE FACE

No one's life is perfect. You have to laugh sometimes!

Catherine Cole

Table Of Contents

Don't be put off by the number of chapters – some of them are very short!

(1) Shauna 6
(2) Email - The Redhead to Isla 12
(3) Shauna 14
(4) George 23
(5) Email - The Redhead to Isla 24
(6) Email – Isla to The Redhead 26
(7) Shauna 29
(8) Email – Beth to Shauna 30
(9) Shauna 33
(10) George 39
(11) Shauna 41
(12) George 45
(13) Ruby 47
(14) Email – Beth to Shauna 50
(15) Email - The Redhead to Isla 51
(16) Email – Beth to Shauna 55
(17) Email - The Redhead to Isla 59

(18) Shauna 60
(19) Email – Beth to Shauna 70
(20) George 76
(21) Shauna 79
(22) George 85
(23) Shauna 90
(24) Email – Beth to Shauna 104
(25) Shauna 111
(26) Email Isla to The Redhead 125
(27 Email Redhead to Isla) 136
(28) Ruby 140
(29) Email - The Redhead to Isla 149
(30) Email – Isla to The Redhead 151
(31) George 155
(32) Email Beth to Shauna) 162
(33) George 168
(34) Email Beth to Shauna) 171
(35) Email Redhead to Isla) 171
(36) Shauna 178
(37) George 193
(38) Email Beth to Shauna 198
(39) Email Redhead to Isla 202

(40) Email Isla to Redhead 204
(41) Shauna 210
(42) Isla to Redhead 223
(43) George 227
(44) Shauna 234
(45) Beth to Shauna 238
(46) Text Shauna to Beth 238
(47) Text Beth to Shauna 239
(48) George 240
(49) Shauna 243
(50) Ruby 252
(51) Shauna 257
(52) Email Redhead to Isla 261
(53) Shauna 265
(54) Ruby 277
(55) Email: The Redhead to Isla 284
(56) Shauna 289
(57) Email Beth to Shauna 296
(58) Conversation between Shauna & Ruby 298
(59) Ruby 300
(60) George 306
(61) Email: The Redhead to Isla 311

(62) Ruby 313
(63) Shauna 315
(64) Email - Redhead to Isla 326
ACKNOWLEDGEMENTS 329
DISCLAIMER/COPYRIGHT 333

You'll be glad to know the book is finally starts on the next page!!!

(1) Shauna

It was Saturday morning. Lewis slowly let go of sleep and floated up to the surface of consciousness, the warmth of the duvet pinning him to the shackles of sleep whilst the early morning sun shining behind the curtains beckoned him into the land of the living.

My life is brilliant he thought to himself and quoting James Blunt. I have a well paid job, a nice car, a pretty good body for a man my age, I make love to an exciting, experimental redhead and…..

"Babe, are you getting out of bed at all"? He was woken from his reverie by Shauna, his wife of almost 3 years, or was it 4? He couldn't remember at the moment "We're supposed to be popping round to Mum and Dads this morning"

"Don't you want a bit of this?" enquired Lewis, gripping his penis and waggling it up and down in the familiar mating ritual performed by men all over the land.

"Not this morning, babe" came the disappointing but predictable reply.

"Hmmmmm, I thought so"

"I'm just not feeling too brilliant this morning" Shauna replied as she gently stroked her belly.

Oh yes, my life is brilliant, thought Lewis, returning to his mental list of things to be grateful for. I make love to an exciting, experimental redhead and my wife is expecting our first baby.

Making a mental note to find some time later to visit a well-known internet porn site, Lewis hauled himself out of bed. Clearing his throat loudly before breaking wind several times, he made his way to the bathroom, scratching his crotch as he went, leaving Shauna to ponder on what had happened to the polite, gentlemanly flatulence-free man she once knew. The man she had once found it so difficult to talk to due to the rapid beating of her heart and the butterflies flickering inside her tummy. At this particular moment in time, he was making her stomach churn. Or was it the morning sickness?

Shauna pottered about in the kitchen, trying to muster up some enthusiasm for breakfast. She was rather accident-prone and, although she tried to be accurate with her actions, inevitably she would drop and spill, clunk and clatter. As she browsed the cupboards for inspiration, she created some kind of one-woman-band with the crashing of plates, bowls, spoons and jars.

"Babe?"

Shauna turned to find Lewis standing in the kitchen doorway, leaning into the frame with his face fixed into a submissive little boy expression. Or was it a pathetic expression? Was he trying to look appealing? I already have one baby to think about, mused Shauna, and now Lewis is acting like another.

Oh God, I hope he's not trying to lull me back into bed with baby-talk.

"Babe?"

"Yesssssss" Shauna dragged out her reply, hoping to play for time and an excuse to avoid returning to their hot, sweaty duvet. Nothing worse than returning to the bedroom to discover anew the smells and fug you've been basking in for the last 8 hours (if you're lucky enough to have had the recommended amount of sleep). It almost chokes you with the stench and embarrassment. Shauna had been surprised to discover that 'morning sickness' was not disabling her as much as the dinner time nausea she seemed to experience after her evening meal. However, returning to the stinkfest that was their bedroom following Lewis's early morning bottom trumpet fanfare would surely send her diving, head first into the bathroom.

"Do I really need to come to your parents this morning?" Lewis almost whined.

What? Cheeky bugger. How was it that he always manages to get out of anything *I* want or need to do but we always do what *he* wants to do? He's always made it quite obvious that he feels my family are below him.

Just because his parents are loaded, their wealth doesn't make them better, it just makes them richer. My parents are richer for the love they have for each other and for their family. Oh, listen to me, Shauna inwardly laughed at herself. I sound like one of those magnets you find in gift shops with soppy sayings. It's true though, she continued with her own personal radiohead. My parents made our lives rich with nurturing, love and shared experiences, despite their meagre income.

"Well, yes I think you should come with me" Shauna found herself already preparing to give in to his plea. Why wasn't she more forceful with him? Why didn't she just say "Yes, you bloody well do have to come to visit my lovely parents who, despite your obvious lack of appreciation for them, actually seem to like you" Or are they just being loyal to me? Maybe they secretly think you're a pompous snob who doesn't treat their daughter the way they think she deserves to be treated.

"It's just that I've got loads of paperwork to catch up on" Lewis began his case "And I thought you could just go on your own and I can get on with all the boring stuff whilst you're out"

By paperwork, he meant the aforementioned porn sight, of course. And by boring stuff, he meant a furtive and dirty text volley to the redhead.

"I know you're busy at work and I know you've been staying late to catch up" Even as she said it out loud, Shauna thought what a cliché it was. Was there something going on? No, we're happy. Aren't we? We're having a baby. Anyway, must soldier on as usual. Haven't got time for doubts. "But could you just have a whole day away from work commitments, relax and……"

Just wait, she thought, she could see his body language change, he's about to start his usual turn-the-tables initiative and make me feel guilty.

"Oh for God's sake. I work so hard for *you*. So hard to make money for *you*. And all you do is nag and moan……."

She didn't hear the rest. Partly because she'd heard this record before. The one he put on when he wanted to get his own way. And partly because she was so distressed by his response, her head had created a protective fuzz to which she withdrew. Her own personal radiohead again, her own safe thoughts. Her own headspace crash helmet.

"No, not just for me. For you too. For all your hobbies, your car, your cigarettes, your drink……." Shauna's voice weakened and petered out.

Hot and flustered, she reached into the fridge whilst trying to hide her face from his now angry eyes. True to form, she caught something on something and pulled out a bucket of Greek yoghurt without meaning to. As she withdrew her arm from the fridge, the bucket of thick, white dairy product followed, crashed to the floor and exploded.

Why does a relatively small amount of liquid travel so far? Why does it cover every surface? Why does it treble in volume when released from its container?

"What did you do that for?"

What a smug bastard!

"I didn't do it on purpose" came Shauna's churlish reply. She inwardly cringed at her response but it was already out. Lewis grabbed her retort and used it against her.

"Oh, you're so bloody moody. I'm definitely not coming with you this morning if you're going to be like this. I'm going to stay here and work hard to make money for *you* whilst you go out and enjoy yourself" Lewis turned away and as he did so, looked round across his shoulder "Try to come home in a better mood" The final arsehole barb grenade was thrown.

He's got what he wanted. How did that happen? The same way it always does.

(2) Email - The Redhead to Isla

Isla, thanks for your last email. So sorry I haven't replied for ages. Been really busy but it sounds like you have too.

I'm still single (kind of – more on that later) but still having fun. I think the problem is that everyone else wants me to find someone and settle down but I'm not really fussed. I'm quite happy with my life – and my sex toys – tee hee!!

Sometimes I get lonely when I'm the only singleton at a party but, to be honest, most of the couples have had more than their fair share of each other so I usually end up having a great flirty chat with one of the men or a real honest heart-to-heart with one of the women. I'm always the life and soul and the one everyone wants to *be* or *be with*. Tee hee!!!

Anyway, I said I was 'kind of' single. Technically and legally I am but recently I've been having a bit of fun with one of the guys at the gym. You've probably guessed but he's married. No, please don't judge me. I know it's wrong and I know he's probably lying when he says he and his wife are more like brother and sister than man and wife. I bet she's gorgeous, intelligent, successful, sophisticated and great in bed. In fact, all the things he is too. She intimidates me and I've never even met her. He doesn't talk about her. Probably guilt. I don't want to hear about her anyway. Well, yes, I do. I want to know everything about her but, by the same token, I don't want to know anything at all. Do you understand what I'm saying?

Sorry to burden you with this secret. You're the only person I can tell. You know me so well and you know I'm a good person really. I hate being 'the bit on the side' but yet I am. If you read about me on paper, you'd hate me. But when you know the person, you know that nobody is one hundred percent good or bad. God, I'm getting deep here, sorry.

Anyway, we must get together soon. In the meantime, I've got a speed-dating event to go to. I'm only going because my work-mates have bugged me so much about finding a man. I'm doing it to shut them up. Bet *his* wife never does things to try to make other people happy. I bet she's relaxed and serene and believes people should be free to make their own decisions. Must stop thinking about her.

I'm thinking of you though, Isla. Give me a call or text or email…… Any form of communication and we'll get together soon, xxx

(3) Shauna

Shauna climbed into the car, predictably catching her handbag strap on the gear stick. Grrrr, Shauna huffed and tugged at the bag, pondering why does this always happen? If you asked me to do it I wouldn't be able to. Almost every time I get out of this car, I catch something on something and end up being jerked back in.

As usual, the car took some starting, which involved initial optimism and patience and ultimately deteriorating into unladylike cursing and swearing. In the past Shauna had tried polite begging and had made wild promises to always love and treasure the car if it would only just start this one more time.

Eventually, the car shook and rattled into noisy combustion in an effort to propel her in a forward motion towards the family nest. Shauna knew the car would cut out at almost every junction and that she would need to be creative with her clutch and gear control on roundabouts to avoid a total breakdown (of the car and herself). Approaching hazards Shauna gripped the steering wheel, hoping and praying the car in front of her wouldn't stop unnecessarily and force her to do the same, resulting in immediate engine death. In the meantime, she tried to relax behind the wheel and look forward to seeing the familiar and comforting faces of her family.

After a predictably precarious journey, Shauna turned into the cosy street she still thought of as home, despite the fact she'd been living with Lewis in a house five miles away for four years, three years next month of which they would have been married. Not that Lewis would remember their wedding anniversary.

The journey conquered and complete, Shauna found herself on the doorstep of the semi-detached home in which she had grown from a wobbly toddler, barely able to walk, into a fully-grown woman who occasionally displayed the same instability of foot. Using the front door key she still retained, Shauna let herself into the hallway, which was unintentionally preserved as homage to the 1980s. Fashion is a fickle thing and styles inevitably come back round again. This hallway was in the waiting room of good taste, waiting to be invited back in again.

Making her way along the corridor of heavily patterned wallpaper and dado rails, she opened the door to the living room. As always, the electric fire in the mock marble fireplace had all five bars pumping out waves of heat. It was stifling but comforting at the same time. The humidity felt high enough to grow tropical plants. In fact, Shauna could almost feel the build-up of a burst of refreshing but warm rain. She imagined the heavy drops falling on the sofa and hissing on the fireplace before immediately evaporating upwards towards the scroll textured ceiling.

Her father, whose frame she had seen silhouetted in the window as she'd arrived, was sitting in his usual comfortable chair, peering over the top of his specs and studying the local paper. No doubt he was bursting with criticisms and witticisms but they would have to wait for a while as the apple of his eye had just walked through the door.

"Come over here chucky egg" he beamed, remaining in his chair but lifting his smiling face up towards his cherished daughter "and give your dad a hug". He wasn't being lazy. George had once been a very athletic and active young man. He had been supremely strong and ever active. He still did his best and pushed himself as much as his body would allow. Sadly, his physical prime had been cut short by an industrial incident at work. This was prior to the "where there's blame there's a claim" era. The company had done their best, probably through guilt, and re-deployed George as a foreman but there was no hefty cheque to take to the bank.

Shauna squeezed her father in a powerful hug. The one man who would never let her down. No man was as good as her father. If her growing baby was born a boy, she would point him in the direction of her father for guidance on life, morals, how to treat a lady like a lady and, of course, how to mend a flat tyre on your bike.

"Would you like a cup of tea love"? Her mother, the gentle matriarch, was always there to dispense hot drinks and offer sustenance at any time of the day or night. "I've got some of that lovely ham from Shaws in the fridge. I could make you a sandwich, if you'd like one? Or there's a nice bit of quiche left. Would you like a bit of quiche?"

Shauna crossed the room to kiss her mother. "It's OK thanks, mum. I've just had breakfast. I'll pop the kettle on though". Shauna was aware that her mother was also unable to easily leave the comfort of her chair.

On this occasion it was nothing to do with any physical impairment. No, Shauna's mother, Dee, was pinned to her seat by the heavy head of Alex, Shauna's younger brother who was fighting with the cat for lap space. As Alex lay with his mop of blonde hair on his mothers lap, he showed no sense of embarrassment that, at the age of nineteen, he still preferred to lay across the sofa like some sort of Roman god, waiting for someone to drop a peeled grape in his mouth.

Alex was beautiful and, Shauna believed, probably gay. The thing is, he hadn't told anybody. Not even himself! Shauna had suspected for years. She'd discussed this with her younger sister, Ruby, but had been met with "no, of course he's not gay, he's got loads of girlfriends".

And this from a girl who works in a high-end hairdressers with more than a trio of gay men strutting around her on a daily basis. Having said that, Shauna's sister was rather
self-absorbed and probably hadn't taken notice of another human being since puberty.

"Do you think you'll get round to see Nana this weekend darling"?

"Yes, mum, I'll do my best. It all depends what plans Lewis has for us. He's very busy doing extra work at home but hopefully we'll get some time"

Lewis was always very uncomfortable around Nana Buckle. She didn't miss a trick and had reached the age where she'd been on earth for so long and seen so much she felt she'd earned the right to say exactly what she thought to whomever she thought deserved it. Shauna was worried that Nana would get herself into trouble but most of the youngsters who lived in the area feared the razor tongue of the old lady who leaned on her garden gate and shouted "You should be at school" to the truants kicking footballs in the street or "He's a bit big for that thing" to the mother pushing a toddler in his buggy "Should be walking at his age"

"Your cousin Martin took his new girlfriend Jackie round there last week. Apparently when she put down the tea and biscuits she looked at Martin and said "Your new young lady won't be needing any biscuits, will she? It looks as if she's had enough already".

It was true. Jackie was well padded around the bottom and thighs but it wasn't down to Nana Buckle to ration her food intake.

Shauna was reluctant to visit Nana Buckle this weekend. Her all-seeing eyes would probably detect the early stages of pregnancy. Shauna was only 11 weeks and hadn't told anybody yet. She wanted to wait for the 12-week stage before announcing the good news.

The only person she had confided in was her best friend, Beth. Shauna told Beth everything. Sadly, many of the confidences were now communicated electronically as Beth had moved to Spain six months ago. Still, sometimes being able to put things in writing was cathartic. Her emails to Beth often became a form of therapy.

Of course, Beth was sworn to secrecy about the

impending baby arrival. Shauna did not need to worry about her secret being spilled by Beth. They both knew things about each other that were locked inside and would never be disclosed. That sort of trust and history is a unique bond to be treasured. Theirs had started early. Their mothers, Dee and Linda were neighbours and went through their pregnancies and anti-natal classes together. The girls were the first babies for Dee and Linda and were raised together every step of the way. Subsequent brothers and sisters followed for Shauna and Beth but their close friendship continued unbroken.

Shauna and Beth had always promised to do the same. To fall pregnant at the same time, carrying virtual twins. To share their morning sickness, maternity clothes, stretch mark stories and to raise their babies together.

Shauna drifted out of her reverie.

She tuned her ears back into the conversation in the room, which appeared to be a friendly discussion between her parents about the previous night in bed. This could have been uncomfortable for Alex and Shauna to hear but it was all good clean fun.

"George, you're a nocturnal bed thief"

George laughed and shook his head as Dee continued.
"You don't know because you're asleep. You steel the bedding and stray from your designated half of the bed over to mine"

More laughter from George "It's not a football pitch,

19

Dee. There is no off-side rule"

Dee was going to have her say.

"I wake up to find myself clinging to the edge of the bed. Freezing cold"

George looked towards Shauna and winked as Dee continued to wind herself up.

"You're snoring away, and defending your territory with bony elbows. Your elbows press into the soft flesh of my shoulder and it hurts"

Alex suddenly raised himself from his reclining position and sat upright on the sofa.

"Oh, I like the sound of the soft flesh" teased George "Is this going to lead to something erotic?"

"I feel like getting out of my side of the bed and climbing into yours. There's always plenty of room there"

"I can see a marketing opportunity here" George was unable to argue the case being made against his sleeping habits but he obviously had a humorous suggestion to help "Maybe bedding manufacturers could print a half-way line on the sheets……."

George continued to discuss all sorts of possibilities. Although she found her father very amusing, Shauna tuned him out at the point he suggested giant coloured circles on the sheet for people wishing to play Twister and started to wonder about her husband and whether it was time to return home.

"Better get going. Hopefully Lewis will have finished his work by now. Mum, are you still up for our trip to Triptees shopping village next week?"

"Striptease"?

"Triptees George" Dee put him straight "Yes darling. I'm looking forward to it".

Shauna circled the room dispensing goodbye kisses.

"Ooooh Shaunie, looks like you and Lewis had a fun start to the day" Alex winked and his eyes gestured towards her breasts.

"What? Oh no, that's Greek yoghurt. It fell out of the fridge and exploded everywhere. Didn't notice that splodge on my top" Shauna replied, spitting on her hands and rubbing at the white stain. Alex raised his eyebrows in a mock knowing way.

Escaping the over-heated house and taking in a much needed breath of fresh air on the doorstep, Shauna returned to her car and commenced the usual ritual of coaxing and foul language to encourage it to start. At these moments, she often recalled the famous scene in the TV show Fawlty Towers where Basil beat his car with a tree branch when it failed to start. They'd been watching the episode as a family, all lined up on their sofa like the Simpsons. George had laughed so hard he rolled off the sofa and landed on the paisley patterned carpet. Shauna had thought that was almost as funny as Basil punishing the car, even if her Dad had slightly exaggerated the experience for comedy effect.

I'm so lucky to have such great parents, she thought. I hope Lewis and I will be as good.

(4) George

Shauna came round today. She looks tired. I wonder if she's pregnant. I know I should be happy for her if she is but I dread to think of that selfish egotist being the father

Alex has been draped on the sofa, cuddling up to Dee all day. I've often wondered if he's gay. Why doesn't he just come out and tell us. None of us would mind. Despite the fact that Alex obviously thinks his mum and I are a pair of old fuddy-duddies, we're actually quite open-minded. We've lived a life, you know, and we've had a lot of fun. Oh yes, we've had fun.

I wish Shauna was as happy as me and her mum were at her age. I can tell she's putting on a brave face much of the time. Why didn't the anti-social so-and-so come round this morning? Shauna said he was catching up on paperwork. Paperwork my arse!

(5) Email - The Redhead to Isla

Isla, hope you're OK. I loved the pictures of you on Facebook in that fancy dress outfit. Very creative!

Well, I went to that speed-dating thing I told you about. It was surprisingly good fun. I thought it would be full of sad, lonely men in raincoats but there was a real mix.

One guy spent ages telling me about an old scooter he was restoring. He was talking engine torque, horse-power and miles per gallon. When the bell rang to move onto the next table, he seemed oblivious to it and launched into a detailed description of the postal charges and comparisons with UK and overseas imported spare parts. I don't think he knows a single thing about me but to be fair it doesn't matter because I won't be riding pillion on his Vespa, despite it's apparent thrust capability.

There was a really nice bloke called Richard in a striped shirt with a gentle voice and a really nice smiley face. He even offered me a lift home at the end of the night. Some of the other party-goers were making it quite obvious that they fancied him. One of them even sidled up to me and said, in an obvious jealous tone, that Richard was obviously going to pick me. I took great pleasure in letting them know he'd already offered me a lift home. I don't know why, but for some stupid reason, I didn't tick Richard on my sheet. Don't ask me why. Sometimes I do things to mix it up a bit but, in this case, I've passed over the opportunity to spend time with a charming gentleman.

Ah, maybe that's the problem. He was too nice and too available.

My only tick went to Rav, a dark and interesting man who was the only one to make me laugh out loud. He was very self-assured and pushed in when I was talking to a group of guys during the warm-up drinks at the bar. Men and their territory, eh! I found it quite rude but also very daring. I was fascinated by his confidence and wanted to see more, hence the tick. I've had an email to say he's ticked me too so we're a match. Wonder how many others he's matched with? Wonder if Richard is charming anyone with his gentlemanly advances tonight?

Don't know why I'm even worrying about any of this. The only man I'm interested in right now is married. All the time I was being chatted up by those guys I kept thinking about *him*. Wondering what he was doing. Was he sitting with his beautiful wife curled up on the sofa beside him? Were they laughing and chatting over a glass of wine? Were they in separate rooms? Were they fighting? Were they making up with slow, romantic love-making. Oh, stop it!

At some point, I need to casually mention my date with Rav – hopefully that will make him jealous.

(6) Email – Isla to The Redhead

Mate, please be careful messing around with a married man. You know it's wrong. You don't know what damage you're doing to his relationship and ultimately to yourself. You deserve so much better. Let's hope this Rav guy turns out to be the one for you. He sounds edgy and different. A head turning redhead like you needs someone dark and daring on your arm.

I've been on another promotional assignment at work. This time it was at a local superstore. I had to stand in the doorway, catching shoppers as they walked in whilst simultaneously catching a cold due to the draught being created by the constantly active automatic doors. In fact, one or two customers (male, of course) leaned in to tell me they could tell I was cold. Should have worn a padded bra!

The promotional item was a well-known family chocolate brand. I was given my script and a tower of tins of the brand to be promoted. Before starting, I checked my appearance in the mirror, fluffed up my hair, pushed up my boobs and fixed the regulation smile on my face. How difficult can this be, I thought to myself? This is a very popular family classic – everyone will want a tin.

As the customers filed through the door, I greeted them with my scripted offer "Can I interest you in half price Wality Road at 5.45?"

In amongst the customers who just plain ignored me

(rude!) there were some very lovely people who declined due to dental or dietary issues – fair enough. However, after several hours, I began to find the smile slipping off my face every time I received one of the following replies.

I'll just remind you of my line first.

Me: Can I interest you in half price Wality Road at 5.45?

Customers: I have plans at that time, can I not just take them now?
Or
Is that the only time I can buy them?
Or
How much are they at 6?

Unbelievably, there was a 50/50 mix. Some of the replies came from jokers and sarcastic buggers but probably half of those replies came from people who genuinely believed there was a time constraint to the bargain.

Honestly mate, I never cease to be amazed by my fellow man. I bet you think the same.

Anyway, the store manager could see I was losing the will to live. Not sure how he'd managed it but I suspect he was watching me on CCTV. Bet he's downloaded a copy and taken it home to watch again in private. I wouldn't mind actually cos he's quite fit. Unfortunately I noticed a gold ring on his wedding finger so he's out of bounds. However, doesn't stop me doing a little bit of cheeky flirting.

Somebody once said to me it doesn't matter where you get your appetite from, as long as you eat at home. Maybe you could apply that to your married man. Watch him work out in the gym, feast your eyes, get hungry for sex and then go and have it with someone who belongs to YOU!

Anyway, the store manager said he'd noticed I was looking a little bit fed up. He actually used more colourful words but I won't elaborate. He's basically given me carte blanche to promote the chocolates *my* way. He said I looked like a pro with lots of experience. He said I obviously know how to please the customer and that I was skilled at persuading them to part with their money for a little treat. At the time I took it to be a genuine compliment but when I was having my Choccywockycappuccino at Ceasars Bar later, I replayed what he'd said in my head and I'm not sure he wasn't being just a little bit facetious.

(7) Shauna

Shauna arrived home to find Lewis in the back garden, smoking and talking on his phone. He was obviously unaware that he was being watched as he slowly paced up and down, occasionally throwing his head back in a real belly laugh and then, suddenly looking almost wistful and sad.

I think you could safely say he jumped out of his skin when he heard the patio door slide open to reveal Shauna's presence. The other participant in the telephone call was dismissed rapidly as Lewis walked back towards the house, stubbing his cigarette out on the patio on the way.

"Hello darling. How are your Mum and Dad?" Lewis snaked his arms around Shauna's waist and kissed her once, twice oh and wow, another one. Lewis was never this demonstrative.

"Yes they're fine thanks" Shauna smiled. She was enjoying the closeness, despite the lingering smell of his last cigarette. "You OK? Did you finish your paperwork?"

Lewis distracted her with some more unexpected but very pleasant kissing. Hmmm, what had brought all this on? Apparently his phone call was to his mother. They were invited for lunch tomorrow. There was no further mention of the paperwork.

(8) Email – Beth to Shauna

Shauna, you're hilarious! You've always been accident prone so I'm not surprised to hear about your latest stumble. It's those big boobs of yours. They make you top heavy. Fancy falling over, not once, but twice. And being helped up both times by two old ladies. Bet they thought you'd been drinking. I can imagine them both watching you walk away with your ripped tights, tutting and making remarks about the youth of today. I hope your baby is OK!

Yes, life continues to be fun here. I've picked up a temporary job at a local car rental company. It's like going back in time to the days I worked for HenryHire. Of course, in those days, most of the customers spoke English. To be fair, a large percentage do here too but I'm also having to resort to my very basic Spanish and lots of hand gestures. You can imagine how unsuccessful that is at times. I'm surprised I haven't been sacked yet!

CostaCoches, yes that's the name of the car rental company I work for, have a nice bright uniform to reflect the sun here. Unlike the HenryHire one which was quite formal and airhostessy, my current uniform is a bright yellow polo shirt and a choice of a very short skirt or a pair or more functional work trousers with funky pockets and zips. Well, you know what I'm like around pockets and zips. I love them. Sadly they are quite hot and sticky in this weather so I tend to wear the short skirt, which makes me look a bit slutty, but at least I'm cool. Temperature wise, not fashion sense wise. The poor boys still have to wear the trousers but I've seen some of them eyeing up my skirt. I know what you're thinking so I'll leave it there!

At least I don't get stopped in supermarkets here and asked where the haemorrhoid cream is. In my HenryHire kit I always being mistaken for a member of staff in chemists and chain stores whereas now I just look like a cheerleader or a children's entertainer.

What makes me laugh is when I'm leaving the house in the morning, dressed in what is clearly a uniform with CostaCoches badges front and back and a neighbour will stop me and ask if I'm on my way to work! I'm not a sarcastic person but I really want to reply "no, I'm going on holiday, I just like wearing this luminous yellow clothing for pleasure". And then when they see me in my shorts and t-shirt or even a bikini they say "not going to work today?" Again, it's very temping to say "Why yes, I'm just off to work now as it happens. We're all dressing as glamour models today".

One of my neighbours is great fun. She's from Newcastle and lives here with her husband who works on the oilrigs. He's only here for a month at a time before going off to the North Sea for a month of work so my neighbour does a bit of villa cleaning to keep herself busy. There's always plenty of villa cleaning here in the summer and we often bump into each other, me dressed to rent cars and her to scrub stains. She once told me if she ever wrote a book about her life she would call it "Sun Cream and Skid Marks."

Have a great time at Triptees with your mum. Say hello from me. I miss your lovely mum. I miss you too, of course, but mummy Dee is like family. Oh, that rhymes!!! Oh and, Shauna, try not to fall over whilst you're there. In fact, don't have any accidents of any sort!!!!!!

(9) Shauna

Shauna was chatting to her workmates. Yes, she should have been working. In fact they all should but sometimes you just need to catch up, bitch, moan and debrief. It's human nature. We have a herd mentality and we all like to collect around the watering hole, or in this case the brightly coloured vending machine.

The Tannoy cracked. An announcement was about to be made. "Would the owner of a blue….." Oh no, that's my car thought Shauna. What have I done wrong? Have I left the lights on again? Have I forgotten to put the handbrake on and it's rolled into the flowerbed again? "……. please come to reception" continued the dulcet tones of Barbara, the receptionist. Barbara was a brisk but efficient lady who was always immaculately groomed, if a little old fashioned in her sartorial choice. Her prime years, Shauna suspected, were the 1980s, judging by her taste in clothes and her daily efforts to preserve that decade in fashion. Her power suits and matching bright coloured accessories, even her eye shadow, were a nod to that period in time. Sadly she frequently resembled an escapee from a fancy dress party.

"Hello love, I'll be with you in a minute" Barbara raised her perfectly coiffured back-combed starched head of platinum blond hair before returning to the telephone switchboard "Peear PR, how can I help yoooooooooooo" She probably didn't realise she did it but Barbara would hang on to the you part of her greeting for ages, decreasing in volume for an inordinate amount of time. Shauna pondered why Barbara never passed out after expelling all that air.

Lisa, Barbara's counterpart receptionist colleague, and a young lady very much up-to-date with fashion appeared at the desk, took her seat and began answering the switchboard, allowing Barbara time to deal with Shauna.

"Oh yes love, a very nice young gentleman came in to ask for the owner of the blue car, in fact your car, love. I'm afraid I was a bit busy here on the switch alone. Someone was doing their make-up or flirting with top management again" Barbara rolled her eyes and nodded in the direction of Lisa "So the gentleman left his number and asked if the owner of the car would give him a call".

Shauna returned to her desk, wondering why someone would be interested in her old blue banger. What should she ask for it? Was she even interested in selling? Lewis would not be impressed if she carried out a financial transaction without his say-so. Yes, it would be an excuse to get a new car but she was quite fond of the shaky old thing. She was thinking about the car now, not Lewis! Mind you, we need a safe car to carry the baby...... Oh shut up Shauna, just pick up the phone and call......

"Sean Robinson, hello" Nice voice but how funny….

"Sean Robinson? That's funny, my maiden name is Shauna Robinson. We're almost name twins" Shauna filled in the gap with a little giggle. Oh My God, what's wrong with me? What a stupid thing to say……. Shauna suspected she should stop rambling and get on with it.

"I've got a message to call you about my car, the one parked in the Peear PR car park" Why do I need to tell him that. He knows that because he wanted to talk to me about it. Stop talking Shauna….

"Oh yes, I'm so sorry. I'm afraid I think I've clipped your car with my works van" His voice was warm and friendly, what a cliché, but Shauna found herself warming to the bad driver. She could hardly say anything. Her driving was not always the most accurate.

"When you say clipped, is it bad or can I keep driving it?"

"Oh God, I think I'm going to have to come clean. I can't keep this up any longer". At this point, Shauna felt her heart race and a feeling of nausea rise in her throat. What was he going to say next? Should she put the phone down?

Daisy, one of the Marketing Department secretaries, came into view with a pile of papers clutched to her chest. She was always photocopying. She must be returning from the photocopier after another session of paper jams, empty toner cartridges and general bad behaviour from the ridiculously expensive and diva-like machine.

Shauna beckoned Daisy over in order to have the presence of a friendly and supportive female, should the call turn nasty.

"I often work across the road in one of the other units and I've seen you getting in and out of your car…. Well, I think you look like a really nice girl….." Shauna looked up and made scary eye faces at Daisy who was unaware of why she was witnessing this one-sided conversation but, hey, she was up for anything! Sean continued "…. and I was wondering if you'd like to go for a drink some time?"

Shauna continued to stare at Daisy. She clasped her hand across her mouth in an effort to stifle the natural giggle that was bubbling up.

"Oh, that's very flattering of you" Shauna exaggerated her response in order to allow Daisy to pick up on the nature of the call "You sound very nice but I'm afraid I'm married"

"Oh, I might have guessed some lucky guy would have snapped you up" Sean sounded disappointed. "Sorry, I sound like I'm talking about a bargain on an on-line auction site"

"What?"

"Bloody Hell, I'm not helping here am I? Look, I'm really not a weirdo. It's just that I really like the look of you. You look fun and happy and…."

"Oh God. I've just remembered I'm pregnant too" blurted Shauna. Oh God, why was she telling a total stranger the news that she and Lewis and, of course Beth, were currently withholding from everyone…….. Except Daisy who was now the one with her hand clapped over her mouth.

"Oh mate, oh mate" Daisy stumbled over her words of excitement, threw the pile of photocopies on Shauna's desk and rushed round to hug her. Was it the heat from the recently processed paperwork, the warm hug from Daisy or was it the embarrassment of the situation making Shauna flush all over. She felt suddenly very overcome and very sick.

"Oh babe, I'm so pleased for you" Daisy was now crushing Shauna. It was genuine emotion but Shauna couldn't breath. She felt faint.

"Hello? Hello? Shauna are you OK" Sean, still on the other line, sounded concerned.

Shauna found herself explaining far more to Sean than she ever expected to. By proxy, Daisy also heard the story. They were both sworn to secrecy.

Phone call over. Game over? Shauna felt hot tears stinging in her eyes. But why? Daisy sensed she should remain silent for once. She stood beside Shauna, rubbing her arm the way a toddler pats a pet. In some respects, it was really annoying and irritating and Shauna just wanted to be alone. But, strangely, the presence of Daisy beside her gave Shauna strength. She didn't know why she needed it and she couldn't understand the tears burning in her eyes but something had stirred up her emotions and she couldn't keep them in check.

(10) George

Just come back from another nightmare supermarket shopping trip. Despite the fact that we do a 'big shop' twice a week, Dee always seems to need 'little bits' during the gaps in between. In fact, pretty much every day we find ourselves in a supermarket queue.

On the way there, we passed a sign saying "Giant Rug Sale". Well, Dee loves a bargain so I enquired "Do we need any Giant rugs darling?" Unfortunately I had to explain the joke to her. Her attention was being directed to her purse as she rummaged through the library of supermarket special offer vouchers and coupons stored in there. Her purse was always stuffed with 'buy one get one free', '20% off if you spend a million pounds', 'buy this product and get that one half price', even if you can't stand the stuff. Inevitably, Dee would find the appropriate voucher in her bulging purse during the journey home. More often than not, this would be on the eve of its expiry by which time we would have already bought and paid full price for the item we probably didn't need in the first place.

As we travelled home from the delights of the shopping aisles, we caught a glimpse of Alex walking down the road with a young lady. Unfortunately the traffic was ridiculously slow due to another set of temporary traffic lights so we never managed to catch up with them before they headed off into the park but we could see his lady friend has, as Dee put it, "a lovely thick head of red hair". Dee said if she had hair like that, she wouldn't tie it back into a ponytail like Alex's girlfriend. Well, we think she's a girlfriend. I'm

39

saying nothing here because Dee thinks the sun shines out of his every orifice so I'm never allowed to give any opinion on our son unless it contains a glowing report.

(11) Shauna

The day had arrived for the Triptees shopping trip and Shauna was storming back into the house, swearing under her breath.

Her car had dug its heels in, or was that wheels in, and absolutely refused to start. Shauna had angry tears stinging in her eyes as she re-entered the hallway to find Lewis already on his bloody phone. Did he really have that much to say?

He seemed quite keen to resolve any issue Shauna had and, once he discovered the problem, he reached into his pocket, pulled out his car keys.

"The petrol tank is full" he said, holding the keys out for Shauna to take "Have fun and remember to use the parking sensors".

Oh wow, Lewis loved his car. Shauna hardly ever had the opportunity to drive it. Well, unless you counted the times Lewis overstepped the drink drive limits, without even checking with her first, and expected Shauna to remain sober and drive him home. On those occasions, he was frequently critical of her driving and would fish for an argument. Shauna would try to limit any conversation whilst she was at the wheel on those occasions and therefore did not have the opportunity to enjoy driving the high-spec beast of a car Lewis loved so much.

Dee was equally surprised when Shauna arrived in Lewis's pride and joy. Not because she was impressed by the sumptuous leather interior or the engineering under the bonnet. No, Dee was just gratified to discover that Lewis had donated his car for their enjoyment that day. He didn't seem to look after her little girl the way George had always treasured her.

"Is Ruby not coming?" Shauna asked her mother as she lowered herself into the passenger seat. I know that may seem a strange question to ask because Ruby clearly wasn't getting into the car at the same time. However, Ruby was a contrary creature. On occasion, she would be the first person, ready and waiting, huffing and puffing and raring to go. On other occasions, she would be quite happy for the rest of the family to wait for her nail varnish to dry or for a stray hair to be ironed into place with endless strokes of the hair straighteners before joining them in the car.

"No darling. She's working later this afternoon but maybe we could pick her up a little treat whilst we're there" Ruby always did well on the 'little treat' front but Shauna wasn't counting!

"Just give me a minute, Mum" Shauna was leaning over to the high-tech satnav mounted on the dashboard. "I just thought that, as we have it, we may as well use this fancy sat-nav to find our way to Triptees" Shauna actually had a very good sense of direction, despite her accident prone nature which wasn't helped by a dreadful sense of balance.

Surely it can't be too difficult she thought. It's just like a giant android phone. Shauna started pressing buttons, muttering under her breath as each screen became more complicated than the other. Dee commenced her usual running commentary of events, a family trait she had inherited from Nana Buckle. Shauna knew exactly what was happening and when, but her mother insisted on reading each screen of the satnav out loud to her. She was just about to give up and rely on her pigeon sense of direction when a screen popped up with the word 'search' on it. Ah, that's more like it.

As Shauna selected the search field, a list of previous destinations automatically appeared, designed to help the driver negotiate their way to frequently visited places. The list included their own home address, presumably from when they were returning from far-flung places. Other familiar and uneventful addresses flashed in front of her eyes but one in particular stood out. The Swan Hotel in Weston Undercroft. How odd. We haven't been there since…. well, two Christmases ago. And not in this car.

"Darling, is everything OK. Shall we go in and ask your father for a map" Shauna's thoughts were interrupted by her mother who was not technology minded and would have preferred to rely on a large map, taking over the entire front console of the car. She would have happily run her finger along the route as Shauna drove, pointing out road names and landmarks. The map would inevitably obscure Shauna's vision at some point as Dee had a habit of opening the map to it's full capacity, making it suitable for use as a sun visor as well as an orienteering aid. Shauna could recall many a family journey with Dee furiously punching at the vast map in front of her, trying to corral it into conformity, whilst her poor father tried to salvage some sort of vision through the front windscreen and safely drive his family to their holiday destination.

Shauna clicked back to the present time. If she wanted to dwell on The Swan Hotel she would need to do it at her leisure and not whilst escorting her mother to a vast out of town shopping centre the size of the Isle of Wight.

As always, Shauna and Dee had a 'lovely time'. The companionship between the two women was relaxed and easy. Dee would point out items of clothing for Shauna, which she would initially turn her nose up at. Dee would utter one of her many catchphrases "it will look better on than off, darling" and would always be proved right. Shauna would be childishly disappointed that her mum was right, again, but she always enjoyed the compliments the clothes chosen by Dee would attract.

The shopping trip was, of course, peppered with frequent stops for coffee and cake and "a nice bit of lunch". George would often joke that he fancied "something absolutely disgusting for lunch" instead. Although, in her present condition, Shauna was avoiding caffeine and choosing to drink herbal teas instead, telling Dee that she was detoxing.

Naturally, due to the large volume of liquid consumed there would be frequent visits to the ladies. It was during one of those visits that, whilst in the cubicle next to Shauna, Dee heard the plaintive voice of her daughter

"Mum, I need to tell you something and then I need your help"

(12) George

I have to confess I'm feeling a bit helpless today. My little girl lost her baby yesterday. I had a feeling she was expecting but she said she was waiting until she was 12 weeks to announce the good news. Unfortunately we found out, sooner than she'd planned. Sadly it also meant we found out that our first grandchild was not going to make it.

Dee called to tell me she was on the way to the hospital with Shauna. Apparently they'd been trying to get hold of Lewis but he wasn't answering his phone. The last thing Shauna, or Dee for that matter, needed to be worrying about was getting hold of him so I told them I'd keep trying.

After getting his voicemail message (smooth, smug bugger he sounds) for the tenth time I began to get quite angry. Why wasn't he answering his bloody phone? He was always furtively looking at it. I'd seen him on many occasions when he didn't know I was watching him, slipping the phone out of his back pocket, his face lighting up as the screen saver faded, smiling or frowning depending on what he'd obviously seen on the screen. He'd look up and check around to see if anyone was watching before continuing to play with the bloody thing or he'd slip it back into his pocket and attempt to re-join the conversation or activity he'd detached himself from.

So why was he not answering when my beautiful daughter was calling him. When she really needed him.

Time to enlist the help of my other beautiful daughter......

(13) Ruby

Dad called to find out where I was and what I was doing. I'd been into work for a couple of hours but I was just on my way home, via the cashpoint where I was checking my balance before withdrawing some money. It turned out I could only withdraw £10. Blimey, that wasn't going to get me far, was it? Looks like I'd be bumming money off Mum, Dad, Shauna or Alex – in that order. I still owe all of them money from previous shortfalls in my budget but I'll pay them back….. one day!

I couldn't believe what Dad was telling me. Poor Shauna. Didn't even realise she was pregnant. Can't believe I didn't notice. I'm usually one of the first to notice when one of the clients is pregnant. Well, when I say one of the first……. Oh well, I did once guess first. Admittedly it was when she'd opened her purse to pay and a baby scan photo had fallen out on the desk in front of me.

As I pulled up to Lewis and Shauna's place, I suddenly felt really shaky and nervous. I hadn't really had time to process the fact that Shauna was pregnant and now I was going to tell Lewis that she wasn't.

As I got out of the car I bumped into an old school friend of Shauna's. Gina Baxter, or Ginger Gina as she was nicknamed by the boys. This was due, as you've probably guessed, to her red hair. Which, by the way, was now a glorious thick mane of amber tresses. Jealous? Me? Yes!!!!!!

47

Gina is also the sister of Trey Baxter (who Shauna believes is really called Terrence!). It's still a small community round here and I often bump into old school friends. Including the other Gina who the boys nicknamed Gina the Screamer. Mine, by the way, if you're interested was Booby Ruby!!

I couldn't work out if Gina was walking towards the house or walking away from it. She seemed to change tack when she saw me get out of the car and ended up walking round in a confused circle. For a while she seemed to be playing for time and then suddenly blurted out a question about the salon. She asked if I still worked there. I'm sure she saw me in there three weeks ago when Fabio was giving her an up-do (that's not a euphemism!) for a wedding she was going to. Anyway, she suddenly pretended to be all casual, even though it was all a bit awkward, and said she might see me in the salon one day. Errrr, yes, you will Gina cos I work there!!!!

Anyway, less of that. I had an errand to run so I despatched Gina off to wherever she was going or wasn't going (I don't think she knew!) and I rang the front door bell. If Shauna was at home I'd just walk in. I know it drives Lewis crazy but that's one of the reasons I do it. I can't stand the bloke. But I knew Shauna wasn't home so I felt obliged to conform to the norms of social grace.

Lewis answered the door with his phone pressed to his ear. What is it with him and that bogging phone? He's always on it. More than me and I'm a pretty heavy user of modern communication technology, I can tell you. By the look on his face and the way he was talking out loud for my benefit, I realised he must be on the phone to Mum. Luckily I didn't have to be the bearer of bad news. Sadly, the news was still true and my kind, gentle, loving sister was still suffering.

(14) Email – Beth to Shauna

Shauna, I'm so sorry to hear you lost your baby. Your mum called to tell me and she said you don't want to talk to anybody at the moment. I understand and I will wait for you. I don't know what to say. It must have been a dreadful time for you both. I don't know what to say. Sorry, I've already said that but it's true. I know it doesn't help you so I'm going to stop saying it. I know it's probably too soon for you to make plans but please think about coming out to Spain for a bit of time away. You can relax in the sun and we'll leave you alone if you want or need that. Anytime you like. Just get on a plane. Please know that I am thinking about you all the time, Shauna, and sending all my love.

(15) Email - The Redhead to Isla

Mate, so sorry, I thought that was a fancy dress costume you were wearing on your Facebook page. You looked great anyway.

Oh my God!! I went on the date with Rav. He wanted to pick me up from home but I suggested we meet at the bar instead. I arrived first. He was late. How rude! He came rushing in, looking like John Travolta in Greece, all leathers, slicked back hair and tight trousers. `Unfortunately I don't look anything like Olivia Newton John ...... in either of her personas from Greece. But I'd be the foxy one at the end rather than the virgin Sandra Dee if I could choose! I felt quite plain in his presence. There was me, him and his huge ego and it was full-on from the start.

The couple on the table next to us must have loved it. They sat in silence and listened to our every word. Rav insisted on ordering a sharing dish, which he also insisted on feeding to me. I hardly know the guy and he's feeding me mouthfuls of messy egg and potato bake, making stupid faces as he did so.

He was pushing me to place some kind of category on our relationship already. How many times a week did I think we should meet? Should we go on holiday? Where would I like to go? Slow down chum. Then he asked what I was looking for out of our relationship.

I didn't realise it was going to be easier to enter Mastermind or University Challenge than to go on a first date with Rav. I told him I was looking for company, fun, maybe...... He interrupted me. What did I mean by fun? Oh, you know.... Then he said, very loudly 'SEX'? I swear the lady on the table next to us choked on her sausage. A sausage, by the way, which she was actually managing to eat all by herself without having it spoon-fed to her by her male companion. To be honest, I think he was too busy staring at me and Rav to feed his wife a sausage.

Erm, yes, maybe some sex but not straight away. What was this? I know he is trying to re-build his life after a split from his ex who seems to have moved on rather quickly. Was he trying to compete? Was he trying to install a ready-made lover into his life immediately so he could flaunt me to his ex? Mind you, I have to confess, I was also hoping to elicit some jealousy from my secret married lover by going on this date so maybe Rav and I were playing the same game. It's just my rules were a bit less overt and desperate.

The constant grilling, mixed with his almost constant boasting about his successful business and, of course, the Ferrari he drove, was becoming frustrating. I suddenly remembered that I needed to visit a friend in hospital. For a minute I thought he was going to offer to come with me to the bogus, just made up, welfare visit. Fortunately he seemed to accept my excuse (wow, I must be a good actor) and escorted me to the door.

In the car park, I looked around for his Ferrari. Not there! I casually enquired. Oh yes, it's at home. I like to use this economical little family hatchback. Hmmmmm, yes, I believe you. Bit like the fish that got away story. Who cares, I've already decided I don't want another date with Rav. I can feed myself and I don't want to feed his ego anymore.

I turn to say thank you and goodbye with a fleeting kiss on his cheek. He turns his face in towards me and moves in with his tongue. I pull my head back in a casual retreat. Don't know why I'm sparing his feelings but people are starting to leave the bar and walk to their respective cars. I'm aware we're being watched by the couple who were sitting next to us. I have a feeling they gulped down their food and paid the bill in double time in order to follow us out and continue their obvious enjoyment of my car-crash of a first date experience in the car park.

Still smiling and being polite, I walk to my little car which I've never pretended is a Ferrari, Porsche, Lamborghini or, in fact, any performance sports car. All of a sudden Rav is there in front of me, asking when we'll see each other again. Oh shit!

I try to pass him off with a promise of being in touch soon, which of course I have absolutely no plans to do. OK, he says. When will that be? Oh, erm, in a couple of days. As I'm still fumbling through my fabricated promises to contact him, he suddenly crushes me in a big bear hug. Really tight. Then he says oooh, you're lovely, aren't you as he grinds his body against mine. I look around to see our table neighbours looking on with continued amusement. Imagine their surprise then when Rav suddenly picks me up! Yes, me, a fully grown adult. I pleaded with him to put me down but he took no notice. I leaned over and clung to the rail on the top of my car. I shouted at him to put me down. I told him that I probably weighed more than my car and that he'd suffer for this display of strength later.

Eventually he allowed me to slide down his body. A strategic move which he clearly enjoyed. Wish I hadn't made eye contact! I fumbled rapidly for my car keys, managed to manoeuvre out of the space without running Rav over, although at that point I wouldn't care or stop even if I had. I raced to the exit, talking to myself under my breath. What a surreal experience. Did it actually happen? It won't be happening again.

Sods law, I could see the lights at the end of the road on my exit route were red. I also knew that he'd be travelling in the same direction. I didn't want his fake Ferrari which was actually a Ford Focus (try saying that after a pint of Pimms) waiting behind me at the lights with his eyes looking longingly at me reflected in my rear view mirror. So I turned in the opposite direction, adding an extra 10 minutes to my journey home. It was worth it though to avoid him. He was displaying stalker tendencies and I didn't want him following me home. It was only later I remembered I was supposed to be visiting a friend in hospital.... In the other direction. Oh well, I'd never see him again so what does it matter.

Dating disaster number....... What number is it now? How many emails have I sent you? It's very therapeutic for me to write it down though. Isla, you are my unwitting agony aunt.

(16) Email – Beth to Shauna

Shauna, thanks for being in touch. It was horrible to hear the sadness in your voice. What a horrible time it is for you. I know you were so grateful for the help and support of your Mum and Dad and Ruby, of course.

I hope you recover in your own time. I hope Lewis becomes more communicative with you soon and is able to support you emotionally too. I know it's a tough time for him too but….. oh, you know. I won't say it but I'm sure you know what I mean.

Things are going well here. I'm still working at CostaCoches. I often feel quite lonely and isolated here though because of the language barrier. I'm trying to learn Spanish and I do a little bit of studying every day. However, when I listen to my colleagues talking amongst themselves, it's like they're talking a totally different language. Yes, I know they are - they're speaking Spanish. What I mean is, I don't recognise any of the words they're using. I stare hard at them and I nod and smile when they talk to me but I really hope they're not getting fed up with me asking them to repeat things or slow down when they talk.

Luckily my colleagues all speak English. How embarrassing is that! I come to live in Spain and I end up speaking to the locals in my native tongue and not theirs. Most of them are really proficient too so it can make me a bit lazy at times. I still have a small amount of basic schoolgirl French stored in my brain so on occasion my sentences contain random Francais too. I've invented a whole new language -

Franish or maybe Spench.

Occasionally when I'm attempting a flurry of Spanish I see rueful smiles on their faces. I wonder what I've actually said? At least I'm making them laugh. Nobody has slapped me in the face yet! I find the Spanish people are very generous with their language. They love it when you try to learn and they genuinely want to help you. Therefore my colleagues are very polite and patient with me and they always make sure I repeat any new words and phrases to ensure I've got it right but I'd love to know what's amusing them on the occasions when they exchange glances and seem to be obviously trying not to laugh.

God, I've just remembered. Do you recall when we were younger and we'd walk home from school pretending to be Spanish with our own made up language? Hilarious. We were just talking a load of utter rubbish and pretending we understood each other. How on earth was anyone overhearing us supposed to believe we were Spanish when the words we were sprouting didn't even exist? Wow, we thought we were so cool then.

I feel much less self-assured now than I did then. The confidence of innocent youth. Ooooh, that sounds like the name of a band or the title of a film. The only films you and I have been in are our own shocking holiday videos or shaky phone footage on hen nights. And our singing is more likely to get us banned than get us into a band. See what I did there!

Oh, talking of embarrassing moments.... We were delivering a car to a customer yesterday whose own car was in for repair at a nearby garage so he'd asked for the rental vehicle to be delivered there. It's a swanky showroom with huge windows and slick salesmen in very white shirts. How do they keep them so crystal clean and bright. My white shirts always go various shades of yellow or grey after a few washes. Ooooh, I sound like someone from a detergent commercial.

Anyway, my colleague Juan was following me in one of the pool cars and I was the glamorous delivery host with the clipboard and paperwork. As we arrived at the garage, I could see a gentleman sitting on one of the squashy sofas in the state-of-the-art showroom who I guessed was our customer.

I walked confidently towards him, thinking how amazing I must look in my uniform, clipboard under my arm and a welcoming smile on my face.

BOOM!

I'd just walked straight into a plate glass window and it hurt. The customer stood up from the squashy sofa and rushed towards me, via the open door on the other side of the window I'd just face planted. At the same time Juan rushed towards me to lay a steadying hand on my arm. I waved them both off with a flippant, gesture as if to suggest I was absolutely fine and perfectly happy to carry on with the transaction.

The truth was I could see cartoon birds flying round my peripheral vision and my teeth were vibrating. Don't ask me why. Maybe they act as some sort of shock absorber during moments of high impact. As I bent forward to point out to the customer the boxes he was required to tick and sign to take possession of his shiny rental car, my nose started throbbing. I couldn't actually see the wording on the paperwork, or the aforementioned signature boxes. Luckily I know where they are, based on previous handovers so I just waved a casual hand in the general area at bit like a TV weather forecaster does over the map. Unfortunately I couldn't stop a dribble of protective saline tears trickling from my eyes, running down my nose and plopping on the paperwork.

Sexy!!

(17) Email - The Redhead to Isla

Thought I'd better get it out of the way so I sent Rav a text this morning: "Rav, thanks for yesterday. You're a great guy but I just don't think we're suited. I wish you luck with finding love, take care x"

Seconds later he replied: "What? I thought we had so much in common. Please can you tell me why you've ended things?"

Ended things? We'd only had one date! We hadn't even *started* things!

Stupidly I engaged further and replied: "Maybe I'm just not ready for a full-on relationship but I think you are and I don't want to hold you back."

Reply: "I can take things slowly, honest."

Yeah, really? After the grilling, intimate questions and the display of lifting skills in the car park, I don't see Rav as being an easy-going guy so I ignore the text.

10 minutes later: "As you seem to be ignoring me now, can you tell me if you have a friend who looks like you, is as beautiful as you and exactly the same as you that I can date?"

I wouldn't even subject an arch-enemy to Rav's brazen chat-up technique so I didn't indulge him with a reply.

(18) Shauna

As often happens when there's a captive audience during a car journey, you talk. Is it the fact that you have a specific time for your journey, traffic jams permitting, and you therefore know roughly how long the conversation is likely to last? Is it something to do with the fact that you are generally facing forward, looking at the road ahead (or you should be if you're the driver!) and therefore able to avoid eye contact? You can be honest and brave whilst avoiding the piercing stare of another. Sometimes the most awkward and difficult conversations take place in a car where there is no escape, unless of course, someone gets out or worse, jumps out!

That thought reminded Shauna of an event in early childhood. In her hazy memory, Shauna couldn't recall where they were going or where they had been but, for some reason, her mother was driving. This normally meant her father had been drinking and Dee had offered to stay sober.

As they drove along, Dee would point things out to the girls "Oh look, there's a heard of cows over there" All eyes were already on the field containing several black and white cows but it was nice of mum to point it out. "Oh look, there's a horse in that field" Again, Shauna and Ruby were more than capable of noticing the roadside animals but, as ever, it was nice of mummy to draw their attention.

"Watch the road, love" George had felt it necessary to point out the obvious to his wife.

"Yes, I'm perfectly capable of doing two things at once" came Dees defence.

The journey continued with more observations and a competition to spot the most red or yellow cars. Shauna couldn't remember who chose which colour and who won but she can remember it was fun.

"Why are you going this way, love, isn't it quicker....."

"I know which way I'm going, thank you. Oh girls, look two red cars together"

"We've finished the game now, Dee" George laughed and shook his head. He looked round at the girls on the back seat and winked.

"Yes, well, I've been concentrating on driving" Dee huffed

"Love, think you've changed gears too soon. The engine is struggling" Shauna and Ruby were totally unaware of the requirement to select the correct gear for the car and their father's helpful remarks seemed more than acceptable to them. However, their mother did not seem to appreciate the assistance.

"Who's driving this car. Me or you?" Dee snapped

"Just saying, love, you're not properly in control of the car when you change up the gears so soon" George continued, totally unfazed by the rise in pitch of his wife's voice "I'm just thinking of our safety. If something happens you won't be able to react quickly ...."

"I'll be able to react to this though" The girls lurched forwards as their mother slammed on the brakes. "If you're so good at driving, do it yourself". Dee furiously fumbled with her safety belt and eventually managed to release herself from the mechanism. She reached between George's knees to retrieve her handbag, tugging it from the foot-well before opening her door and giving it a good slam as she abandoned the car. Dee stomped away, muttering under her breath. Although Shauna did think she'd overheard a few naughty words in there!

The intervening events were a blur but Shauna could remember finding herself sitting at Nana Buckle's kitchen table. Nana was fussing over Shauna and Ruby, making them feel safe with her comforting presence, juice and home-make cake.

Through the crack in the door, Shauna could hear her grandad (now sadly departed) talking to her father in deep tones. "George, you have to remember, her hormones are all over the place with the baby on the way" Ah, yes, Shauna remembered now. Her mother was expecting Alex at the time.

"Give her a few minutes to calm down and we'll get you all back to the car" Granddad Buckle opened the door, before looking back over his shoulder towards George "And when Dee gets back behind the wheel, just be her husband and not her driving instructor" Granddad chuckled "I tried to teach her to drive when she was a teenager, remember, and that didn't go well either. She's sweet and sour, that one"

Meanwhile, back in the present, back in another captive car capsule of conversation!

Lewis had suddenly become surprisingly supportive over the loss of the baby. Yes, it was his baby too but he was now focussing on Shauna's grief. Shauna suspected his mother had had a gentle but timely word with her son.

Lewis knew about the pain of losing a baby and potentially being a childless couple. His parents had struggled to conceive. His mother had a series of miscarriages and, tragically, their first born, a daughter named Caitlin, lost her life to cot death at three months old. Lewis knew his mother had never fully recovered from the horrific loss of the tiny, vulnerable bundle of joy Caitlin had been. As a small boy, Lewis could remember being taken to the cemetery by his mother to lay flowers on Caitlin's grave.

Exhausted with sadness, his parents had resigned themselves to being a childless couple. They decided to do something to make the lives of vulnerable or suffering children easier. They threw themselves into charity work and eventually found fostering a rewarding way to express their need to nurture.

Their first placement was a four-year-old Nigerian girl named Amadia. They were told her name meant 'lightening spirit' and it certainly suited her. Amadia's parents were still in Nigeria and, as is often the custom, she and her brothers and sisters had been sent to live with family in the United Kingdom to give them a 'better life'. Through a series of events, the

63

young family found themselves displaced. The agency told Bob and Carole that Amadia would shortly be placed with another branch of her family, ideally alongside some of her siblings, or members of the Nigerian community as they felt this was appropriate for her identity. Bob and Carole understood.

Several attempts were made in the first year to find a suitable permanent home for Amadia but nothing seemed to fit. In fact, the only fit all three of them could attest to was the one that already existed. Amadia was a spirited, energetic young lady. She was highly intelligent and did not take any prisoners! Bob absolutely delighted in being challenged by her razor sharp wit and no nonsense questioning.

Carole took a little more time to acclimatise. Partly because she didn't want to fall in love with the little girl too easily for fear she would be taken away from them soon and partly because Amadia was not an overtly affectionate child. Carole wanted a baby to hold, to hug, to squeeze. Amadia would not stand for too much affection. Bob seemed to be able to display his love and care with playful hair ruffling, high fives and general teasing. Bob became a child himself around Amadia and she loved it. She loved being the superior one as Bob clowned around and Amadia put him in his place. Carole watched them. No, she wasn't jealous. She loved the effect Amadia had on Bob. She loved watching them play. But she really wanted a baby who adored her and needed her.

Then along came Lewis. Totally unexpected. They'd taken their eye off the ball. Bob's balls, as he often joked. They'd stopped trying for a baby. Carole didn't even realise she was expecting Lewis until she was five months pregnant. Yes, people said she *must* have known. There must have been signs. She'd been pregnant before. Carole explained that her body had never conformed to the normal biological clock most women's bodies ticked to. She thought she would never carry a child again. She was not looking for signs and symptoms. She was busy with her family and her charity work. A visit to the doctor for what Carole thought was persistent and embarrassing indigestion evolved into an antenatal visit. She returned home with tears of joy and some very unexpected good news for Bob and the ever-inquisitive Amadia.

Of course, as soon as she realised she was expecting again, Carole went into immediate worry mode. Fortunately she didn't have to wait too long. Lewis was born at 38 weeks and Carole finally had her baby to love and cherish. She had the baby who would need, love and adore her.

Amadia was wonderful with Lewis. She was six years old when he was born. He was her baby brother and, in her usual matter-of-fact way, she took it all in her stride. She was quite bossy with Bob and Carole and would insist they dealt with his every need immediately.

The two grew up as brother and sister. Amadia released all her hidden affection on baby Lewis. He was treated to all the hugs and kisses Bob and Carole were rationed with.

Life seemed idyllic until, aged ten, Amadia was taken from Bob and Carole and, even worse, from Lewis. Amadia was placed with a Nigerian family member living a five-hour drive away. Yes, they could visit and yes, Amadia could come and stay in school holidays if she wished but it wasn't the same. As far as they were concerned, Amadia *was their family* and they were distraught.

Carole had always dreaded this happening and had steeled herself against it in the early years. But Amadia had been in their family nest for six years now. Carole had begun to relax. She had assumed Amadia would only leave their house as a grown woman making her own way into the adult world. Not this way. Ripped from them as she approached the often-traumatic teenage years.

Little did they know, as they parted, that Amadia would be back in their family unit within the year. Two more separations would follow, for insignificant periods of time, but all very significant in the development of this displaced young lady. Fortunately her strong and stoic nature meant she appeared to cope with the disruption. Bob and Carole weren't so sure but it was always difficult to gauge Amadia's true feelings.

As a toddler, Lewis struggled to understand why his big sister was taken from him. He was heartbroken when she first left. Carole was angry about the entire situation. It was not only affecting Amadia, it was affecting the whole family, including her precious baby Lewis. Her excessive mothering of him ramped up several degrees during this time. Lewis picked up on his mother's anxiety and unwittingly fed it by becoming clingy and even more dependant on her.

As a grown man, Lewis was still very close to his

mother and, through her, had understood the heart wrenching pain of losing a child. As he drove, he let his thoughts float back to conversations he'd had with Carole, the visits to Caitlin's grave, the need for time and patience and understanding.

He wanted to make things better for Shauna. He knew he wasn't always the most sympathetic husband but, in this situation, he felt he had the insight and empathy to be strong for her and help her through. By the same token, he was a rather selfish, self-indulgent man and he wanted to do all of this *his* way, to suit *him*.

"Well, how about going somewhere fairly local if you don't want to be away from work for too long"?

Even though Lewis had suggested they get-away for a break, he seemed reluctant to go too far afield. Shauna was hoping for somewhere warm and sunny but, as usual, she found herself lowering her own expectations and settling for those of her husband.

"What about The Swan Hotel in Weston Undercroft? " Shauna tentatively suggested "That's a nice little country hideaway"

"Errrrrr" Lewis seemed to be playing for time "Well, we could but we haven't been there since Christmas two years ago and we don't know what it's like these days. It may have changed. It may be dreadful now"

Why is he trying to put me off, thought Shauna? You could say that about any venue you haven't visited to for several years. It's like saying "I'm not going on holiday to France because I went there on a school

67

trip ten years ago and I'm worried it's deteriorated".

"We don't know that though, do we? And your satnav history shows you went there last month"

"What? Are you spying on me? Lewis was not known for controlling his anger and it was beginning to surface. Shauna wondered if it was guilt but as he continued and gathered his thoughts, his voice became smooth and almost patronising,

"Oh well, of course, I went there for a business meeting"

Shauna sat in silence, digging her nails into her palm as some sort of perverted comfort mechanism, a pain she could control. She didn't want to be suspicious but she was.

"Hey, do you remember when people used to deface the village sign for Weston Undercroft and change it to Vest and Underpants?" Lewis managed a weak laugh in his attempt to throw Shauna off the scent "In fact, I think my mate ...."

Shauna tuned Lewis out and tuned up her personal radiohead. The angel inside was telling her that Lewis was probably telling the truth. He did work hard and he was always doing extra work to make a comfortable life for them. However, the devil inside was screaming "Wake up you stupid girl. He's lying. Ask him more. Don't let him get away with that pathetic, stereotypical excuse". But Shauna knew she'd already pushed Lewis to her own comfort level. She knew further questioning at this time would result in him shouting and screaming at her. She didn't want to arrive at Lewis's works 'do' with red, puffy eyes and she didn't want Lewis to throw himself into an angry drinking bout".

(19) Email – Beth to Shauna

Hola Shauna! See how good my Spanish is?!

I'm trying really hard to learn the local language, as you know. One of the problems I have is that my colleagues and a large percentage of our customers want to improve their (already very good) English. I start off talking Spanish, peppered with English words for the things I don't know in the local tongue, which results in a verbal soup of different tenses and dialects. It's hilarious and very confusing for my workmates who are still endlessly kind to me. They wait patiently for me to stumble my way through a sentence before replying in perfect English.

Anyway, I must keep trying. I mustn't be lazy. If we live in Spain then the least we can do, in exchange for the almost constant sunshine, is to make an effort to speak their language.

We've had a few disasters with ordering food here though. We felt we should embrace the tapas lifestyle. When you look at the menu, it's difficult to determine the size of the portion. For our first attempt, we guessed our way around the menu, using the prices as an indication as to the imagined size. Our strategy was to order six little taster things and then order more if we fancied it……….

After the fourth dish of six arrived, we realised our eyes were bigger than our British bellies. The establishment we'd chosen to eat in obviously catered for those on a budget. The portions were huge. I thought tapas was traditionally dainty little mouthfuls to accompany your refreshment of choice. Oh no, not at this place. Dish five came out and we were both sweating like the proverbial pig, which we also seemed to have eaten most of!

We tried to remember what the sixth and final plate would contain but it was all Spanish to us. Based on the fact that three of the dishes so far seemed to contain pork, we also realised our Spanish was even worse than we thought it was. I'm not vegetarian, as you know, but the excessive consumption of pork on this particular evening has turned my stomach for any more in the foreseeable future.

Working for CostaCoches continues to be fun and random in equal measure.

The majority of our car rental business is walk-in or pre-booked holidaymakers. However, we do provide deliveries to car servicing and repair centres. As you know, I left a print of my nose on the shiny glass of a car showroom during one such delivery. Yesterday morning, we were delivering a car to a school in a nearby village. I was driving the shiny rental car and the ever-gorgeous Juan was in the 'runner' car.

I'm learning my way around the area but I still get lost in the intricate urbanisations. It doesn't help that Juan drives so erratically. I won't make any sweeping statements about the local drivers but I will just say I've become accustomed to people driving towards me in the middle of the road, pulling out right in front of me only to drive at five miles per hour thereafter, parking on roundabouts or just stopping dead without pulling over to drop someone off, completely blocking the road. Instead of the passenger leaping out and moving out of the way so the flow of traffic can continue, they will sit and chat to the driver for a bit, maybe have a little kiss and just generally pass away the time they could have been passing earlier. Eventually and very slowly they will get out of the car without a backward glance or thank you to the motorists waiting patiently behind.

Anyway, back to my story……. Juan was hurtling along the little lanes. I lost sight of him a few times and when I caught up with him, he proceeded to drive like a little old lady, barely picking up enough speed to prevent the car from stalling all together. Sometimes Juan would be in the middle of the road, sometimes he'd be breaking hard and then he'd race off again. Very stressful for me trying to follow behind. I never knew if I was going to lose him or rear end him!!!!! No rude remarks from you here, young lady!

The other thing that was making me uncomfortable was my bladder. I'd been drinking copious amounts of coffee from the vending machine in the rental office. It's horrible but it's free and it fills a hole, as they say.

Now, as you know, I'm a lady. No, don't laugh! Yes, I'm a lady and I would normally wait until I'm surrounded by perfectly plumbed porcelain before carrying out certain bodily functions. However, on this occasion, I was so desperate I could actually feel things popping and banging inside me. It didn't feel good and I was worried about causing long-term damage.

There was nothing for it. I would have to bob down

behind a bush somewhere in this beautiful Spanish scenery. Unfortunately, this would mean lowering myself (in more ways than one!) in front of the beautiful Juan. My feminine persona was about to be shattered. But so was my bladder.

Juan was now on one of his racing spurts. Oooh, that's an unfortunate description as I was desperate for a spurt myself!! I put my foot down and eventually rounded a corner where I saw the rear tailgate of his car bouncing along at speed. Phew. Keep up, keep up. I started flashing my lights to draw attention to myself. I was hoping he'd understand. You don't need languages for this, surely.

Juan continued to race along the road. My light flashing became frantic. Surely he must have seen me by now? More frustrated flashing. Flash, flash, FLASH, FLASH, FLASH, FFFFFFFFFFFFLLLLLLLAAAAAASSSSHHHHHHH!!!

Juan eventually slowed down. I was close behind him now and I could see his beautiful smiling brown eyes in his rear view mirror. He made eye contact with me, waved his hand in a friendly way and....... Noooooooooo!!! He put his foot down and raced off again.

Surely my bladder was going to explode all over the upholstery now?

Fortunately, several minutes later, the school loomed into sight. I had managed to arrive at the delivery address with a dry seat. Blushes spared.

I walked as fast as I could towards Juan, trying to

73

keep my legs together. Not easy. I don't know why but even my voice had changed. The effort of concentrating on containing my bladder was restricting the flow of blood to my vocal chords. With gritted teeth, I explained my predicament to Juan and asked him to enquire of the lovely teachers standing outside in the school playground where I may find a banos = bathroom. There's a Spanish lesson for you!

Juan seemed in no immediate hurry. I watched with agony as he wandered over to the prettiest young female – of course! I watched with horror as he seemed to be engaging in an epic flirting session. Both of them laughed and chatted with ease, apparently unaware of the bloated bag of urine buckling at the knees nearby.

"Juan"? My voice came out as a cry.

Finally, he seemed to focus on my desperation. A series of conversations followed between the teachers and eventually a gentleman approached me with a large bunch of keys in his hands. It appeared the school was closed today but the teachers were off somewhere and needed a hire car.

The gentleman walked me to a door and inserted a key in the lock. I could already feel my internal muscles relax. Hmmmmm, the key didn't appear to be the one. The gentleman examined it in some detail as if this was going to fix the problem. I could see several other keys on the key ring. My fingers were itching to wrench it from his hands and try them all. I was now gritting my teeth so hard, a headache was forming in my temples. Was I about to wet myself in a school playground. Something I hadn't done since I was five.

Eventually, after two more failed attempts, the door was thrown open to reveal a small internal corridor with the Holy Grail at the end of it. No time for manners, discretion, privacy or dignity. I ran with my knees together, almost bent double, frantically tugging at my knickers and finally threw myself on the beautiful piece of pottery.

So great was my need, I hadn't bothered to close the door. At this point, I really didn't care. It was a battle between Mother Nature and self-respect and Mother Nature was winning. I suppose I should have been embarrassed but I was so relieved (excuse the pun) I didn't have the energy to feel any shame at all. However, as I looked up to see the stunned face of the very kind gentleman, still standing in the doorway with the keys in his hand, I could tell *he* was very embarrassed. The steam emitting from me and the Niagra Falls sound effects must have finished off his day. He walked away, probably in disgust, and fortunately I never saw him again. Unfortunately, as he walked away from the doorway he had previously been blocking with his frame, he allowed the gathered teachers in the playground a full view of me on the loo. Why did I feel the need to give a little wave?

(20) George

Dee wasn't my first girlfriend but she was the first (and last) one I *loved*. I love her more every day to the point I just don't think I could love her any more than I do. Yes, I know that sounds soppy for a bloke but Dee is very special.

My first girlfriend? Wow, what a naughty girl she was. My mother and father worked several jobs in the local area. One of these was a joint working venture within a large house owned by an affluent family with three well-educated daughters. My father was a general gardener and handyman and my mother cleaned the home twice a week. It all sounds like a cliché, doesn't it? Something from a Bronte novel or a glossy weekly TV drama. Well it get's worse!

Occasionally I would find myself at the big house, killing time whilst I waited for my parents to finish. I enjoyed helping my dad in the garden but I particularly enjoyed the fettling and mending tasks he would undertake around the house.

On the occasions where my father was working elsewhere, I would sit inside the house, idly waiting for my mother, pretending to do my homework. Aged fifteen, this was a fairly boring venue. I wasn't a good son in those days. I could have helped my mother but, instead, I would constantly ask her how much longer she was going to be. I sighed so hard I almost fainted.

However, things brightened up during the school holidays. The three sisters would return home from boarding school. Two of them would immediately disappear to the riding stables to spend the majority of the holidays on horseback. When not riding their steeds, they would be reading horsey books or cutting and sticking horsey pictures and posters on their bedroom walls.

Lucy, however, was a different story. Yes, I think there was a pony with her name on it somewhere but she showed very little interest in him. Oh no, she preferred her stud to possess two legs rather than four. She preferred a "real man" as she flatteringly described the skinny, spotty me on whom she could practise the human biology she had been studying at school.
Yes, I know this is controversial. We were both fifteen and, as the father of two daughters, I hope and pray Shauna and Ruby were a little more patient with their ardour but that's something I can't bear to think about.

Lucy tried to romanticise our relationship. She was very bossy and I was a lamb to the slaughter. I would say or do anything she asked me to. She once told me we were living out the story of Lady Chatterley's Lover. Unfortunately, the itchy and scratchy carpet tiles on the conservatory floor were no substitute for the lowly but romantic garden shed favoured by Mellors and Lady C.

Two things there. The carpet burns were acquired without me noticing, such was the thrill and excitement of the moment. It was only later I would feel the incessant burning on my knees and would have to fabricate stories of hard tackles in football. Yes, I bet you're thinking it was a different type of hard tackle that generated the red scabs on my elbows and shoulder blades. I'm being very descriptive here, I know, but that probably explains how demonstrative and, quite frankly, rough, Lucy was.

The other problem with a conservatory, of course, is that fact that a large percentage of it is....... glass. I really don't know who I would have chosen to discover us if I'd had that luxury. Lucy's mother was a very polite and well-mannered lady. I know she had three daughters but it would be hard to imagine her ever taking part in anything as basic as sexual intercourse. Lucy's father? I don't know. I'd never met him and I really didn't want to be introduced with my pants down, bunched around my ankles. Lucy's sisters? Well, I suppose that would have been the better of all evils. You would hope they would protect their sibling from the wrath of the parents. Yes, I suppose I would have chosen one or even both of them. But, no, it was *my* mother who found us. Oh the shame. She didn't say a word. The look on her face as she turned and left the room said it all. I've often used that look on my three. On Ruby more than Alex and Shauna, it has to be said. But sometimes silence really is golden.

My mother never referred to what she had seen. Her silence was almost loud, if that's possible. I really wished she would say something to break the tension. As the days went by, we slipped into uneasy conversation and eventually things returned to normal. I was never taken to the house again to wait for my mother to finish. Sadly, I was never taken to work there with my father either. Maybe that's why I went into engineering. I needed to complete the practical education my father had been passing down to me. Lucy and I had taught each other a different kind of lesson. I suppose you could call it human engineering! I really hope she passed her biology exam!

(21) Shauna

Nana Buckle had made some of her coconut tarts. Shauna's favourites. Shauna was usually quite careful about what and how much she ate but she could easily polish off a whole tin of Nana Buckles home-made coconut tarts in one sitting.

Nana didn't make them often enough. When Shauna asked, she would say they were too much trouble to make these days but Nana had made a special effort for Shauna this morning. The tarts were misshapen, the pastry was thick and the coconut mix was probably a little bit too dry and would often get stuck in the roof of her mouth, rendering speech and even breathing difficult but Shauna loved them.

The taste of the salty tears running down Shauna's cheeks mixed with the heavenly sweet coconut and pastry reminders of her childhood. Light and shade, she thought.

"Darling, I wish I could make it better for you" Nana buckle put another cup of tea down in front of Shauna. "Time heals. Things obviously weren't meant to be this time. It will happen for you one day, when it's right" From anyone else, this would have sounded boring and patronising. Shauna had heard it so many times. But from Nana Buckle it was what she needed to hear. "You have a baby in the plan but not in the pram"

Nana Buckle, as ever, seemed to see the real picture. Was she telling Shauna that one day she would become a mother, maybe in another life?

Nana Buckle had certainly lived a life. She was what you'd call a character. Her daughter, Dee, Shauna's mother, was one of four children born to Nana Buckle.

Dee would often recount stories of her childhood to Shauna, Ruby and Alex. She would sometimes turn the more appropriate ones into bedtime stories. The children thought their mother was a great storyteller. Little did they know, many of the adventures were based on some of the amazing or magical things that happened when Nana Buckle was your mother.

Dee told a story about the time Nana Buckle had taken her young family away in their battered campervan. Grandad Buckle was alive in those days but he couldn't take time away from work. Nana was a strong, independent lady and thought nothing of bundling the children into the van and taking off for an adventure.

Unfortunately, funds were tight. On one occasion, the van broke down. The children didn't realise at first. They assumed they hadn't moved on because Nana loved the friendly campsite so much.

Dee told the story of her mother setting up their camping table at the side of the road. She laid out her precious books on a tablecloth. Nana Buckle was an avid reader. A real bookworm. She would read anything and pass it on to another keen reader. She would always endeavour to inspire the pleasure of reading in others. There were some books, though, that Nana Buckle never passed on. Her favourites. Some classics. Some that had inspired her or touched her heart.

Dee saw her mother had placed those books, along with the remainder of their collected reading matter, on the tablecloth with a hand written sign above advertising them for sale. As often happened wherever she went, Nana Buckle became a well-known figure and the campsite was no exception. The other campers marvelled at her strength and resourcefulness. They were awed by how happy and carefree the children were and how their mother would play with them rather than fussing and cleaning the campervan like so many of the other mothers.

The books sold. Did the buyers really want them? Would they ever read them? Maybe not, but they knew they were helping this one-of-a-kind, special lady return safely home with her four lucky offspring. They even turned a blind eye to the fact that some of the books were marked "Property of Chaucer Primary School"

"Your mum and dad tell me Alex has a girlfriend" Nana Buckle licked the end of her finger and dabbed at a crumb on the table. The crumb attached itself to the end of her finger and Nan popped it into her mouth as she winked cheekily at Shauna. "Apparently they saw him with a young lady with lovely long red hair" Nan toyed with another crumb on the table. Was she waiting for Shauna to say something? "Do you know, I always thought Alex would be the sort of boy who preferred other boys but maybe I'm wrong".

Nana Buckle was known for being outspoken at times. She was kind hearted and open minded but had an increasing tendency to speak her mind. Shauna held her breath waiting for a potential remark about her brother Alex but it didn't come. Nana changed the subject and, instead, enquired about Beth. Shauna happily updated Nana with a potted history of Beth's time in Spain so far.

Beth was very much part of the family and had always been a frequent visitor and consumer of Nana's coconut tarts. Although Shauna loved Beth to bits, she was often aggrieved at the quantity of coconut tarts Beth could put away.

Nana was very generous with her time and possessions. As youngsters, Dee and her siblings were always encouraged to have friends round to play and often stay. Beth's mother, Linda, had stayed with the family for an entire summer during a traumatic time in her parent's marriage.

Linda was not the only guest to have benefited from Nana's hospitality. Nana had a tendency to take in waifs and strays. The children were accustomed to returning from school to find an extra mouth sitting at the kitchen table or to find a stranger using all the hot water whilst enjoying a steaming hot bath. The children were brought up to be tolerant and were taught to share.

This was all well and good until, on one occasion, Nana took in a local tramp and his Jack Russell. Nana told the children it was only for one night until the gentleman was able to source alternative accommodation the following day. Hmmmm, the gentleman, however, seemed to know on which side his bread was buttered. He made himself more than comfortable in the house and seemed to be showing little sign of moving on after a week.

Dee was more inconvenienced than most, however, as it was her bed the gentleman had been given to sleep in, forcing her to sleep on a camping mattress on the floor of her little brother's bedroom. Her toddler brother loved having his big sister in the room to ward off any monsters that crept about in the night. However, for Dee, the monster was now in *her* bedroom and she wanted it back. What would her friends at school say if they knew? Not cool. An old tramp in your bedroom. Linda knew, of course, but knowing what Dee's mother was like she took it all in her stride, secretly wishing she had a slightly eccentric mother and a house full of strange and interesting people.

This particular gentleman was finally asked to politely leave when, after a night of drinking from a brown paper bag, he wet the bed. Dee's bed!! Dee was horrified and begged her mother not to let anyone else sleep in her bed again.

The bedwetting gentleman moved on, grateful for the sanctuary he had been afforded but obviously aware he had outstayed his welcome. He picked some daffodils from Nana Buckle's front garden and presented them back to her as a parting gift. Dee did not miss him but she missed his comical Jack Russell. She hoped JR (as she had named him) would be OK and she hoped his master would not get them into too much trouble in the future. As it was, they would often encounter the pair in town. When he was sober, the gentleman would be very quiet and unobtrusive. On brown paper bag occasions, he would be loud and gregarious with his greetings.

Years later, when Dee was on a first date with a young man she was trying very hard to impress, they passed JR and his owner sheltering in a shop doorway. "Good evening DeeDee, most lovely to see you" he beamed and bowed "And I hope the young gentleman is going to treat you to a good evening" He winked, wobbled and broke wind. Treating them both to a slightly toothless grin (he'd lost some teeth since Dee last saw him) he picked up the ageing JR and held up one of his front paws. "JR wants to say hello too" he said, waggling the dogs paw up and down in a waving motion. Dee couldn't resist the tatty old Jack Russell. She knew she was potentially giving the tramp the means to top up his liver destruction when she gave him £5 to buy food for the dog but what could she do?

Her date stood silently throughout the entire performance. Inadvertently, he'd failed the test. If he couldn't think of anything to do or say in a situation like this, he wasn't the man for her!

(22) George

Shauna went to visit 'Nana Buckle' today. Dee's mother can be a bit frightening for some but she's always had a soft spot for Shauna and I'm really grateful to her for that.

Many a visitor to Nana Buckle has come away with unsolicited advice about losing weight, polishing their shoes, improving their manners and even changing their partners. Fortunately, Nana Buckle took to me from the start. I think it's because we share the same sense of humour and I used that to fight my way through her initial scrutiny.

Dee tells me that her mother had frightened off several suitors before me. Dee's siblings had similar experiences with their love matches. I can't speak for the durability of their relationships but Dee and I have had a good strong marriage overall. Yes, there have been a few bumps in the road along the way and we've had to pull over into a matrimonial service station or two to look at the map and get ourselves heading in the right direction (ooooh, getting deep here) but, on the whole, Nana Buckle gave her seal of approval to a good match.

By the way, you've probably noticed I refer to my mother-in-law as Nana Buckle. Yes, she has a Christian name but as soon as Shauna was born, making Dee's mother a Grandmother, I have always referred to her in this way. Initially it made it less confusing for the children but, later in life, created questions. How come she is our Nana Buckle? She can't be *your* nana too! I have to say, that was one of the easier kids questions to answer.

The 'where did I come from' question is inevitable from most children at some point. Shauna and Ruby both came to me for the source of that one. Dee's question master was Alex. Of course, Dee and I put our heads together before and after to make sure we'd given the correct information in a palatable fashion. We hoped we'd been as relaxed and open in our teachings to ensure our children did not go through life horrified by the prospect of finding love, making love and maybe making a baby.

Shauna had obviously been telling Nana Buckle about the loss of her baby. Knowing Nana B, she would have guessed Shauna was pregnant long before anyone else. She may be forgetting the odd thing or two but her sixth sense is certainly still in tact. Shauna would have been comforted by the fact that she wouldn't have to say too much to her Nana. Her thoughts and feelings would be understood.

Nana would probably have made some of her coconut tarts. A rare treat these days. I'm not taking anything away from Mr Kipling who knocks up a great batch of cakes for every occasion. All I'm saying is that, if Nana Buckle put six coconut tarts in a cardboard box they would fly off every supermarket shelf faster than boxes stuffed with ten pound notes. Well, I'm biased, aren't I? The tarts are a bit rustic in appearance and texture but it's the taste of nostalgia that gets me every time.

Nana is still quite old fashioned with her taste in food. Recently, one of Shauna's cousins had taken a new boyfriend round to meet Nana and was probably hoping the smell of baking coconut was in the air! Anyway, apparently Nana started telling them about a lunch date she'd had recently with a local gentleman who is showing quite a bit of interest in her. He'll have to be a strong and sturdy chap because she'll certainly be putting him through his paces and if he's found wanting, she will let him know in no uncertain terms.

For the moment, the local gentleman seems to be surviving and he'd taken Nana to a popular Italian café, which offered a filling lunch menu. Nana was recounting their choices "There was a little bowl of olives to start with. They look like grapes, don't they, but they taste like soap. And then we had fuckyouare bread, followed by….."

Shauna's cousin enquired about the bread again.

"Fuckyouare bread. You know, flat……"

Shauna's cousin tried to put Nana straight but was struggling to speak for laughing. Eventually her new boyfriend stepped in with a helpful suggestion of "Focaccia" bread?

To cap off the visit, Nana Buckle explained to the visiting pair that she had been struggling with stubborn ear-wax recently. New boyfriend halted the direction of the marzipan fancy he was moving towards his mouth and placed it back on the plate. Yes, Nana was saying, she was trying some ear drops which dissolved the wax but, apparently, it was a very noisy process as you could actually hear it breaking up the hard wax within your ear canal. At this point,

Shauna's cousin could not even have managed one of Nana's coconut tarts, even if she'd made a fresh batch and placed it on the table in front of her, still warm and wafting delicious sweet scents. All that talk of waxy build-up had made her feel more than a little bit queasy.

Apparently, Nana completed the hilarity of the visit with one final remark "Well, I won't keep you two any longer. You've probably got things to do. And anyway, the sound of this popping and crackling must be driving you mad"

Cousin and boyfriend looked at each other, confused. They looked back to Nana and found her pointing towards her ear. Cousin opened her mouth to explain that only Nana would be able to hear the crackling as it was in her ear canal but she gave up. As ever, Nana was a mixture of switched on and switched off.

Nana stood up to see them to the door. As she walked across the room, she let out a couple of small farts. Parp, parp, parp as she moved across the room. This was not uncommon. After the gunfire of wind effect, Nana would speed up and trot towards her destination, as if running away from her own bottom.

New boyfriend folded up with laughter. He could contain his manners no longer. This had been an excellent treat for him. He loved Nana Buckle. He would have loved her even more if she'd presented him with a plate of her coconut tarts but that was a delight he would have to wait for.

Luckily the treat was already allocated to him. Nana gave Shauna's cousin a wink at the door "He can come again" she said, nodding towards new boyfriend before turning to the young man and planting a big kiss on his cheek, inadvertently branding him with her shade of bright red (and almost indelible as he found out when he tried to wash his face later) lipstick.

(23) Shauna

When Shauna arrived at the doctor's surgery and presented herself at the desk, she was advised that the doctor was running late. About twenty minutes. Maybe thirty. Unlike the stereotype of stern and impenetrable harridans, the receptionists at Shauna's surgery were generally very amenable. Shauna didn't mean to add to the pressure the staff were obviously already being put under but she couldn't stop herself letting out a small groan. She had gone to a great deal of trouble to finish work early in order to make the late afternoon appointment. Shauna was a hard worker but tended to take her foot off the accelerator towards the end of the day. Today, however, knowing she was required to finish early, she put her foot down and almost broke her own land speed record for administration duties in order to ensure she was able to get away an hour early. That vital hour would allow time to start the car (not always guaranteed) and to find a parking space in the surgery car park (not always guaranteed either).

The surgery had stood on the same spot since the mid sixties and was therefore designed to accommodate a handful of vehicles which, in those days, would have predominantly been driven by the doctors themselves. Nowadays almost every patient over the age of seventeen seemed to arrive in his or her own car. Shauna suspected, it probably wouldn't be long before babies were monitored and observed by their mothers using overhead drones and placed in remote control buggies to make their own way to the weekly weigh-ins.

Shauna bent over the coffee table below the fish tank to select an easy-read magazine to flick through whilst she waited. Easy-read selected, Shauna raised her head to search for somewhere to place her bottom, knowing several sets of eyes were watching her and hoping she wouldn't try to sit next to them. Or even worse, try to talk to them!

As usual, the waiting patients had seated themselves with what seemed to be the regulation empty chair between each individual or group. No one, it seemed, ever filled up the entire row before moving on to fill up another one. No, everybody wanted his or her own personal space, sandwiched by an empty chair on either side. Each individual seemed to require a barrier between themselves and the bugs and germs their fellow man had checked in with.

Shauna pondered the idea of introducing airline style seating. On check-in, you would be given a row and seat number, window, middle or aisle. That's if you go for economy. First class would see you being ushered behind a curtain and served champagne. No, how would that work? We're all equal here. That's the one leveller. We share the common bond of seeking help with our health. Shauna dismissed the concept of allocated seating from her mind and instead turned her attention to finding somewhere to sit.

Being slightly short-sighted, Shauna squinted round the room but could see no isolated empty chairs. The only vacancies appeared to be between other groups, thereby meaning she would have to sit on the virtual fence between personal space phobics. Oh well, nothing to it. She only had a potential wait of thirty minutes. Not entirely a lifetime. She was a big girl. She could do it! Shauna reversed into an empty chair, repeating the usual "excuse me, sorry, excuse me, sorry" mantra of the British.

Shauna looked around, making eye contact with an occasional brave soul who was prepared to acknowledge their shared presence in this room full of woes and viruses. She was slightly saddened to see several tiny babies and, even worse, a young lady who appeared to be about five months pregnant. Shauna didn't want to feel ungracious. She wanted to be happy for them. She didn't want to feel resentment or jealousy. Her time would come. One day she would be the glowing mum-to-be, sitting proudly, feeling the flutters of her unborn baby as he or she somersaulted inside. She would want to laugh out loud and tell everyone waiting that her baby was busy today. Really moving around and kicking. I can't wait to meet the little one who is so active today. I can't wait to see their face.

Not today though. Shauna was empty. She looked away and let her gaze mist over as she turned to the window, tears stinging in her eyes. Just to make things that little bit more poignant, Shauna's allocated doctor was currently away on maternity leave. One of her last consultations, before taking her baby bump home to await the new arrival had been to confirm Shauna's pregnancy and to congratulate her on the good news. The lucky doctor would return to the practise as new mother. Would she be thinking of Shauna? Would she wonder how Shauna was coping with her pregnancy? Would she hurry back to check her patient records to see if Shauna had delivered a boy or a girl? Would she feel sad for Shauna when she discovered the baby was not destined to become a patient with a name and number on the surgery register.

Shauna mentally slapped herself in the face. Come on. Don't sit here dwelling or you'll end up welling. Was that a Nana Buckle expression? She looked down at the glossy magazine. On the glossy front cover a premier league footballer was featured, dressed head-to-toe in cream and white. His beautiful wife sat next to him, similarly dressed in creams and soft whites. On her lap sat a tiny baby, also, yes you've guessed it, dressed in ivory.

This was too much for Shauna. She angrily flicked thorough the magazine, generating startled looks from the waiting patients around her. On page thirty-five she found an innocent looking wordsearch. Before rooting through her bag for a pen, Shauna checked the subject matter of the wordsearch. Knowing her luck, this one would contain forty words relating to childbirth and motherhood. No, she was in luck. The hidden words were all flowers, flora and fauna. I can handle this, she thought, bending her head over the jumble of letters and carrying out an early scan for any words that might jump out before she started working her way down the official list.

Almost immediately she found the word 'bum' written backwards and horizontally. She'd never heard of the bum flower and, sure enough, it was not featured in the search list. 'Rose' was in there. Yes, list checked. All good, she was off to a good start. Shauna loved a good wordsearch. They were always so easy to pick up and put down. Sometimes a short break would result in Shauna returning to the search with fresh

93

eyes and successfully locating elusive words. Every now and again Shauna looked up to scan the waiting room. Some people seemed content to just sit and stare into space. Occasionally, Shauna felt eyes on her but, every time she looked up, the suspect's eyes would suddenly find something interesting to examine on the floor or the ceiling.

As she glanced over the wordsearch, Shauna unconsciously slipped her pen into her hair. Her eyes moved over the jumble of letters. Every now and then she would identify a run or a pattern showing promise. The letters would get off to a good start but ultimately fizzle out into an unofficial word or something that sounded good but wasn't correct. A potential GLADIOLI ran into GLADALLOVER. Nice, she thought, but not correct. What initially appeared to be CANDYTUFT was actually CANDYCRUSH. Isn't that another game altogether, she thought? Shauna straightened up. The word 'ivy' materialised from the page. She attempted to retrieve the pen to circle it before she forgot where it was. Unknowingly and distracted by the concentration required to locate a garden full of greenery, Shauna had been twisting her pen round and round in her hair. It was now entwined like the ivy she had found in the alphabet soup.

As she tugged at the pen, little strands of hair clung to the mechanism. And it hurt. Those fine strands of hair suddenly took on the consistency of knives digging into her scalp. Shauna began to panic. Would she ever be able to remove the pen? How had it become so tangled? The adrenalin started to flow. How long should she leave it before asking the receptionist for a pair of scissors? Thinking she may be called in to see the doctor at any minute, Shauna decided to go for bust and jerked repeatedly on the pen. It eventually gave up its hold on her hair but not before grabbing at several strands to retain within its clip mechanism. What sort of sick writing implement was this? Shauna studied the pen, tears of pain stinging her eyes and a fierce headache forming in the plucked roots. She scanned the room to see if anyone had noticed. Of course they had. Several pairs of eyes darted away quickly as she met them. Shauna set about removing the lengths of hair from the pen. There was enough to knit a jumper for a gerbil.

Back to the wordsearch. Shauna started to set herself targets. I need to find the word 'primrose' before my name is called. Word found. Not called. OK, how about 'chrysanthemum'. Big word but they're often easier to find. Shauna found herself becoming excited. The pressure was on. She wanted to be called in to see the doctor but now she had a goal. She searched frantically for the chrysanthemum. She moved her pen up and down, horizontally and vertically. Inadvertently she found 'daisy' and 'busy lizzy' but not the word she wanted. As excitement mounted, Shauna started to think she may need to go to the toilet. Was this real or was it built up tension? Did she really need to go?

"I have an appointment at 5pm" The voice of another patient checking in, only to be told to expect a twenty to thirty minute wait. To be honest, due to the cumulative delay, the receptionists should be advising of a potential wait of at least an hour. They could start serving evening meals and bring in some extra revenue for the surgery.

The patient was asked for his name.

"Sean Robinson"

Sean Robinson? The guy who'd called me at work to ask me out? Shauna tried to keep her head bowed whilst simultaneously turning to the right to afford herself a view of the man waiting at the desk. She must have resembled a caricature of an undercover spy. A comic exaggeration, like something from a Pink Panther movie. She might just as well have cut two round spy holes in the magazine and held it up to her face in order to fully observe Sean Robinson.

Well, he didn't look bad at all. Lewis was a big man. Tall and well built and, Shauna thought, a very good-looking man. Sean appeared to be shorter in height with a mop of dark hair and, oh look at that, a beautiful pert bottom. Shauna was not one of those women who was permanently on heat. She could happily go out for a night with the girls and spend the entire evening chatting to her friends without a glance towards the male population surrounding them. Some of her friends were constantly scanning the pub, bar, night club or kebab stand for talent. Whilst Shauna chatted to these friends, she would be aware of their eyes roving the room, looking over her shoulder to make eye contact and flirt with the person with a penis behind her. Shauna was a one-man-girl. When she had her man, she locked herself into him and was unaffected by the testosterone carriers around her.

Shauna often marvelled at Mother Nature. Why was it that one particular man could make one specific woman weak at the knees and almost sick with desire? Why can one human-being make another human-being blush and overheat so much they almost set off the fire alarm? Why does one person render another person speechless? They open their mouths and say the most ridiculous things in a squeaky dry voice. The same individual leaves another individual totally void of feeling. They are totally unaffected by the presence of someone else's idol and therefore able to carry on an articulate conversation without hesitation, without breaking into a sweat or without breaking nervous wind.

The fact that Shauna found Sean attractive was surprising to her but not an unpleasant feeling. She followed his route to the row of seats behind to the point her bone and muscle structure would not allow her head to turn any further. She returned to the wordsearch. Her eyes travelled over the garden of letters on the page but she was unable to unearth any more flowers. She was so aware of the man behind her. She wasn't sure exactly where he was seated but she felt as though she could feel him breathing down her neck. She could almost feel the tingle of his breath on her skin.

"Shauna Robinson"? The doctor stood at the entrance to the consulting room.

"Yes"

"Yes"

Shauna turned to see that Sean had also risen from his seat.

The doctor looked down at her notes "Sean Robinson"?

"Yes, that's me" Sean Robinson replied. Oh, how embarrassing. Shauna cringed. She had obviously misheard but, by doing so, had waved an enormous flag to identify herself and her location. Sean was not only gorgeous, he appeared to be gracious too. He turned towards Shauna and made a little bow. "You've obviously been waiting much longer than I have and I'd be happy to let you go before me if the doctor would allow us to swap"? He looked in the direction of the waiting doctor who shrugged as if to say why not.

Shauna mumbled something about being rather busy with a wordsearch and said she was happy to wait her turn. Was it just her imagination or was every single pair of eyes in the waiting room focussed on the impromptu stage play unfolding in front of them? "And actually my name is Shauna Robertson" Why did she feel the need to say this. She was making things worse. "Well, actually, I used to be Shauna Robinson but then I got married and……" Oh help "And I still think I'm Shauna Robinson sometimes but….."

"I'll catch you later maybe" Sean winked and made his way towards the consulting rooms, leaving Shauna alone and upright. "Sorry" she said to the room in general before sitting down again. Why was she apologising to them? What for?

Shauna was now full of nervous energy. She was more constricted than ever by her chair neighbours who had used the opportunity of finding a vacant seat between them during Shauna's display to mark their territory with bony protruding elbows. Shauna was forced to sit with her shoulders hunched forward in order to fit her arms into the limited space. This in turn was restricting her airway. Shauna felt dizzy and light-headed. Obviously nothing to do with her encounter with the gorgeous Sean!

There was no way she would be able to focus on the worsearch now. She fiddled with the buttons on her coat, twiddled her wedding ring and then began an on off on off routine with the rigid wooden bracelet on her wrist. It was a gift from Daisy at work who had kindly returned from a recent holiday with name bracelets for all the girls in their department. Shauna studied the bracelet as if she had never seen it before. Never had a wooden, cylindrical object been so fascinating.

For some strange reason, Shauna slipped the bracelet into her mouth. Sideways. She looked like the wide-mouth-frog. When they were younger, Shauna, Ruby and Alex would place a Ki-Kat in their mouths in the same fashion and compete to see who could keep it in that position for the longest. Who would snap it with their tongue and eat it? Who would spit it out? Who would sit there with the chocolate melting, dribbling spit mixed with the brown chocolate down their chins, onto their clothes and invariably onto their mothers cream sofa. Oh dear!

"Shauna Robertson"?

A different voice. A different doctor.

"Shauna Robertson"?

Shauna couldn't speak. She had risen to her feet but, as she'd opened her mouth to retrieve the bracelet, it had slipped further into her mouth and down towards the back of her throat. Oh God! Shauna was going to choke to death right here in front of the fish tank. The waiting room audience would have paid money to see this show. Shauna's heart started beating fast. Was anybody aware of her plight? Time seemed to stand still. Shauna reached into her mouth and tugged hard at the bracelet. Her gag reflect was normally good but this was extreme circumstances. She wretched and burped but fortunately managed to save the waiting room carpet from a coating of her afternoon tea and biscuit. Well, two biscuits! Almost on the brink of fainting, Shauna made her way towards the startled doctor who asked her if she was okay?

The truth was no, she was not okay but, true to form, Shauna put on a brave face and said yes, she was okay. She was about to ask this doctor, a lady she had never met before, what her chances were of conceiving again? Should she be trying for another baby? Why did she lose the last baby?
.....

Shauna walked towards her car, lost in thought. The locum doctor had been kind and sympathetic and, most importantly, honest. She herself had suffered two miscarriages before going on to carry her now two-year-old son full-term. She told Shauna that "fifteen to twenty percent of known pregnancies end in miscarriage" and that "about one in a hundred women in the UK experience recurrent miscarriages." Shauna had felt like reaching out and holding the doctors hand. She wanted to connect with her in some way but felt it would not be appropriate. Shauna's tactile and loving nature was a hindrance at times. She craved closeness and affection like a child on occasion, something that was belied by her mature and confident outward appearance.

…..

"Probably a good job we didn't swap appointments" Sean was leaning against Shauna's car. "You would have ended up with hay fever medication and I would have been given an ante-natal once over" How did he know which car she drove? Oh, of course, he had been watching her in the car park from his vantage point across the road. "How are things with you"?

Shauna couldn't stop herself. He was so gorgeous and so inviting. No, she didn't kiss him. She cried. The dam of sadness and tears broke and released its contents on the unsuspecting young man standing in front of her.

Thankfully he didn't say a word. He stood silently, watching the heart-breaking display of emotion from the girl he had once hoped to get to know over a drink in a pub. Maybe see a movie at the multiplex? Maybe see a live band. After their telephone conversation, he had never expected to be close to her. He hated to see her so distressed. He wanted to reach out and hold her but he didn't want to overstep the mark. Suddenly Shauna flung herself towards him, wracked with sobs, she rested her head on his shoulder and completely let go. Sean could feel his shoulder becoming wet from tears and….. oh dear, snot. Never mind, she obviously needed to do this.

Shauna was exhausted. She had been holding so much in for so long. She really needed to do this. After a while, her sobs abated and she became conscious of the scene they must be presenting. She was also aware that a large amount of bodily fluids had been smeared on Sean's jacket. How to get out of this one.

Was there a dignified way? Shauna slowly pulled away and watched, to her horror, as a trail of snot stretched and snapped between the end of her nose and the fabric on Sean's shoulder. Shauna stepped back, revealing her wet face and began frantically rummaging in her pockets for a tissue. Empty. Oh bugger! She wiped her nose on the sleeve of her coat like a toddler. She looked down at the shiny slug she had created. A constant stream of fluid was still escaping unabated from her orifices. Where was it all coming from? Did the human distress reflex perform like the windscreen washer system in a car? Was there a plastic container secreted about her person housing the liquid supply for her tear ducts and nasal passages? Sean began patting his pockets in order to locate something suitable to clear up the excess fluid. Empty too. Oh bugger!

He turned and walked away. Shauna believed he'd done so in horror and disgust. She saw him open the door of a car nearby and reach into the glove box. Sean returned with a cloth. In a former life, it had obviously been white in colour. It was now almost grey and peppered with black streaks. It must have wiped many a dusty windscreen but, at that point in time, it was the most luxurious item of fabric Shauna had ever seen. She heartily blew her nose into the grubby cloth. And again. And again. She dabbed at the tears running down her face. Any vestiges of make-up were now eliminated. Even the waterproof mascara she wore had found the challenge too much. Shauna sported the dreaded panda eyes any self-respecting woman fought hard to avoid.

"Oh God, I'm so sorry" Shauna sniffed hard, producing an awful snot inhalation sound effect. Sean, rather than being disgusted, seemed to find this quite endearing. He looked on, smiling sympathetically. "Everything's gone a bit wrong. I had a miscarriage and Lewis got really drunk the other night and called me a barren tart" Sean wouldn't know who Lewis was but Shauna didn't really think about that. He seemed like an intelligent man. He could work it out "I'm trying hard not to make him angry but he's so short tempered these days. He makes me feel it's all my fault. And I miss Beth. Yes, I can talk to Ruby but Beth is….."

All these names. Sean was trying hard to keep up but Shauna was becoming distraught and starting to become incoherent. Without thinking, Shauna launched herself on Sean's other shoulder and commenced further fluid out-pouring.

When Shauna had suitably recovered, Sean suggested coffee or a drink somewhere nearby. Shauna would love to have sat quietly with this gentle soul but she knew Lewis would be home waiting for her return. Yes, he would probably be on his dratted phone as usual, but he would still be making a note of the time and monitoring her absence from their home. She had already been missing for more time than was comfortable. He would never believe her truthful account of the extended delays and waiting time. Imagine if she had extended that time by having a clandestine drink with a good-looking stranger.

Leaving Sean coated in drying snot and saline, Shauna climbed into her car and puttered, spluttered and backfired out of the car park. She imagined the waiting room occupants watching from the window, on their feet applauding and calling for an encore!

(24) Email – Beth to Shauna

Shauna! Thanks for your email. Your trip to the doctors sounds informative, positive, emotional and hilarious. Not necessarily, but probably, in that order.

Fancy that guy, Sean Robinson, sharing the same doctors surgery as you. At least you had the chance to put a face to the voice on the end of the phone. It must have been a bit like Blind Date. Here's the one you turned down.

I almost got myself into a spot of bother at work yesterday. I was in the front rental office, working hard, as usual. Tee hee! Gary, our Branch Manager, came and stood next to me and started huffing and puffing. He's English. Well, Welsh actually. A mans man. A big rugby player. Yes, another British person living and working in Spain. How am I supposed to immerse myself in Spanish culture when so many of the people I interact with are British? Anyway, I could see he was working himself up a bit and it was most unnerving.

Eventually I realised his pent-up frustration was aimed at Juan who was innocently and beautifully cleaning one of the rental cars outside. Gary kept staring at him through the window. More huffing and puffing before he turned to me and said

"I need to have a word with Juan"

From Gary's tone, I was obviously expected to say something. Quick, think……. My mouth opened…….

"Oh"

"Yes, I've had a complaint from the Regional Manager" Gary continued "Someone was seen, erm, well, basically having-it-off in one of our cars during the open evening last week".

"Oh" Me speaking eloquently again, if you haven't guessed. And who says *having-it-off* these days? Think he was trying to be polite when talking to a female colleague but he didn't need to protect my ears. Anyway, I swallowed hard and asked Gary "How did you know"?

"Well, he stupidly hung his CostaCoches shirt up at the window to hide behind and the Regional Manager saw it".

What a snake. The Regional Manager saw it because he was with that flirty little tart from the local car dealership responsible for servicing and repairing our fleet. He was checking out her bodywork and revving up her engine in the car next to us.

I took a deep breath and said "It wasn't Juan. I can see you glaring at him but it wasn't him"

"Oh" Gary's turn to be creative with words now

"It wasn't Juan's shirt. It was mine"

"You were with Juan"?

"Oh God! No! With Steve. My boyfriend"

Steve had come down to the open evening, partly to see me because I was working late and partly to take advantage of the free wine and tapas. Probably the latter more, actually!!! Anyway, at the end of the night when the guests had left and we were surrounded by valeted vehicles we got a bit carried away in one of the small, affordable hatchbacks. You can guess the rest.

The Branch Manager laughed. So did the Regional Manager when I stood in front of him to apologise later that afternoon. He took it really well. Not sure if he was laughing at my attempts at Spanish or about the situation. Mind you, I'd also found *him* in a compromising position with Little Miss Flirty Pants but he was keeping quiet about that.

All-in-all it's been an eventful time here at CostaCoches. After my time at HenryHire in the UK, observing the ways management harnessed the opportunities available to them, I'm more than familiar with the quirks of mankind. It was a real eye opener.

I remember once, during my HenryHire days, we hired out a virtually brand new car to a family who came into the branch to collect the car. They seemed an average group with three slightly overactive but cute children. I remember they were particularly keen to ensure no additional costs would be incurred and charged to their card at the end of the hire. To be fair, that's always a concern when hiring a car and I'm just as bad when I do it myself.

At the end of their rental period, the family called to say they wouldn't be returning the car direct to the branch but that it was ready for collection in a nearby car park. I was working behind the desk that day when the delivery drivers returned with the vehicle.

They were shaking their heads as they entered the office and suggested I might like to have a look at the car. As I walked towards it, the car looked in good shape, rather like myself. Tee hee! Seriously though, Shauna, I used to look hot in that HenryHire uniform.

The inside of the car was a different story. It was totally chewed up. No more comparisons to me, please! The seats were ripped and bits of foam were bulging out everywhere. The gearstick was covered in teeth marks. The dashboard was scratched and clawed. Unbelievable. I know the children of the family were energetic and excitable but this was beyond acceptable.

I picked up the phone. When I announced who I was, the mother, who had answered the call, rapidly disappeared and handed the phone over to the father. In the background I could clearly hear the sound of what appeared to be an enormous hound barking and growling. The father feigned surprise when I told him about the upholstery damage. It was difficult to hear his excuses due to the background barks, which I guessed were from the dog and not the boisterous children. Can you believe the cheek of the man? He told me the car was in that condition when they picked it up.

I was expecting some sort of pleading and grovelling apology. An explanation as to why their family pet had obviously been allowed to make a meal of the inside of a 1.4 petrol driven four-door saloon. Fortunately we were backed by a very proficient legal team who provided us with the necessary tools to deal with the first stage of a grievance. I slipped into auto pilot mode and advised the customer that this case would be passed on to our insurance department for further action and advised him of his rights. Something like the traditional "I am arresting you for allowing your hungry four legged friend to consume the interior of ...."

More loud barking in the background, partly masked by the sound of marauding children. I continued....

"You do not have to say anything, but it may harm your defense if you do not mention, when questioned, something which you later rely on in court. Anything you do say may be given in evidence. Do you understand?"

"What the Hell?" Came his reply "What the fuck are you talking about. Who do you think you are"?

Oh dear. I think I went off script there. I'd been watching a great deal of TV crime dramas at that time and I obviously got carried away with the wording of the insurance claim notification.

"Erm, someone from our insurance department will be in touch with you soon" I mumbled as I cleared the line.

I was hoping I'd got away with it but when I looked up to see my colleagues gaping at me, eyebrows raised in askance, I realised they had heard every word. I'd turned into a frustrated Charge Sergeant and they seemed highly amused.

You would think I'd have learned. I did the same thing a month before when a rental customer clearly replaced the expensive stereo in his rented vehicle with a knackered, broken old thing from the beginning of time. He had the bare faced cheek to tell us the car was delivered with the stereo hanging out of the dashboard complete with wires dangling from the gaping sides like tangled electrical spaghetti.

That was then and this is now. I'm renting cars in Spain but the public continues to amuse and amaze me.

I have to confess to moments of homesickness here, Shauna. I miss the natural and easy conversations you have with someone you know and love. Someone who understands you and your past. I wish there was someone I could talk to honestly about how I feel about life. Don't get me wrong. I love it here. It's a great place to live and life is so relaxed but I don't feel that I fully belong here and I'm wondering if I ever will.

Sometimes I find the pace of life here frustrating. I'm accustomed to everything being open all the time in the UK. I'm used to ordering a parcel on-line and it being delivered to my door the next day. I'm used to buying everything in one big supermarket, rather than driving round to several smaller shops and taking an entire morning to do it.

As I read back what I've just written, it sounds really churlish, spoiled and materialistic. Yes, life here is simpler. It's not competitive and people here live to socialise, relax and spend time with their family. Yes, they work long hours but when they finish work, they chill out and spend time eating and drinking together.

Possessions are not prized as much as family. That's how it should be. I suppose I'm just jealous because my family is not here with me.

Think I need to count some blessings here. Two different worlds. Two different ways of doing things. And I'm lucky to be in a position to experience both.

It's like you always say. Life is not one hundred percent perfect. It's all about 'light and shade'.

Shauna, please come out and see me if you can. I'd love to see you again.

Hastas and Hugs, xxx

(25) Shauna

Shauna, once more, was allowed behind the wheel of Lewis's car. There was a typical reason for this though. It was the end of the evening. They were on their way home from an award ceremony. Lewis and his team had hit their sales targets and the company, as usual, provided plentiful food and alcohol to thank them all. Lewis had been 'working the room' or 'networking' as he called it. He saw himself as a witty, charming and approachable benefactor. Shauna wondered what his staff and contemporaries really thought of him but, whilst the complimentary drinks were flowing, to his face they seemed to approve of his style. She suspected, behind his back, the word 'wanker' was often used to describe their smarmy colleague. She had certainly privately used that term herself on more than one occasion!

As usual, before leaving home, Shauna and Lewis had discussed the drinking and driving plans. Lewis had offered to drive, albeit in a rather sulky tone. Shauna said yes, she would like to have a few drinks and relax. She hadn't had a drink since falling pregnant and sadly losing the baby. It would be nice to have a couple of glasses of something. However, as the evening progressed, from experience she knew it was necessary to monitor Lewis's alcohol intake. In fact, scrub that. She knew he would exceed the drink drive limit in the first fifteen minutes, therefore forcing Shauna to drive home as she was a slow drinker and would not have thrown herself at the complimentary bar with quite as much enthusiasm as her husband.

Lewis would never suggest a taxi. Despite his reasonable salary and the fact that his team had been awarded a healthy bonus, he would never consider spending a small amount of his income on the expenditure of a taxi. The only time he succumbed to this was when a group of friends would suggest sharing. On those occasions, Lewis would put on a jolly smile and pile into the taxi, knowing that the cost was going to be split and, if he planned it carefully, he could get away without paying his fair share. He would often choose these moments to pick an argument with the innocent taxi driver. Shauna would sit red faced in the back whilst Lewis slurred some sort of sarcastic taunt. If she dared to intervene, he would turn on her and embarrass their fellow passengers. Shauna learned it was better to sit silently and grit her teeth, often retreating to her radiohead.

Shauna was always nervous driving the car with Lewis as a passenger. He would frequently criticise her driving. Yes, this sort of thing was not unusual amongst couples. She had witnessed her parents bickering on family holidays. The disagreements over Dee's negotiation technique and map reading skills often provoked heated discussions. However, her father would eventually look good-humouredly in the rear view mirror to catch the eye of his children on the back seat. He would wink and by the 'crinkles' Shauna could see in the corner of his eyes, she knew he was being playful.

Shauna was aware that Lewis was scrutinising her handling of his precious car. Even worse, she noticed he was balling his fists and his head was beginning to nod slightly in the way she knew meant he was brewing up for some kind of angry onslaught. History had told her to remain quiet and to avoid any form of confrontation. It was always a balancing act. Lewis could go either way after one of these excessive drinking binges.

"I see you were getting on well with Stuart" came his sneering opening provocation.

Oh God, here we go.

"No more than anyone else" Oh no, Shauna regretted that response immediately but it was out.

"Ah, so who else were you flirting with then?" He'd got what he wanted. The start of an argument. He must be delighted.

"I was mixing with your colleagues to help you, darling" She hated having to use an endearment but hopefully it would soothe him.

"How the fuck is you flashing your tits at my colleagues supposed to help me?" Lewis was almost screaming. His normally deep, manly voice was now unflatteringly hysterical.

Any self-respecting woman would stand up for herself here. Not Shauna. Why? She was scared, that's why. She knew she had to keep him calm. Why was she with him? Why did she marry a man like this? What would her father say if he knew Lewis was talking to her this way? Her father would never talk to her mother like this. Shauna knew if she confronted Lewis about this conversation in the morning he would deny it had happened. If she pushed it to the point he had to begrudgingly accept the truth, he would deliver his classic line "I was drunk. You know I didn't mean it".

Not good enough Lewis. He was never like this at the start of their relationship. He was easy going, relaxed even good fun after a few drinks. A *few* drinks. Was that it? True, his alcohol intake was higher these days and it seemed increasingly fuelled by anger. Lewis would always order his own drink first. Strategy. He would stand at the bar and throw back his first drink whilst the barman was pouring Shauna's. As soon as hers was placed on the bar in front of her, Lewis would be ordering his second. Shauna used to joke and ask if it was a race. Not now. She would occasionally give Lewis's second drink 'a look' as it was placed on the bar in front of him but this would inevitably make him angry and an evening could easily be destroyed before it had even started.

Shauna wished she could share hilarious stories with Beth about amusing car journeys. She really missed Beth at times like this and turned to her own headspace for comfort. In this alternative world, Shauna imagined Beth was watching her live on some kind of screen, remotely observing her dramas. Shauna felt comforted by the fact (imaginary of course) that Beth was watching over her and witnessing the events in her life. It made her feel safe and gave her strength when she needed it.

Shauna thought back to the early years with Lewis, to happier times, to their honeymoon in Bali. An idyllic destination, paid for by his parents as their wedding gift. The trip included visits to some of the smaller Indonesian islands. Gili Trawangan, known as Gili T, became Shauna's favourite. The only form of transport on the island, other than your own two feet, was by horse and cart or push bike. No motorised vehicles, no noisy whining scooters. Their apartment accommodation was located only a few metres from the sandy beach, bordered by bars, their decks and floors dusted with sand blown from the beech.

Their apartment was located within a beautiful complex of similar apartments nestled around a central courtyard. When checking in, Shauna and Lewis were advised that the beautiful courtyard was used for yoga classes, art workshops and various other "weird hippy shit" as summarised by the cynical Lewis. Shauna momentarily found herself wishing she were here with someone else. Beth or Ruby perhaps. Someone who would love to take part in the Pilates, pottery and bead making. Glancing at Lewis, who was looking particularly gorgeous during his honeymoon, she acknowledged there were things Lewis could do for her that Beth or Ruby certainly couldn't or wouldn't. In fact, Lewis had been particularly attentive during their honeymoon. They were married now and both consenting adults but Lewis was behaving as if he was starring in his own personal porno movie. At times Shauna hardly recognised him and occasionally found herself feeling a little bit shocked and embarrassed by their exploits.

Their apartment was single storey, spacious and open plan. The only exception to the open plan living was the bathroom, for obvious reasons. However, even that still strived to aspire to the concept of 'open plan'. The bathroom was partly covered by a short canopy to shelter occupants from the regular afternoon rains. The shower area, however, was open to the elements. Shauna loved the feeling of standing under the cascade of hot water, looking up towards blue skies by day or stars by night. Something about this form of bathing, naked outdoors but hidden from view felt very liberating.

On more than one occasion, Shauna had been revelling in the feeling of showering al fresco when she became aware of a fellow guest in the apartment next door enjoying the same experience. It was surreal to be standing, totally naked, knowing the gentleman she shared a brief hello with when meeting in the courtyard, was now standing with his bits coated in shower gel only a few inches away. The same thoughts went through her head when sitting on the outdoor toilet. Hmmm, too much information? Shauna preferred not to imagine what that would look like!

Many happy memories were made during their time in Indonesia but more than most were made on Gili T. Shauna was in heaven here. It was so removed from the rat race. She would describe herself as a 'people person' but there was a side to her that craved privacy and anonymity. As newlyweds, Shauna and Lewis enjoyed the luxury of their surroundings and basked in each other's company.

One of Shauna's Bali memories was a funny one. Their first Indonesian hotel had been in the beach resort of Kuta. The newlyweds had chosen a delightful and rustic beachfront location. Feeling excited and slightly childlike on their arrival, Lewis and Shauna had been delighted to discover the huge wooden bed in the centre of the beautiful bedroom. Lewis had encouraged an impromptu game of kiss-chase, which resulted in Shauna dissolving into fits of shrieks and giggles as Lewis chased her round and round the large room.

The game sparked something evolutionary in Shauna. The fight, flight, fear and fiasco mechanism was thrilling. Shauna almost wet her pants with excitement. Lewis played the predator and, in Shauna's eyes, became sexy and scary at the same time. Her only escape route frequently involved a dart across the large wooden bed. Lewis would follow with a more heavy-footed gallop across the mattress. The couple found themselves recreating a kind of speeded-up farce from a 1970s comedy sketch show.

Shauna became breathless with laughter. The exertion of running around the room and jumping onto the bed was exhausting. Her adrenaline levels were high and her cheeks were flushed. Lewis revelled in the hunter-gatherer role and began to close in on her. This meant that, at times, they would both be running across the top of the big bed at the same time.

'Crack'

They both stopped in their tracks. Shauna's excited laughter faded as she carefully eased herself down to the floor. Lewis was already down on his hands and knees inspecting the bed.

The friendly and gentle hotel receptionist took in the information he was being given. Should he believe the teenage kiss-chase story from the exhausted, breathless and red faced newlyweds or should he assume, as most of us would, that they had been engaging in an enthusiastic and vigorous love-making session at the start of their honeymoon?

To an onlooker, the perception of the couple as a free spirited and rather rampant pair was no doubt enhanced by a subsequent event, which was also innocent but may have appeared otherwise.

When checking into their apartment on Gili T, Shauna and Lewis had received verbal instruction and guidance on a variety of things. The use of wi-fi, local bars, cafes, how to post a letter, something about yoga and Pilates classes and the best places to hire scuba equipment. As often happens, the couple nodded and smiled as the stream of information poured out, both hoping the other one was listening and, more importantly, remembering the imparted information.

Obviously not!

On returning to their apartment one evening, Shauna had carried out a quick stock-take of her clean underwear supply and discovered she was down to her last pair of clean pants. No problem, she would wash them in the sink and hang them out to dry in the warm evening air. In fact, why not wash a few bits and bobs to keep her going. And, whilst she was feeling generous with her laundry prowess, she would offer to wash some of Lewis's pants too. The one's she really liked. The tight little jersey trunk-style ones that enhanced his bottom and cupped his man package so well.

It had been a lovely evening. One of those effortless times when natural conversation flowed. No snagging arguments. No incendiary remarks thrown in to skew the happiness or incite an argument. Shauna had been giggly and Lewis was in a frame of mind to enjoy it. He had also been happy to revel in the fact that he was predominantly the source of the laughter. Puffing his chest out each time he made a remark that reduced Shauna to fits of laughter, he felt empowered and made a mental note to himself to make Shauna laugh more. It was such a lovely sound and very infectious. Even better when he was the one who was making her laugh.

So, back to the laundry. Shauna selected two pairs of her own knickers, her favourite bra and two pairs of the sexiest package hugging pants Lewis owned. After washing the items in the complimentary shower gel and making sure they were all thoroughly rinsed (Shauna didn't want to create a biological hazard in the gusset area during her honeymoon) she hung the underwear on the rail above the indoor/outdoor shower. Perfect, she thought, the gentle breeze and warm evening air would dry the dripping articles overnight, ready to be slipped on in the morning.

Shauna and Lewis were woken the following morning by the sound of several voices chatting nearby. Very nearby. As he was the man and therefore her protector, Shauna indicated with her eyes and subtle nod of her head, that Lewis should be the one to investigate the potential intruders.

Lewis wrapped the bed sheet around himself, leaving Shauna naked and vulnerable on the bed. Hmmm, what a gentleman, she thought sarcastically to herself. Does he realise what he's done? Not wishing to lay on the bed displaying all her bare flesh and female accessories, Shauna climbed out of bed and pulled on a bathrobe. Why didn't Lewis just do that, she mused? As she was now up and out of bed, Shauna decided to follow Lewis to the door.

Together, the newlyweds discovered the source of the multiple voices, which had now grown to become more plentiful and excitable. A group of people, dressed for yoga or Pilates (it was hard to tell from their clothing) had gathered in the central courtyard outside their apartment. This was obviously one of the resort activities recommended by the receptionist when they had checked-in. Definitely should have paid more attention to the specifics of date, time and location! Oh well, never mind. They were awake now anyway. The dilemma now was whether to join in or go back to bed and practise their own private form of body contortion.

From within the group, a gentleman exhibiting the healthy air and confidence of a fitness instructor appeared, daintily holding a pair of knickers, which he gracefully offered to Shauna. As he moved towards her, in the corner of her eye Shauna spotted a large and lacy bra dangling from the corner of a stone carving on the wall behind him. The instructor followed her gaze and proceeded to retrieve the bra. How did he know these items were hers? How embarrassing. Why was everyone staring? Shouldn't they be limbering up or doing the downward dog or something?

Shauna smiled and bowed as her scattered underwear was presented. She wanted to ask if he'd found anything else as there appeared to be a couple of items missing. The evening wind must have whipped up and blown the washing from the shower rail. Her lingerie could be scattered all over Indonesia by now. Shauna had a flash thought in which she imagined the holidaymaker in the apartment next door enjoying an alfresco shower, gazing up at the clear blue sky to see a pair of pants descending from the heavens above. Shauna came out of her reverie to discover the fitness fanatics patiently waiting for her next move. Best to get out of here and leave them to the bending, folding and contorting of limbs.

Shauna and Lewis turned to make a hasty retreat to their apartment. As they did so, they heard a cough from within the collective gathering of limber and flexible holidaymakers. They turned to discover a very attractive young lady (too attractive for Shauna's liking) holding aloft a pair of 'bulge bags'. Oh, that was another name Shauna had created for Lewis's tight underpants. The very pretty lady seemed quite amused by the pants, particularly the Superman logo printed on the front. Lewis couldn't resist a flirty little wink as he retrieved his pants from the young lady. And then, to make matters worse, he kissed the back of her hand in an exaggerated gesture. Very gallant, even though he was holding what appeared to be a pair of pants suitable for a seven year old!

The other missing items of underwear were never found. Shauna preferred to imagine they had been blown out to sea rather than the more disturbing thought that someone else had them in their possession.

Another one of Shauna's Gili T memories became an uncomfortable one – literally! In order to explore the tiny island, Shauna and Lewis had hired pushbikes from an obliging gentleman within their complex. The pricing seemed very vague, as did the duration of the rental but the couple had come to appreciate the relaxed, trusting nature of the friendly staff.

They set off on the track, which appeared to run round the circumference of the island, villas on one side, bars and cafes on the other. The track was busy. Horse and carts rattled along, bouncing over pot holes. Cyclists negotiated their way through the crowds, ringing their bells when required to advise others of their presence. Pedestrians took their lives into their own hands, darting between the various obstacles, their only advantage being the agility afforded by those on foot to jump out of the way in a hurry when required.

As they moved away from the crowds and towards a quieter part of the island, the track became thicker and deeper with sand making the sheer effort of pedalling hard work. Lewis appeared to have a better bike, more suited to the sandy terrain, and was making greater progress. Shauna was struggling. The effort of pushing down hard on the pedals made her head feel like it was about to burst.

Without meaning to, Lewis would gain distance and leave Shauna behind. Every now and again he would stop and turn to see his wife puffing, panting and emitting a variety of rude four letter words. It was quite funny but he could see she wasn't enjoying herself.

In an attempt to help, Lewis suggested they swap bikes. Shauna agreed. Just a small matter of adjusting the saddle to allow for Shauna's shorter legs and they were off. Yes, this was better. Not much but at least Shauna could project the cycle in a forward motion.

Annoyingly, Lewis seemed to be just as capable on

the bike previously ridden by Shauna and very quickly began gaining furlongs. The sandy coating on the track continued to hamper Shauna's progress to a lesser extent than before but still enough to frustrate the heck out of her.

Shauna had observed Lewis standing up from the saddle and pushing down hard on the pedals during the more challenging sections of the track. As a young girl, Shauna had pretty much exclusively ridden her bike this way but it was many years since she had been on two wheels. Shauna had therefore elected to sit sedately in the saddle rather than challenging her poor balance by standing up.

However, as the terrain became even more difficult there was nothing for it. Raising herself up, Shauna found the exertion and weight she was able to force down on the pedals assisted greatly and she finally found herself almost able to keep up with Lewis.

Shauna found herself really enjoying the experience. It was exhilarating. What an amazing place. Look at the sea, the beautiful beach and …. Oh, it was getting easier here. The sand had turned to dust, Shauna felt she could lower herself down onto saddle again. Owwwwwwwwwww!!! Oh my Goddddd!!!!! That hurt.

Lewis must have left the saddle a little loose when it was lowered for Shauna's shorter legs. It had tipped back and was pointing upwards like a sharks fin, black and terrifying, Yes, men have a couple of particularly sensitive items between their legs which cause exclamations of agony when punched, knocked or squashed. But the intimate part of Shauna's body, which had made contact with the tip of the upturned seat, was not the area you would choose, as a woman, to be out of action during your honeymoon.

Shauna immediately threw the bike to one side and cupped herself between the legs. She tried to walk in a straight line but this was made difficult by the presence of her palm. Shauna staggered along the path for a short while before turning and running towards the abandoned bike. Lewis had stopped by now and turned to see Shauna kicking the innocent push-bike. He couldn't understand the reason for the remonstration but Shauna was calling the cycle all sorts of very unladylike names. He couldn't make out every single word but he was sure, at one point, he heard his new bride shouting "heap of junk" something something something "cut my cu........." something something something

(26) Email Isla to The Redhead

I'm typing this quietly cos I've got a bit of a hangover and the keyboard is a bit too loud for my delicate head. I've turned the screen brightness down too because it was making my dry eyes burn!

Last night, our work team were invited to an awards ceremony, which incorporated several of the businesses we've done promotional work for in the past.

Do you remember me telling you about that fit store manager in the supermarket where I had to promote those tins of chocolates? Well he was there with his wife. I didn't see her but some of my teammates met her and said she seems like a nice lady. He, on the other hand, was really working the room and flirting with everyone. I was no exception. He seemed to thoroughly enjoy the conversation he had with my breasts. Not sure if he saw my face at all which is annoying because I spent ages on my hair and make-up. I'm not blessed with luscious shiny red locks like you, Red, so I have to put in a bit more effort with my hair. I thought I'd pulled it off. Think he just wanted me to pull him...... No, I won't say it. I'm a lady! No comments from you, cheeky monkey!

Red, I hope you've heard the last of Rav. Unfortunately when you go fishing in the sea of love, you occasionally pull up a clingy squid or a smelly old trout. I've had my fair share of octopuses too. Is that the plural? Or is it octopi? Anyway, blokes with seemingly eight arms, constantly grabbing at you.

When you move one hand away, another one appears somewhere even more inappropriate. Sometimes it's not an arm in an inappropriate place, if you get what I mean – LOL! Sometimes I love the chase and the fun of it but only when I'm in the mood. Sometimes I want to be the predator and not the prey, raarrrgh!!

Anyway, on to your life now Red!

Looking at your Facebook page, you certainly seem to be having fun and your frequent visits to the gym are really paying off. I know you're visiting the gym more often in the hope of bumping into your married lover – BAD. But you're toning up and looking amazing – GOOD.

I think you need to get away for a while. Get away from the married man, the places you secretly go to meet him and the constant uncertainty of what he's doing and with who. Or is it whom? Anyway, you should have come away to Greece with Daisy and me last week.

The hotel was really cheap. The entire holiday was a bargain actually. My brother helped keep the cost down by giving us a lift to the airport. I couldn't believe how much Daisy flirted with him. Luckily he didn't seem interested but, at that point, the holiday wasn't the only cheap thing!

We were both on a budget so we weren't surprised to find ourselves dropped off the coach in the early hours outside the shabbiest hotel in the street. We said we didn't care and we kept telling each other we were only there for the sun but, in the dark morning gloom, it all looked a bit grim.

It was obviously that limbo time of day where everyone has just come back from the clubs and crashed out. The shops and cafes hadn't opened yet so the streets were deserted. We made our way down to the beach. It didn't look too bad actually. Phew! Then suddenly we heard barking and turned to see a pack wild dogs running towards us. Five fearful hounds heading in our direction.

Oh My God! I was so scared. I'm not very good with dogs and these didn't look anything like those fluffy things people carry around in their handbags these days. They were really snarly and skinny. And Greek! They looked hungry. No worries, I thought, Daisy always talks about her horse-riding childhood, mounted on her very own rosette-winning pony. Her sister had a pony too, of course. The sisters grew up in affluent comfort, surrounded by lush countryside and blessed with an abundance of freedom and a series of Labradors as four legged companions. I was sure Daisy would know what to do.

I turned to her for reassurance………….

I could just about see her in the gloom, running away as fast as her toned pony riding thighs would allow.

Oh God Red, I almost wet my pants. I just stood there with my fingers stuffed in my mouth (don't ask me why) and my knees knocking together. I thought I was going to be savaged and eaten alive before I'd even managed one day of topping up my tan. Yes, I know it's a fake tan but my plan was to get a *real* one!

I just stood there, clenching and pulling up my pelvic

floor, trying so hard not to wee. I knew the dogs could smell my fear, I didn't want to demonstrate any further weakness by wetting myself……. or worse!

Well, I'd like to say I was saved by a gorgeous Greek Adonis who swept me up to safety in his arms. The truth is my saviour was a little old Greek lady who barked a selection of local words at the dogs. She began lurching towards them and waving her arms the way my Nan does to the school kids who sit smoking on her front wall. Unfortunately, in my Nan's case, the teenagers shuffle off slowly whilst mumbling four letter words she probably doesn't understand. The little old Greek lady had a bit more instant success and the dogs dispersed as swiftly as they had appeared. I suppose they may have been swearing under their doggy breath but I don't speak Greek!

I thanked her over and over. I couldn't stop myself. It must have been nerves. Unfortunately I couldn't remember the Greek word for thank you so I resorted to English and then French. Is that what we all do? The little old lady just looked at me and shrugged and carried on walking. As I followed her with my eyes, I could see Daisy making her way back towards me. Yeah, thanks for your help Daisy!

We decided to go back to the hotel and have a baby nap. After a few hours sleep we arose to discover the town had also woken up and the sun was out. Yaaaay!!!! We put our bikinis on, packed our bags with towels, trashy books and sun cream and headed down to the pool, so beautifully depicted on the hotel website where it was described as a 'glistening azure paradise'. It was green – YUK!!!! Really green. Like a pond. It looked as though it had been like that for years. No chance of it being recovered whilst we were there then!

To cut a long story short, we spent every day on the beach. It was great. Really soft sand, loads of bars and places to eat. Loads of people our age. Loads of Greek blokes strolling up and down in their tiny trunks. You would have loved it.

The local guys obviously wait for the next wave of totty to arrive so they can show them the local beauty spots and point out areas of historical activity and architecture. Hmmmm! Alternatively, they want to show you their own beauty spots and take part in some current activity around their own personal architecture!

Despite supposedly having a boyfriend in the UK, Daisy was more than happy to pair up for a holiday romance with Dimitrius, one of the local water ski instructors. He was pretty gorgeous, I have to say, but I didn't get a look in regardless of the fact that I was the single one and therefore available for a bit of fun with a seemingly well endowed Greek God. It's those tiny posing pouches. They've probably got a mobile phone in there too but the lycra of their Speedos always seems to be stretched to eye-watering bursting point by the contents.

Daisy, of course, could water-ski. Annoyingly to a very high standard. It turns out her father owns a speed boat (of course!) which means Daisy and her sister spent half their lives on horseback and the other half performing difficult and challenging manoeuvres whilst being towed round the lake behind Daddy's power boat.

Daisy looked great, gracefully gliding on the water with her blonde locks blowing in the breeze. The only thing I could top her with was the size of my boobs so I made sure I flashed mine as much as possible. I'm used to competing with you for the best hair, Red, and you nearly always win but at least I have the biggest boobies!!

My ability on the water was pretty much beginners luck. Somehow I managed to pop up out of the water like a cork and remain upright for at least five minutes before losing concentration and tipping forward for a fall. Daisy and Dimitrius kindly refrained from heavy petting in the boat long enough to haul me back in, exhausted and preparing for a huge bruise on my right thigh.

Later on, back in our room, Daisy showed me the footage she had managed to take on her phone in between snogging and groping sessions with Dimitrius. Oh God, in my head I thought I'd look quite cool on skis. No, not true. My face was frozen in a permanent, unflattering grimace and my knees were clamped close together. It's almost a blessing when I tip over sideways and slap the water hard with my right thigh. Ouch!

One night we were invited to a barbeque by Dimitrius and his fellow water-ski instructors at their base on the beach. What an idyllic location. So cool. We really felt part of the gang particularly as Daisy was Dimitrius's girlfriend (albeit it temporary).

For some reason, we'd decided to take up smoking. We were surprised the boys smoked so heavily, considering their healthy sporty lifestyles but we wanted to fit in with them so we took up the habit too. Daisy and I bought a pack of 20 to share between us and tried to sit nonchalantly inhaling and sexily blowing smoke through our pouty lips. How embarrassing. We must have looked so fake. Two slightly sun burnt English girls, too self-conscious to be cool, hanging out with the local Lotharios. Well, we thought we looked great and the boys clearly did too because we got loads of attention.

Looking fabulous (of course) I wiggled my way to the barbeque area and loaded my plate with enough food to fill me up but not too much to make me look like a greedy pig. I found somewhere to sit and prepared to tuck in. Suddenly a guy appeared and sat right next to me (almost on top of me!) and studied every single thing I put into my mouth whilst constantly nodding and smiling at me. He kept raising his eyebrows too. Weird. I assumed he couldn't speak a word of English, hence the visual communication tactic. I'd just slipped a piece of lamb off my kebab stick and popped it in my mouth when he leaned in even closer (if that's possible) and said "bet that's not the first time you've had a big piece of meat in your mouth" Eh! And then, even worse "How about the lady tries a portion of my big meat in her mouth?" Eh! "Very satisfying" For who?.... or is that whom?

I was saved by Daisy who had abandoned me at the start of the night. I'd seen her wrapping her toned water skiing thighs around Dimitrius as they sat in a sexual position sharing the same chair. The only thing preventing it being an indecent sex act was the tiny pair of white shorts Daisy was covering her pert little bottom with.

God, listen to me. I sound so old fashioned and disapproving. You know I'm not like that, Red, but Daisy was bringing out something in me. I hate to admit it but I think it might have been the green-eyed monster. She looked great in those little white shorts. In fact, she looked great in everything. I'm not used to coming second to another woman. I'm not used to coming second at all. And, yes, I mean in bed too!!!

Anyway, Daisy leaned in to whisper that she needed to go to the loo and would I come with her. She seemed quite distressed and in a bit of a hurry. She glanced at the gent almost sitting on my knee and raised her eyebrows in askance. The expression on her face then clouded and turned to one of pain. She turned back to me and raised those eyebrows again in an 'are you coming..... now now NOW?' way. I was glad to have the excuse to leave the bloke and the offer of a portion of his meat so I climbed out of the tight bench seat and followed Daisy who, by now, was already making her way out of the ski school shack and heading off to the dark beach.

Daisy started to run along the beach and I was struggling to keep up with her. She turned round at one point and shouted at me to hurry up.

We knew the toilet block was some way down the beach but I couldn't really see the problem. Whilst running after her, I suggested she just squat down and wee on the beach. It was dark enough and nobody would see. They probably wouldn't care anyway.

Daisy was almost crying now. She ran along the sand

shouting "noooooooooooo"

So then I suggested she just go in the sea, but received another "nooooooo" to that one. Turns out she wanted more than a wee and she wasn't going to go on the beach or in the sea. She was determined to make it to the toilet block.

I was falling behind, partly because my shoes had heels and I hadn't had time to take them off and partly because I was laughing so much. All I could see was a little bouncy bum, clad in a tiny pair of white shorts, disappearing down the beach in the moonlight with Daisy repeatedly crying "nooooooooo".

Eventually we reached the toilet block. Typically the lights were out. It was pitch black. Daisy disappeared into the gloom and almost immediately Dimitrius appeared. How on earth did he catch up so quickly?

He ran passed me and headed for the toilet block, calling "Daisy, I love you". Did he think he was Romeo or something?!?

From inside the dark toilet block I could hear Daisy's plaintive voice "Isla, get rid of him pleeeeaaase".

"Daisy, I love you"

"Isla, please please please get rid of him"

Hilarious. I couldn't stop laughing. I hadn't recovered from the image of Daisy, little white shorts bobbing along in the moonlight, attempting to run along the beach whilst keeping her legs together and clenching her bum cheeks as she darted between the choice she had of going in the sea, on the beach or pursuing the route to the toilet block.

Why did she insist on the toilet block?

Eventually I managed to persuade Dimitrius to return to the ski shack and wait for us to return.

In the darkness I could hear Daisy groaning. Oh dear, she must have been in pain. Eventually I heard the toilet flush followed by the sound of the tap running. For a long time. For ages actually. Turns out she was trying to wash her white shorts. Oh!!! Don't think Dimitrius would have been feeling quite so romantic if he'd seen his holiday lover, stripped to the waist, rinsing her shit soiled shorts in the sink. Try saying that after a pint of Pimms!!

Sorry mate, I've waffled on a bit here but I hopefully I've made you laugh. A few other things happened on that holiday but nothing quite so funny. I did manage to blow the fuse for the entire hotel with my hair straighteners though. As I plugged them in there was a bright spark, a crackle, then a fizz followed by total darkness. Hmmmm, I've had that feeling before – Tee Hee!! The hotel manager even knocked on our door. I thought he'd pinpointed the cause to our room, especially as my straighteners were in my hand when I answered his knock. He'd only come to apologise and to re-assure us the power would be re-connected again soon. We were even given a free drink at the bar that night as compensation.

On our last night, I caught Daisy staring at her phone. She seemed to be a bit upset but, when I asked her if she was OK, she put on an obvious fake smile and said she had decided to finish with her boyfriend because he wasn't exciting enough. Hmmmm, I made a big pretence of agreeing with her but I suspect I was witnessing her being dumped by text. What a coward, whoever he is. Yes, Daisy is a high-maintenance drama queen but she has a real heart of gold too and nobody deserves the phone finishing treatment. Having said that, she had been having more than her fair share of fun with a Greek God so maybe it was karma.

Despite that, we had a great holiday and managed to stay friends. Not always easy when you go away with another female. It would have been great with you though, Red. Anyway, as the coach took us back to the airport we realised the driver was taking a different route to the one who dropped us off. As we headed away from town we passed some amazing shops, cool bars and clubs. Can you believe it? We'd spent the entire week walking down towards the beach and hanging out in the basic cafes and shitty restaurants there whilst everyone else was obviously living it up in style a few metres away in the other direction. Mind you, on our limited budget, we probably couldn't afford those places. But could *they* afford *us*, Red?!?

Stop waiting for that married man and go there with me sometime.

(27 Email Redhead to Isla)

Bloody Hell Isla, that water skiing session must have been the first time your legs were together for years!!!

Your email really made me laugh. I could do with a bit of cheering up actually.

The other day, I was spending a bit of time with the married man. Yes, I know you don't approve but you are the only one I can talk to so I hope you don't mind me off-loading a bit.

We were in the back of his car and yours truly was indulging in a bit of oral pleasure. So, you weren't the only one with a big piece of meat in your mouth last week. Actually, he's not that big. Dare I say it, he's a shower, not a grower but there's enough for a mouthful! It was late afternoon so we had to be careful not to be seen. I know it sounds a bit cheap, sneaking away in a car park to have a quick bit of fun together but I'll take what I can get of him. Excuse the pun!!!

Oh, that reminds me, one night last week, my little sister and her boyfriend were on the drive in his old banger. My mum kept looking out of the window and tutting. It was really getting on my nerves and then suddenly she stormed out of the front door. My sister told me later that mum had knocked on the car window and shouted "Hurry up and come in, you've got school in the morning". Then my sister told me what they were doing at the time. Bloody Hell, can you believe it?! The youngest siblings always get away with murder. Can you imagine what my mum would have said if *I'd* been on the drive, sucking off some bloke when I was her age?

So, back to my story. We had the radio on in the car. I'd just finished his happy ending. I'm really good at it and he was in a really chilled state. He never reciprocates the act though. Bit mean but I'm happy being the giver, as it were. He said his wife never goes down on him. Not sure if that's true but I'm happy to believe that *I'm* the special one who really knows what he wants.
Then 'Goodbye My Lover' by James Blunt came on the radio. I've never really listened to the lyrics before but I was enjoying the slow gentle pace of it so I said I liked it, even though it is a sad song.

I was expecting him to agree with me and maybe say something romantic. Instead, he said that when our relationship ends, he hopes it's for a good reason and not because we've been discovered or caught out and forced to end it. He said 'Goodbye My Lover' would become our relationship break-up song.

I was so hurt. What a cruel thing to say. I can't believe he's already predicting the end of our relationship. He obviously doesn't think it's going to last. At that point, I wished I still had his tiny willy in my mouth so I could bite the bloody thing off. What a cocky pig. If anyone's going to end our relationship, it's going to be me. He's never going to have anyone who knows what he wants as much as I do. He will be begging me to stay.

I almost wanted to get hold of Rav and tell him I've changed my mind just so I could flaunt him in front of married man but that would just be opening a portal to a nightmare I may never wake up from! And then I thought, I've got nothing to lose, I could just tell his wife about us and show the cocky bugger that he's not indispensible.

Then he told me how special I am. How much he looks forward to our moments together. How he thinks about me all the time – even when he's in bed with his wife. Ouuucccchhh!! He did it again. I think he realised he'd said the wrong thing again so he brought it back round by telling me he's thinking of leaving his wife. He said there are a few things he needs to consider and work out but ……..

At that point he glazed over and stopped talking. I didn't know what to think. Part of me was really excited but another part of me was still hurt and reeling from the things he'd accidentally said. I'm always at his beck and call and dancing to his tune. He thrives on the power he has to pick me up and play with me and then drop me to return to his wife. I suppose, doing what I'm doing, and getting involved with a married man, means I'm permanently setting myself up to be hurt and rejected.

Anyway, Babe, thank you so much for the suggestion that we go away together for a break. Yes, I'd love to do that. Let's sort something out. Daisy sounds fun and interesting but I bet you and I could really paint the town RED!!! Get it?

And, by the way, YOU would be the one turning heads. Yes, Daisy has the poise of a little rich girl but you have a couple of really good points and I hope you treated them to a bit of topless sunbathing!! I will certainly be topless when we hit the beach in order to impress those Greek Gods. Hope they like the look of my bottom too!

(28) Ruby

I tried to talk to Shauna yesterday. She's doing her usual thing of keeping things to herself. She never wants to burden anyone with her worries. I think she tries to protect others and spare their feelings. The thing is, I'm stronger than her. Well, on the surface. Deep down Shauna is actually a lot stronger than me. Once, during an argument, Alex accused me of being 'all volume and attitude'. I hate to admit it but he's right. I know exactly what I'm like but, the thing is, I don't care what other people think about me and Shauna cares *too much* about what people think of her.

I don't think she's happy. Not just about losing the baby. That's obvious. I mean life in general. She always brushes off any attempts at getting to the heart of anything and ends up trying to make a joke about it. Yes, life is a mix of sad and happy. Nobody's life is one hundred percent perfect and you've go to laugh sometimes. Shauna keeps referring to 'light and shade' but, in my opinion, outwardly she focuses too much on the light. I have a horrible feeling that inwardly she spends more time in the shade. Me? I'm loud and outspoken. If I have something to say I say it. I know I can be volatile and difficult to talk to but I'm not going to let anyone get me down.

I even suggested Shauna joined me last night when I did a spot of babysitting. A chance to get out of the house, away from Lewis and for us to have a chat. It's an easy 'gig'. I walk next door, watch what I want to watch on their massive TV, eat the nibbles they leave out for me and generally have the place to myself. Well, once the children are in bed.

Shauna started the local babysitting round thing when she lived at home. Most of the children are old enough to look after themselves now but I took over the babysitting baton for those families who still needed someone to look after their youngsters and inherited a few new ones of my own.

The parents in the house next door are really cool. I hope to be that type of parent if I ever have children of my own. Mr and Mrs Next-door go out and obviously have a great time. They don't even mind if I bring a boyfriend with me. The dad once said to one of my boyfriends "I don't care what you get up to, just don't wipe your willy on the curtains". So cool!!

Anyway, it turned into a bit of an interesting evening. I thought I was going to be downstairs on my own with a bowl of Pringles on my lap, watching Celebrity Bad Hair Days by nine o'clock at the latest. Wrong. The children were a bit more pumped up than usual. The family are looking after a large Labrador by the name of Larry. Larry the Labrador.

The mum and dad did the usual hand-over stuff. Pointed out where the complimentary food and drink was, told me the children should be in bed by nine (good) and introduced me to Larry. Woof! As they left, their final words were "we won't be late". Well, I've heard that before. In fact, they say it every time. And they're always late. Never mind, they pay me well so I can't complain. It tops up my hairdressing wage nicely.

From the beginning, it was obvious the children had surplus energy to expire. I organised a few boisterous games in an effort to burn them out and get them into bed on or before the nine o'clock deadline. Larry joined in the fun, including the jump rope skipping. He was actually quite good at that, considering he had four legs to manoeuvre over the spinning rope rather than our mere two!

The children taught me a game involving the swapping of hats and shoes. Their vague knowledge of the rules made the game very difficult to follow but what they revealed during the game was quite interesting.

They told me they'd seen my dad's socks. Yes, I said, probably on the washing line? "No, when you go on holiday and mummy and daddy look after your cat, they look through all your drawers and cupboards" came the innocent answer. Bloomin cheek but they're probably not the first people to do something like that. Even worse, they wouldn't just find socks in my drawers. They certainly wouldn't find the sort of toys their children would be allowed to play with!

The subsequent game of hide-and-seek seemed to confuse Larry. He was either found whining and lost in the hallway or on the landing (despite the fact that mum and dad had said Larry wasn't allowed upstairs) or he would find one of the hiders and stand barking, noisily giving away their hiding place.

At one point, I was hiding behind the curtains in the dining room. I had sneaked away whilst Larry was distracted elsewhere. I stood as still as possible and tried not to giggle or move the curtains. I made sure my feet were well hidden and not sticking out from under the hem of the fabric. The children love a bit of pantomime overacting when I'm the seeker but when I'm the hider, I try to give them a bit of a challenge. Don't want to make it too easy and I don't want the game to end too soon.

My cover was blown by Larry, of course. His four paws came pattering across the wooden floor and made their way towards my curtained concealment, his wet nose nudging the drapes to gain access. I was expecting whining or barking. But no, he rose up on his rear legs, placing his front paws on my chest and then. Well, I can only describe it in terms of my first fumbled teenage encounters with the youths at school discos. Larry's tongue lolled from the side of his mouth and he began to grind up and down against me. Ah, right. Let's stop this right now. I'm not that sort of girl. Not the sort you want anyway, Larry.

Due to my predicament, I hadn't noticed but the children had obviously discovered me in my awkward hiding position. "Ooooh, Larry likes you, doesn't he". They were delighted to see Larry and me getting on so well. I didn't want to be too rough with my amorous four-legged friend in front of them but, like the aforementioned teenage boys, Larry needed a bit of manhandling to get him down. I couldn't help hearing the dad's previous warning "I don't care what you get up to, just don't wipe your willy on the curtains". Not so cool now. Maybe he should have had that conversation with Larry.

I needed to create a new game. Something to calm us all down. Maybe noughts and crosses, or hangman? Something to educate the children whilst keeping us

143

all out in the open. I couldn't see any obvious supplies of stationery in the living room but I knew I had a pen and some paper in my bag, which was hanging on a peg in the hall. A brand new leather bag. A gift from Fabio who recently visited the souks in Marrakech and bartered like crazy to bring back gifts for all in the salon. I wouldn't normally have chosen a bag like this. It's constructed of unlined, raw leather and it stinks. I'm not a vegetarian but this bag makes me feel a bit guilty. I've been taking it to work this week so Fabio can see me using it but I plan to take it out of action any day now. I can't wait to say goodbye to the awful smell.

I brought my bag into the sitting room, knelt down and put it on the floor in front of me. The smell wafted up from inside. "Pooh" said the children "Pooh, it smells of poo". They thought they'd just said the funniest thing in the world and started giggling uncontrollably.

Attracted by their laughter, Larry returned to the living room from the kitchen where he had been heard slurping loudly from his water bowl. I can only assume it was the smell of animal that excited him so much but, before I could pull it out of the way, Larry was growling and barking at my new bag whilst tugging the decorative tassels that dangled from it. Larry's own doggy dangling tassels were obviously aroused again too. He didn't know what to do with himself. Still kneeling down, I tried to raise the bag in the air before Larry chewed it into something unrecognisable. He paced around me, obviously trying to find the best angle at which to munch, chew or mate my recently acquired leather gift. Suddenly, from the rear, I felt Larry's front paws land on my shoulder. I felt the hot breath and heard the pants of Larry in my ear as he attempted to re-kindle our earlier relationship using the rather appropriately named doggy fashion.

"Oh, he really does love you" one of the observant children exclaimed as I tried to rise to my feet and hold my bag aloft in one fell swoop. Well, fell swoop sounds graceful and efficient. I was neither of those things. I staggered and stumbled to my feet. Larry was a jilted lover, once more, but was determined to have some fun somewhere. He continued his attempt to mount me, whilst simultaneously sinking his teeth into the bag. I tugged the handle, Larry growled, I spun round, Larry followed.

"Get down. Do it again" came the cries of the children "Do it again, again".

Larry needed some fresh air. I told the children he needed to go outside after drinking all that water and instructed them to lead Larry to the back garden for a moment on the lawn. After all his efforts, he probably felt like a post-coital cigarette to relax and unwind but I wasn't going to oblige his cravings anymore.

During the peace and quiet, I tried to text Shauna to let her know just what her abandonment of me had lead to. I swear I typed "Been mounted by Larry" but, when I looked at it later, my predictive text had sent "My mound is hairy" Even worse, it didn't go to Shauna, I'd sent it to Trey Baxter by mistake.

I just wanted to get out of there but I couldn't leave those innocent (or not so innocent after Larry's amorous exploits) children alone. It was definitely time for bed. Nine o'clock or not, I was going to calm things down now so I could calm my nerves. As a sweetener,

I told the children I would allow Larry to lay on the landing to keep guard over them. Yes, I know their parents had left strict instructions not to allow Larry upstairs but his 'downstairs' was becoming a real problem for me and I was getting tired of telling him "it's not you, it's me. I'm just not that into you". His lack of comprehension was frustrating and tiring.

The children agreed to my terms. However, my final negotiation revolved around the closing of their bedroom doors at opposite sides of the landing.

"Close my door last"

"No, close *my* door last"

"I'm the oldest so I go to bed after you"

I could see this one running and running. OK, Larry, don't get the wrong idea here. I removed my top. Fortunately Larry didn't seem too bothered about the sight of me in my push up bra. I think he prefers his females with at least eight teats.

I tied one sleeve to one door handle and the other sleeve stretched across the landing to the door handle opposite. OK, one, two, three, pull. Both doors closed at the same time. The end.

It was almost the end of me. I was hot, bothered, violated and humiliated. I made a quick exit whilst Larry was distracted by the muffled voices of the children from behind opposing doors. The deal was struck. They were in bed and I was not prepared to negotiate bedtime story reading. Besides, I think they'd seen enough to stimulate their young imaginations. I didn't want to induce nightmares with stories of big bad wolves getting up to all sorts of tricks or wicked stepmothers with poisoned fruit.

Hot and bothered, I flopped on the sofa, switched on the TV and prepared for a relaxed evening of trashy TV.

I must have fallen asleep at some point. The reason I know this is because I found myself waking up, freezing cold with a crick in my neck and a dribble soaked cushion pressed against my face. The mum and dad and another very friendly and slightly drunk couple were all standing round the sofa staring down at me with stupid grins on their alcohol flushed faces.

As I sat up, rubbing my neck and wiping the dribble from my cheek the foursome started laughing. Oh my God!!! In my desperation to get away from Larry the lover on the landing, I'd forgotten to put my top back on. It was still holding the bedroom doors closed. Well, I thought it was but apparently Larry had detected my scent on the fabric and established some sort of friendship with it. Keep it. It's all yours Larry. You may even get the leather bag one day very soon too!

The cheery couples obviously wanted to sit and chat and encouraged me to join them. I declined, darting for my coat in the hallway in order to cover my modesty. I left before they even had chance to pay me. On reflection, they owed me a great deal more than the standard evening fee. There was the danger money, a negotiation skills fee and exhibitionist fee to be considered.

When I woke up the following morning, as I do every morning, I picked up my phone to check the time and address any waiting messages. Only one text, really? I'm normally more popular than that. It was from Trey Baxter in response to my hairy mound declaration and it read:

"It's been a while darling but, being a hairdresser, you were always well groomed".

Don't know if that's cool or not!

(29) Email - The Redhead to Isla

OMG! I've got a right one here. Despite the fact that I'm ignoring Rav, he continues to text me. Got another one yesterday whilst I was working out the in the gym. There was a really fit guy on the cross-trainer next to me and I was admiring his stamina, as well as a couple of his other qualities, when my phone lit up.

It was another text from Rav: 'Hey you! Hope you're OK. Just to let you know, I had a party at my house on Saturday. Loads of people came, including my ex and we had a fantastic time'.

Why do I need to know that? Does he want me to be jealous because I'm missing all the fun of his lame party? I looked across at fit cross-training guy next to me and laughed out loud to get his attention. Well, you lose some you win some. Maybe I could use this as an opportunity to get chatting. Admittedly I was slightly red in the face and probably more than a little bit sweaty. I was also running short of the required amount of oxygen to maintain life, never mind having enough breath to hold down a conversation. However, I wasn't going to miss the opportunity to engage with my tasty gym buddy so I laughed out loud again. Surely he'd look across now……

Yes! It worked. Long story short, I explained the story behind my fake laughter, obviously embellishing it where necessary to make me sound absolutely fantastic. Gorgeous gym guy seemed mildly amused but, to be honest, slightly disinterested.

"Tell him you're shagging your boss" was his

suggestion before pressing the stop button on the cross-trainer and taking his hot, Adonis body off to another piece of gym equipment. Oh what I'd give to be the leather padded seat underneath his pert bottom!!!

(30) Email – Isla to The Redhead

Red, your speed dater has turned into a cyber stalker. I would normally use that word cautiously but, in this case, I'd be careful. I know you're taking it all in your stride and seeing the funny side but he's getting a bit too much. Let me know if you need my help. I know you'll say no but the offer is there.

And talking about over-enthusiastic admirers, I met an old friend from a previous work assignment the other day. A bloke friend. We met at a garden centre for coffee. Not very rock-and-roll, I know, but I always think a garden centre is a good neutral first date venue. For a start, it's daylight. You are surrounded by plants, pottery and pensioners so the atmosphere isn't too sexually charged. Unless you like that sort of thing! Normally you are both sober too so there's none of that dark, fumbling drunkenness that can lead you to remove one too many items of clothing. I'm mainly talking about other people here but I can't deny it's happened to me too on occasion…. OK, yes, you know me well, Red. I won't protest my total innocence anymore.

Anyway, we had a chat and a catch-up in the conservatory café. I had a cappuccino and ended up with a dried milk moustache. He did that thing where he rubbed his thumb across my top lip to remove it. I think he thought it was seductive like a scene in a movie. I just hoped he'd washed his hands after going to the toilet.

Yes, you've guessed it. I wasn't as in to him as I thought I was. I was trying to keep the conversation

151

neutral whilst wracking my brains for an excuse to leave. He insisted on a second round. Oh no! This time I went for an Americano. I wasn't going to risk any more contact between his digits and my lips. RED! I know what you're thinking with your innuendo filled mind!!!

Eventually I found an excuse. Something I thought would turn him off. I told him I had promised to go and watch my brother play football. For one horrific moment, he was considering joining me. Bloody Hell! That would mean I would *actually* have to watch my brother play football. I only do that when I'm trying to impress a bloke and I really didn't want to impress this one. Quick, quick think. I said, yes, it would be great if he could join me – why did I say that – but I just had to pick my mum up on the way. Ah, that did it. He suddenly looked at his watch and remembered a prior engagement. Phew!!

We get to our cars in the car park. Dangerous places these car parks. Something about the finality of it. The fact that your meeting is over and you are both going your own separate ways seems to bring out blind boldness in people.

I say my goodbyes and try not to promise any further garden centre get-togethers. He seems hesitant to leave. I take the bull by the horns and lean in for a goodbye kiss on the cheek. Somehow he swerves, dives over (should be a goalie) and attaches his mouth to mine. His arms are immediately round my waist and then his tongue starts to knock at the firmly closed doors of my lips.

Urgh! I push or pull away, can't remember which, and

turn to open my car door. I notice an elderly couple, pushing a trolley full of plants towards their car, looking on with wistful looks and smiles on their faces. They are obviously heartened to see what appears to be young love. Perhaps they see a couple, unable to be together, parting with a passionate kiss. How wrong can they be?

Anyway, as well as my garden centre groper, I've had a funny few days. Oh yes! I've been on another promotional assignment. This time was for a sex toy manufacturer. What a great gig, hey! The venue was the Triptees Shopping Centre and my assignment was the promotion of their latest range of 'ladies leisure items' and we all know what that means.

I was met by Stacey, a ladies party planner with the biggest boobs you've ever seen. She helped set up my stall, gave me a few hints and tips and dashed off to her next event. Her life may seem fun and fluffy on the surface but I suspect she works very hard. At the end of the day, it's a job and, whether your product is stocks, shares or sex toys, it's bound to have its challenges.

As a bonus though, Stacey did tell me she gets great discount and really enjoys trying out the products at home with her boyfriend. I have to say, as the fabulously voluptuous Stacey clacked away on her high heels, I found it hard to imagine how the delicate lace of the all-in-one nipple tassel body stocking would contain all of her loveliness.

Before she departed, Stacey had informed me we were targeting the 30 plus age group. My script for the approachable or cheeky looking ones was:

"As a young, vibrant woman (flattery will get you everywhere) when would you say is your sexual peek"?

One of my first potential customers responded "About 4.30 in the afternoon"

I couldn't stop laughing. I dropped the toy I had been holding on the floor, which turned it on, excuse the pun. It began vibrating round in rapid circles like a Jack Russell chasing its own tail. The woman, who was lovely by the way, looked quizzically at me and I finally managed to explain that I meant at what *age* would you say is your sexual peek, not what time of day!

Her reply? "Oh well, in that case, I hope I'm still climbing the hill and I'm nowhere near the peek yet!" What a game gal she was. I love my job sometimes.

(31) George

The chap from next door caught me this morning as I was getting in the car. He gave me some money for Ruby. Apparently she'd left their house in a bit of a hurry the other night and they hadn't got round to paying her for babysitting. He said something about a bit extra to pay for the damage Larry had done to her bag. I have absolutely no idea who Larry is or what he was talking about but, by the look on his face, it was a dinner party story. I hope Ruby is OK. Must ask her. Or I'll ask Dee to do it.

Of my three children, Ruby is the one I find the hardest to connect with. I know she's a softie inside but her exterior is tough and slightly scary. Shauna is gentle and open. She appears to be more vulnerable on the outside but I know, inside, she's strong.

Alex is more like Shauna but he's incredibly private. He comes and goes but we are never privy to what's going on in his life. Well, when I say that, I mean *I* am never included. Dee has a special relationship with Alex. It's been that way since he was a baby. I've always hoped we'd have a more traditional father son relationship but Alex just isn't interested in the things I've tried to involve him in.

Shauna once suggested I should try to connect with Alex on his level. The trouble is, I don't know what level that is. I'm obviously on the ground floor and Alex has pressed the lift button to the penthouse. We are so far apart. When I try to take the lift up to his floor he runs down the fire escape to avoid my attempts to bond.

Alex puts up shutters when I ask him where he's going, what his friends are doing, how his studies are progressing. Listen to me! I sound so old fashioned. Next thing, I'll be asking him if he's walking out with anyone. If he's dating a nice young lady from a good home? Maybe a Lucy with highly charged libido like I did all those years ago!

We haven't seen anymore of that girl with the ponytail Dee did find a long red hair on his jacket but he just said he'd loaned the jacket to a friend. Oh well, we can only try!

When Dee and I find ourselves alone we naturally migrate to conversations involving our children. We've spent so much time raising them and supporting their move into adulthood and beyond. You would think that, when Dee and I have time away from that responsibility, we'd think about ourselves but no, eventually one of us will say something about one of our trio and we will revert to Mum and Dad mode without thinking.

During a recent weekend walk, our conversation was brought to a halt by an amusing incident.

Age is relative, isn't it? When I was nine, my schoolmate had a brother who was eleven and about to start secondary school. At the time, I thought his older brother was a *man*. I thought we'd lost him from our gang and he would be married with kids before I ever caught up with him again.

I'm sure our three think Dee and I are old and past it,

particularly Ruby who constantly huffs, puffs and rolls her eyes when I ask her for help with the TV remote, my stupid phone with tiny buttons or the laptop with it's unexpected errors.

So when presented with someone who appears to be in their eighties, I defer to them as my elders and extend the usual level of respect afforded to someone senior to me in age and experience. I wish the generation below me would do the same. Some do, please don't get me wrong. Alert! I'm turning into a grumpy old man.

Anyway, back to my day off with Dee. We were out for a stroll in the sun. My back and knee were in good shape and I was able to walk with reasonable comfort. We'd taken a bag of bread. Yes, it probably should have been stale but Dee purchases a small mountain of bread products every day so there is always a plentiful supply of fresh loaves. I'm not sure how many people she caters for, but a hungry Scout troop would survive a weekend camp living off the contents of our bread bin and still have enough for a family sized bread and butter pudding at the end.

As we made our way along the riverbank, dispensing bite sized chunks of sliced white, wholemeal and rustic artisan bread (what is that?) to the waiting bills of the ducks and swans, we came across a well-dressed elderly lady who was also stuffing the bellies of the birds with small perfectly cut squares of bread.

The distinguished lady was wrapped up warm, despite the sunny day, in a smart raincoat. On her left arm, at the crook of her elbow, hung an enormous stiff black leather handbag, the kind my grandmother and her sisters used to own. One of those ones that closes with a loud click and crack, so fierce it would echo around the bingo hall or frighten birds from the trees.

It was one of those events you could see happening in slow motion. As the smartly dressed lady flung the bread portions into the water, her bag, which was located on the throwing arm, took flight and propelled itself onto the surface of the water a few feet from the edge. I'm using imperial measurements here but please feel free to substitute feet for metres if you are a metric measurer. Anyway, back to the story....

Due to the size and structure of the bag, it landed with a loud plop but did not immediately sink. It bobbed about like a fearsome black ship, refusing to sink without a dignified farewell.

Dee and I were dumbstruck for a few seconds. Time seemed to stand still. We looked towards the elderly lady who seemed unfazed.

Taking on the role of responsible adults, Dee and I rallied ourselves and started to look about for something with which to hook and retrieve the bag.

"Oh, please don't worry about it" came the serene voice of the lady in the raincoat.

I looked down to see Dee laying on her belly, desperately trying to extend her body to reach the bag. What a game bird she is. Must get it from her mother!

Sadly, I'm not quite as mobile as my wife. My knee was good in the sun but I wouldn't have been unable to launch myself on the riverbank with such speed and agility. I scanned around. The only thing I could see was a discarded shopping trolley, partly submerged in the reeds at the side of the river. Whilst being disgusted by the person who had wilfully abandoned the trolley in the beautiful river, I also saw an opportunity to harness the strength of the wheeled wonder to encourage the sinking bag back to shore.

I swung the trolley round in an arc in the water, creating a wave motion. The bag slowly moved towards the bank, just out of reach of Dee's waiting hands. My knowledge of physics is reasonable. I could see that the body to weight ratio of my lovely wife was tipping precariously with the water winning favour over the riverbank as her final destination. It was a bit like the final scene in *The Italian Job*. Dee was the overhanging bus. Was she going to tip over and spill her contents into the flowing river?

"Oh please don't worry" came the plaintive voice of Mrs Raincoat. "Really, there's nothing in there of any value".

Dee is a tenacious character. She never gives up. Believe me, I know. You should try having an argument with her. You can see where Ruby gets her feisty nature from! They both have a tough exterior with the softest, kindest most loyal centre. Most people only see the exterior. I am one of the privileged few who are gifted with access to the inner core of these two complicated females.

The elderly lady moved along the bank and, unbelievably, re-commenced her bird-feeding task.

Risking further pain in my back, I struggled with the trolley in an attempt to return it to its original location in order to recreate my arc style wave creation. As I did so, my focus was obviously directed to the task in hand. Therefore I did not observe Dee rotating her body one hundred and eighty degrees on the bank. She was still laying prone on the grass. However, this time it was her legs overhanging the water. Using some kind of pincer movement, she grabbed the rigid handles of the bag between her boots and eased it back towards the bank, moving her legs towards her body like a frog. She barely touched the water. Only the toes of her boots gently sailed through the water as she carefully dragged herself further onto dry land. Amazing. What a girl.

Dee slowly eased herself further away from the bank in order to prevent the bag from returning to the water. As she moved to safety, I bent down to retrieve the bag from between her clenched feet. Unfortunately after my efforts with the shopping trolley my damaged back would only allow me to lower myself so far, but not far enough. I couldn't make the full reach. How frustrating. I felt helpless.

Dee came to my rescue, as she often does. She could see I was struggling to reach the bag. In one final act of genius, she bent her legs and flicked the bag up backwards and over her head. I managed to catch it. A skill I retained from my old rugby days. Fortunately I didn't instinctively drop kick it. I know that's a classic old joke but it still makes me laugh.

As Dee stood on the riverbank, brushing her grass stained knees I looked at her with total love. No rude remarks about the grass stains please! What a delightful lady she is. My wife, the mother of my children. So unassuming but so capable.

"Hmmmm, better get rid of these grass stains before we get home" she looked up, smiled and gave me a crafty wink.

Mrs Raincoat was reunited with her handbag. At that instant, a young lady (well, someone my age!) came running towards us.

"Oh God" she puffed "I'm so sorry. It's my mother. She does this sort of thing all the time"

Dee and I smiled and nodded and said it was really no problem. We told her that her mother had been quite happy for the bag to sink and that it was us who had decided to rescue it. We told her that Mrs Raincoat had declared the bag of no value.

"Really"? Daughter with raised eyebrows "She carries all her wordily goods in that bag. "It's only because it's so big and full of air that it didn't sink."

With more thanks and apologies from the frazzled daughter, we left the pair to sort themselves out and continued on our walk. It seems we can't even have a quiet day out without becoming involved in a drama of some sort.

(32) Email Beth to Shauna)

Hola Shauna and greetings from a hot and humid Spain. Don't want to rub it in but I spend most of my days in a bikini. I've lost all my inhibitions and I don't care who sees me semi-naked anymore with my bumps, blemishes, mosquito bites (grrr!) and cellulite bared for all to see. Obviously I still wear clothes at work but I'd be the first to applaud if CostaCoches launched a new uniform in the form of two small pieces of lycra with the company logo displayed in the appropriate places, of course!

Unfortunately, this means I'm also privy to seeing other people in small items of clothing in a way you wouldn't normally do in your home in the UK.

Steve's mum is visiting us at the moment. She's bought her friend Val along. Val is a lovely lady, full of life, very bubbly and full of fun. When I first met her, I thought she seemed like the kind of lady who would once have been a pub landlady. Massive jiggly bosoms, bright red (chemically enhanced) big hair-do and a roaring laugh. I was almost right. It turns out, in a previous life she was a night club owner. Sadly for Val, times changed and her brand of night club with its dark swirly carpets and cheesy entertainment went out of fashion. She pulled out just in time and sold the club. It has subsequently been pulled down and now forms part of a new exclusive apartment block for the type of people who wouldn't be seen dead in that sort of evening entertainment venue.

Val's experience has left her with a very open and

realistic approach to life but, predominantly, her attitude is one of 'you only live once so get on with it'. Getting on with it involves Val, sitting by the pool in bright coloured swimsuits and, even worse, the odd bikini. She doesn't care and why should she? She has a body she seems to be perfectly proud of. Unfortunately there's quite a lot of it and we've become almost blind to the massive wobbling buzoomas straining to escape from her floral swimwear.

I think, if you asked any ex-pat living in a hot holiday destination, most of them would say the same things about visiting friends and family. What's theirs is theirs but what's yours is theirs too. These sun-seeking visitors use all your towels, shampoo, eat your food and borrow your clothes. You find yourself repeatedly overeating in places you wouldn't normally go. You end up exhausted from entertaining. The guests slob about by the pool or sit expectantly in the back of the car whilst you act as tour guide. You knock yourself out juggling work and housework to keep them happy and entertained. They fly home. You regain control of your digestive system and the next guests fly in.

I'm more than happy to welcome people to our place. We are the ones who moved away. They didn't ask us to. When we moved away, we offered all our family and close friends free accommodation and invited them to come and see us as often as they could. What we didn't foresee was just how time consuming, intrusive and relentless it would be. At home in the UK, these people have never come to stay in our house and observe us getting on with daily life. Suddenly, here in Spain, we're rubbing along cheek by jowl with people we would never normally share a bathroom with, let alone see them in Speedos!

Val has arms of a generous circumference. I'm trying to be polite here. She borrows all my tops and stretches them. Steve told me I should chill out and be more gracious. I agreed. She's a lovely lady and I'm sure she would welcome me to her home and allow me to borrow all her bright and cheerful clothes. I try to be less anal. Then Steve freaks out one day and says in hushed tones, through gritted teeth, that she's wearing *HIS* top. He keeps trying to gently persuade her to wear something else but she insists his top is fine, as if she's doing him a favour by wearing it. Fine? It's more than bloody fine! It's a really expensive designer top. I'm sure that woman would wear absolutely anything. She would definitely slip a stranger's flip-flops on if she found them on the beach.

Then one day, Steve's mum and Val return from a day on the beach and she hangs a pink children's cartoon towel on the balcony. Annoying in itself. Val insists on hanging her damp washing all over the place. I'm sick of seeing her bra and pants flapping and billowing on the pool railings in the early morning breeze whilst I eat my breakfast. I joked with Val about the cartoon towel and told her it complimented her young-at-heart approach to life. Val seemed confused and then revealed she thought it was *our* towel. No! Why would we have a pink cartoon towel suitable for an eight-year-old girl? OMG! Two days later I found myself asking her about the boy band towel that was hanging over the shower curtain rail. Grrrrr! Not ours either! Val just shrugs and says oh well. Steve and I openly discussed the poor child who is missing their favourite towel. Val just chuckled, causing a Mexican wave of bosom action within her bikini top, and said something about what comes around goes around. Hmmm, what will those poor children inherit in this deal? Bright orange lipstick? A copy of the bonk buster beach read Val seemed so engrossed in? The towel she borrowed from our bathroom that has never returned from the same beach?

Another trait that seems to become apparent for many holiday-makers is an increased lack of spatial awareness and volume control. Steve's mum and Val treat us to bursts of hysterical cackling laughter. Most of the time, the source of amusement is unknown but occasionally we overhear their conversations. One of them was particularly disturbing.

I overheard Steve's mum chatting to Val and really wished I hadn't when I heard her say "I have the power. If he's annoyed me or upset me I can withhold my orgasm. I don't want him feeling smug by making me come. If he starts to try to make me come or rubs me hard when I'm dry, I roll him onto his back and suck his willy instead. I know he loves it and it always works and, afterwards, I can go back to reading my book. Urrrgh! Shauna, I really wished I'd lost the gift of hearing. Can you believe how horrific that was to hear?

You can imagine my relief when, the following day, I was treating myself to a bit of guilty pleasure. No, not that!! I was reading the problem page of one of the magazines the ladies brought over with them. UK magazines are more expensive in Spain so I tend to rely on reading the ones our visitors bring with them. I even find myself reading fishing magazines, ones for coin collectors, truck restorers or ones about building your own dolls house. I'm sure the skills I've learned will come in handy one day.

Anyway, one of the problem page letters was from a woman, clearly unhappy in her marriage and finding the sadness is reflected in her lack of libido. Some of the words stood out and attracted me to read further.

"We've stopped kissing. We used to kiss all the time. Now he only kisses when he wants to make love or, should I say F...!" The poor lady continued with the story of her angry, selfish, spoiled, controlling husband. Later in her cry for help letter I read the words "I have the power. If he's annoyed me or upset me I can withhold my orgasm. ………….. I roll him onto his back and suck …….and, afterwards, I can go back to reading my book" Familiar? Phew, thank God for that. Steve's mum was obviously reading this aloud to Val when I mistook it for a moan about Steve's Dad.

I can't tell you how relieved I was. I really like Steve's Dad so I'm really pleased to hear he's none of the horrible things described in the anonymous letter. He's quite fit actually in an older man way. Probably why I've gone for Steve – they are very similar. No, nothing weird, honest but I can see what Steve will look like when he's a more mature man and it's not something I'm dreading, let's put it that way. I just hope the poor lady in the problem page letter bites her husband's willy off next time!

Anyway Shauna, despite everything I've said about the habits of visiting guests. I really really really want you to come out here and stay with us. Honestly, you can borrow all my clothes. And Steve's! You can sit by the pool laughing out loud whilst you drink the special bottle of flavoured vodka I've set aside for a little treat to myself. You can smash my glasses, break my plates, and wear my brand new sunglasses before I've had the opportunity to wear them myself. You can borrow my nail varnish and leave the lid off so it dries up in the bottle. You can stay up late with all the lights on and air-conditioning running full blast before eventually falling asleep and snoring loudly all night. Oh stop me. I'm getting carried away again. Just get on a plane and come out here now!

(33) George

Why, when you're painting a closed door, do people suddenly feel the desire to push through it? I love my Dee to bits but sometimes she amazes me. I was feeling quite fit and well today so I decided to tackle a bit of painting. Dee normally does those jobs these days and I feel really bad about it. I was always the DIY king but, after my accident, my back makes even minor repairs very difficult and uncomfortable at times.

Anyway, as I said, I was feeling up to a bit of painting so I decided to tackle the glossing of the bathroom woodwork. Dee knew I was doing it. She was delighted because the white paint had deteriorated to a dull yellow over the years, not to mention all the chips and knocks. Sounds like I'm describing myself, doesn't it?

During the rubbing down process, Dee was ferrying backwards and forwards with cups of tea, collecting empty tea cups, offers of more cups of tea, refilling them, despite the fact I said I'd had enough thank you. Good job I was in the bathroom. I certainly needed to use it more than once during this task.

Skirting boards complete, I moved on to the back of the bathroom door and the painted panel above it. Door closed, dustsheets on the floor, I'm standing on a step-stool, the smell of gloss paint wafting through the entire house. A bit of an indication that the back of the bathroom door was now being painted. My waitress for the day, in the form of the lovely Dee, failed to spot the clues. Suddenly I'm aware of her efforts to turn the bathroom handle whilst applying all her weight to the other side of the door in an attempt to open it and get in, probably on another tea related errand.

Dee is certainly a determined character and possibly a little bit hard of hearing. Yes, I had the radio on but, even over the nostalgic sounds of the seventies, she should have been able to hear my protests. Still not picking up on the clues, Dee set up a rocking motion of force on the door, which caused the small stool I was balancing on to tip onto two legs. Paint kettle in one hand, charged paint brush in the other, I tried desperately to maintain my balance but my vulnerable back was losing the battle and I fell backwards, taking the paint paraphernalia with me. As a young man, I've had more than one encounter whereby I've slipped or fallen with pint of beer in my hand. Any man will tell you about the pride he feels when he discovers the glass is still almost full after such an event. A paint kettle, swinging from its thin metal handle does not have the same physical make up. The white gloss slopped over the top and splashed all over the bathroom floor. Ironically some of it splashed into an empty teacup waiting patiently for its next refill.

Dee eventually managed to prize her way through the restricted door access to survey the scene. The floor, walls and sanitary ware were all splashed with white gloss. I was laying flat on my back, legs splayed, and arms outwards. The stool, which was designed in the style of a bright red mushroom and had belonged to one of the girls when they were younger, now only possessed two legs instead of the original three. I must have flung the paint brush as I fell. It had landed in the bath and created a long strip of colour as it slid down the side before resting in the bottom. Dee initially demonstrated concern but, once she had established no bones were broken, she declared I looked as though I was creating a snow angel. Giving me instructions not to move and to stay where I was, Dee rushed off to find her phone to take a photo for Facespace or whatever it's called. She said the kids would love it. Apparently it would go viral. What on earth is she talking about? Just get me up from this gloss gore and let's get down to the nearest floor specialist to finally replace this hideous bathroom floor. We've been meaning to do it for years and now we have an excuse. Sometimes it takes a disaster to force you to move on. There, that's my thought for the day!

(34) Email Beth to Shauna)

Oh God Shauna! I'm so sorry. I didn't realise that problem page letter was from you. I'm so sorry things are that bad for you. Why didn't you talk to me?

(35) Email Redhead to Isla)

OMG Isla. What's wrong with me? As usual I've reacted quickly and regretted later. What is it my mum used to say? Something about act in haste, repent at leisure. Well, I'm repenting now!

It's about my married guy again. We were snatching a bit of time alone. Well, to be fair we were in the gym but we'd got ourselves in a quiet corner and we were flirting whilst working out. I hope they don't have microphones on the CCTV cameras! Anyway, the chat was getting steamy. I could tell it was turning him on. It's my own fault. I was trying to fish for compliments and I wanted to hear that he was having more fun with me than her. His wife. I dropped in a question about them having sex, assuming he'd say they hadn't done anything in ages. Then he said something about it just being, you know and dropping his eyes to his crotch.

Why did I pursue it? It was painful enough as it was. Oh no, not me. I asked what he meant and he said she'd turned him down for the full performance the other day but offered to give him a blow job instead which he obviously accepted. He said he almost prefers it that way, particularly as she's so good at it. He expected me to be pleased with this information and couldn't understand the tears that sprang into my eyes. Hurtful bastard. Why did he tell me that? Yes, I know I asked the question and I know she's his wife and I'm technically a nobody, but he should have lied. That's the rule, isn't it?

As if setting myself up for that hurt wasn't enough, I responded by picking up my phone and sending a message to Rav. Yes, Rav. The guy I've been trying to avoid for ages. I wanted to let married man know that he wasn't my only source of pleasure so I turned to someone I knew would want me and would react to my message. It was only a quick hello I hope you're OK type of message but it worked. Within minutes Rav was on the phone. I know it's frowned upon to take calls in the gym but this was the fish I wanted on the line and I wanted married man to hear me chatting effortlessly with a mystery man. I needed married man to watch me reel in the flirty caller and realise that, if he didn't haul me in quick, I may one day be the one that got away.

Dinner. Tonight? Yes Rav, I'd love to. Lots of giggling and throwing my head back with fake laughter. Married guy was doing that thing of pretending not to be listening whilst actually listening to every word. He nonchalantly wandered over to the free weights and started lifting some heavy loads to demonstrate his prowess. It was so obvious he'd bitten off more than he could chew. He seemed to be really struggling and I swear I heard him fart as he straightened up but I was trying to act as if I'd forgotten he was in the room. More giggling from me. More suggestive deep talking and the deed was done. Dinner with Rav….. Oh shit!!!!!

Isla, you have no idea how painful that meal was. Rav was like the cat that had the cream. Little did he know it but he was never going to lick my cream. Oh, sorry. Gone too far again? Anyway, he was painfully proud of the fact that I'd been back in touch. He kept going on about how I must have realised what a catch he was.

We'd gone to an Indian restaurant. It's one of those ones favoured by hen nights before hitting the town. There were several tables of young ladies having a great time and I really wanted to join them but I had to sit there and listen to Rav blowing his own trumpet again. I was hoping married guy would stroll passed the window and at least see me to make all this worth it. But why would he? He was probably at home with his penis in his wife's mouth!

Due to the other large parties in the restaurant, Rav and I were given a small table with very little room for all the dishes he'd insisted on ordering. He implied he was some sort of culinary expert (of course!) but in reality he knew as much about the origin and contents of each dish as I did.

The waiter kept bringing out more and more bowls and plates until there was barely any room for the glass of wine I desperately needed to get me through this ordeal. Rav suggested to the waiter that he may want to put some of our plates on the table behind which appeared to be empty. The waiter very politely explained that the table behind was booked and about to be occupied. Rav obviously didn't like being declined – I should know that – so he pursued with his quest. The waiter, again very politely, explained that he couldn't put our food on another table but offered to clear away some of the plates if we'd finished with them. There was, after all, a small mountain of dishes crowding the table with more to come. Enough food to feed the entire restaurant. What was Rav trying to do? Impress me with his generosity or the capacity of his intestines to process all this rich and spicy food?

Isla, I was trying to shrink into my chair. By now, I desperately wanted to join one of the hen party tables. They were having great fun. Most of them were unaware of the scene Rav was creating but a few of the diners nearest to us had stopped talking and were listening to the proceedings. Oh God! Not again. This is the second meal I've had with Rav that has become the source of entertainment for fellow diners. At least he hadn't asked me when we were going to have sex. Well, not yet, at least!

Unbelievably, he asked the waiter if he could speak to the manager. At no point did he look towards me and apologise for ruining my enjoyment of the meal. Enjoyment is probably a bit of an exaggeration. Yes, the food was lovely but the company was not!

The manager duly appeared at the table and Rav asked, in all seriousness, if we could have a new waiter because he did not like the attitude of the one we had.

Can you believe it? So embarrassing. I was trying to catch the eye of the poor waiter to let him know I was not in on this and that I also thought Rav was a complete and utter twonk. The poor waiter stood with his head bowed, staring at the floor. Fortunately his manager backed him up and advised Rav that no change of staff would take place and that, if sir wished to make a complaint, he could do so. However, sir may wish to allow his staff to clear the table and make more room for the next six dishes.

SIX?

What an ordeal. I couldn't face any more of this. Talking of 'face', mine was bright red and, even worse, I realised my top lip was forming an unattractive dew of sweat. I was about to excuse myself when Rav declared he needed to do the same. It would have looked strange if we'd both left the table and gone to the toilet at the same time, particularly as I didn't want anyone, and especially Rav, thinking there would be any hanky-panky anywhere. I remained stoically at the table, surrounded by food I no longer had a desire for and watched Rav as he walked towards the facilities. I had once felt a fleeting appetite for him but right now he made my stomach churn.

There was nothing left to do. I had to get my sweaty self out of this restaurant and away from randy Rav. The curry wasn't the only hot dish in this place. Rav fancied himself more than ever and had been licking his lips whilst gazing into my eyes over the steaming crucibles of curry. I knew I was in for more of the hard sell. Hard being the operative word. I couldn't face the sensation of his crotch pressing into me in yet another car park.

I pressed the home key on my phone to check the time. The phone screen came to life and suddenly I had an idea. I picked up the phone and started a fake conversation. I even convinced myself. I pretended I was talking to you, babe, so it was easy. In the corner of my eye I could see Rav returning to the table. He was adopting some kind of self-assured swagger. My stomach lurched a bit and I let out an involuntary burp – ooops! Mind you, I didn't care, I wasn't trying to impress Rav, in fact I didn't want him to fancy me at all. I just felt sorry for the other diners who had already been treated to a fair bit of bad behaviour from our table. I turned round and smiled my apologies to the tables nearest to us.

Rav slipped into his seat in front of me, obviously disappointed to note I'd managed to make or receive a call in his absence.

I went into full drama mode and started saying things like "Oh no, babe, how awful….. no, stay there……. don't do anything……… I'm on my way……" Rav started shifting uncomfortably in his seat. He wasn't stupid. He knew my responses meant I would be leaving the table and his amazing company. He looked around the restaurant to see the reactions on the other tables. Many diners were pretending not to be listening but they obviously were. I suspect Rav must have been gutted to be seen in public as the bloke who was left to pay the bill whilst his lover dashed off to help someone more important.

I stood up whilst making I'm sorry faces at Rav. As I walked to the door I continued to talk into the phone "No, don't touch anything babe…… just leave everything as it is…..…… I'm on the way……….." All very convincing, if I say so myself. Until MY PHONE RANG! Oh yeah. The phone I was talking on starting ringing in my ear. Oh shit! Playing for time, I feigned surprise and confusion and started shaking the phone as if I didn't know what was going on. I looked at the screen. It was my mum calling. I had to answer it to shut the phone up and keep myself occupied whilst I made my final escape. I was almost through the door now. I pressed the accept button and, before my mum had chance to say anything, I shouted "Sorry about that babe. We must have lost the signal. No, I've told you don't touch it or pick it. You'll just make it worse……."

(36) Shauna

Shauna found herself at a 'ladies night'. That didn't necessarily mean all the guests were ladies in the manners and behaviour sense of the word. It's amazing what you learn about your fellow woman when she is presented with teambuilding challenges and a plethora of plastic penises. Yes, it was one of those parties.

The hostess was a Lisa from work. Lisa who sat side-by-side with Barbara on reception, welcoming guests, accepting parcels, booking taxis and, on occasion, receiving a large bunch of flowers for a lucky recipient. I suppose that depends on why the flowers were sent. Not to be cynical but, sometimes a bunch of flowers can mean sorry. Sorry for your loss or just plain sorry I was an arse!!!

Back in the room...... Lisa's sitting room to be precise. A very small sitting room in her parent's semi-detached home. The room had once been a through lounge dinning room but somewhere along the way, Lisa's parents had inserted patterned glass double doors between the two rooms to create two small separate spaces.

On this particular evening, Lisa's father and younger brother had been dispatched to the dining room on the other side of the obscure glass. This didn't prevent them from overhearing the cackles and screams of the women in the room next door, nor did it prevent distorted images of their goings-on being made quite apparent when viewed through the crazy glass.

However, to all intents and purposes, the men were unaware of what was taking place in the cosy sitting room full of females. Lisa's father was given the important role of standing by with his wallet, should his wife wish to purchase something tantalising to spice up their bedroom activities.

Lisa, of course, would receive a hostess gift and a large percentage discount from any purchases she wished to make. She felt it would be inappropriate to ask her father to pay for any of her chosen items!

Due to the restricted proportions of the room, three ladies were squashed on each of the two-seater sofas, whilst others perched on the arms or sat on the spare dining room chairs not required by Lisa's father and brother next door. The room may have had restricted proportions but Stacey, the party planner, certainly didn't. She was a very comfortably built young lady with a waterfall bosom that seemed to be permanently on the precipice of her low cut top. Shauna felt, at any moment, there would be an almighty whoosh before Stacey's breasts overflowed from the straining garment and spilled out, cascading over her rotund tummy below.

Stacey handed out blank pieces of A4 paper to each guest and directed them to sit with the paper behind their backs.

"Now ladies, the aim of this game is to rip and tear your piece of paper into the shape of a willy" Lots of ooohs, and aarrrrssss and far too much loud laughter.

"You have all seen a willy before, haven't you"

More ooohs, arrssss and even louder laughter.

Shauna surprised herself by winning this game. Her paper penis was very large and messy with one testicle much larger than the other but, for comedy value, it was voted number one, thereby earning Shauna a lucky-dip prize. She reached inside the bag and retrieved a jigsaw puzzle with a very well equipped naked man as the featured image.

Lisa's mum and Meera from accounts came joint first in the general knowledge quiz. The younger members of the group were astounded just how much these ladies knew. Shauna wondered whether her mother, Dee, would have been a match for them....... Probably!!!

The next game involved Stacey reading out a list of exploits, pre-fixed by the line "sit down if you have never".

"OK, off we go ladies" Stacey dramatically raised the list above her enormous bosom and began "Sit down if you have never kissed a man"

Everyone remained standing

"Sit down if you have never given fellatio"

Lisa's mum sat down.

"Sit down if you have never had a one night stand"

Meera sat down

The list continued, causing raised eyebrows and

raucous laughter, occasionally deteriorating to some very daring and smutty suggestions. By now, only Daisy and Barbara remained standing. They turned to smile at each other.

"Sit down if you have never had sex in the back of a taxi"

Daisy waivered, obviously thinking about it, almost sat down but then straightened her knees to stand erect again.

"Sit down if you have never had sex on a desk at work"

"Sit down if you have never had sex on your bosses desk"

"Sit down if you have never had sex with your boss"

Daisy reluctantly sat down, leaving Barbara remaining.

The onlookers were amazed. "Really, Barbara, you've done all those things?"

"What!" Barbara looked up from her prize, a box of willy shaped chocolates "No, I've NEVER done any of those things"

This was priceless. Clearly Barbara had misunderstood the negative positive question element. Everyone fell about laughing. It didn't matter that Barbara had accidentally bluffed her way to a box of chocolate penises, the entertainment she had provided was worth it. Secretly, Shauna suspected that Daisy's life was not as varied as she may have implied either so probably neither of them deserved the free phallic chocs.

"Not even fellatio Barbara"? asked one of the women "You've never given head"?

"I don't like too much Italian pasta stuff" Barbara shook her head to emphasise her response.

Stacey became bright red and sweaty from laughing so much. This sort of thing must make her job worthwhile. She pleaded with Lisa's mother to explain what fellatio really meant.

"Not me, you're the one with all the toys" came her quick reply

Another wave of laughter over which someone could be overheard saying "Make sure you wash it first, you don't know where it's been"

A short break was taken. Lisa's mum passed round plates of quiche and sandwiches. Lisa topped up drinks. Everyone offered to help out but the mother and daughter hostesses declined. They explained it's always easier to do it yourself because you know where everything is. Fair point. Someone made a crude remark to ask if the same rule applies to masturbation. Ear piercing shrieks of laughter followed.

Shauna made the effort to make small talk with the ladies she was sharing a sofa with. The lady to her right was a neighbour and friend of the family from way back. The lady to her left worked with Lisa's mother. Both women obviously knew each other very well and displayed an easy-company nature to their friendship. Shauna enjoyed listening to their matter-of-fact approach to life.

From the hallway, Shauna could hear Lisa arguing with her brother.

"Go away bum fluff boy"

Shauna smiled. This was Lisa, the glamorous girl from reception, suddenly sounding like a truculent teenager.

"Mum, tell him to go away" Whining now. Attractive! "This is *my* party"

The sound of pushing and pulling followed. It was difficult to tell who was winning.

Lisa returned to the room, looking slightly flushed with tousled hair.

"Sorry about that everyone" She stroked the side of her head in an effort to smooth down the ruffled locks of her hair "My annoying little brother thinks he can eat our sausage rolls"

"Lisa fancies Meera's son" Little brother managed to shout through the sitting room door before being pushed backwards by his embarrassed sister.

"Oh My God" wailed Lisa "Muuum. Stop him please. I'm so sorry about my annoying brother everyone"

Shauna consoled Lisa buy telling her that Ruby and

Alex were exactly the same. She wasn't sure it had the effect she had intended but at least it restored the light-hearted atmosphere and allowed Stacey the opportunity to display her wares.

No, not the wobbly breasts that still threatened to burst like air bags into the room. The wares she hoped to display to the lovely ladies were items designed to introduce fun and passion into the bedroom. Why those emotions and feelings couldn't be incorporated into a loving relationship without the aid of all this paraphernalia probably perplexed many women but a whole industry was built around this sort of event so best go with it whilst you're here!

"Now ladies, I'm going to begin with the rack here" Shauna laughed inside. Was Stacey referring to her own personal mammary rack? Her breasts seemed too large to be described as such. They were more like a bouncy castle than a pert rack….. Shauna found her inability to focus and concentrate annoying at times. Someone would say something that would create an associated chain of thoughts in her mind and distract her totally from the subject in hand. Very frustrating if she was the person allocated to take minutes in a meeting. At the end of the meeting she would review the pad in front of her. Beautifully titled with the date, attendees, apologies for absence and a few random words of relevant information. Then….. nothing. A few doodles and a coffee cup stain but…. nothing tangible to type into the minutes. Shauna would spend hours after the meeting casually asking all attendees for their thoughts and opinions in order to fluff up the document she was producing.

Focus focus………

Stacey was talking in a soft voice, which was probably aimed at enhancing the alluring nature of the items. What didn't help was her occasional declaration that she and her boyfriend particularly favoured a certain garment. Shauna found it hard to imagine how the delicate lace of the all-in-one crutchless body stocking would contain all of Stacey's loveliness.

Emboldened by the raised eyebrows around the room, Stacey continued to describe the advantages of certain easy-access items of lingerie. Shauna's eyes wandered round the room, surveying the faces of the mixed bag of attendees. Would Barbara be able to understand what Stacey was implying here?

Shauna also noticed that Stacey's voice had risen from the breathy, lispy innocent to the slightly bawdy barmaid style. One item of faux leather beginner's bondage resulted in a story from Stacey about a recent love-making session with her (fortunately anonymous) boyfriend. The recounting of the event made Shauna look at the plated sausage rolls on the coffee table in front of her in a whole new light. Lisa's brother was welcome to as many sausage rolls as he wanted now. Shauna wouldn't be touching them now and maybe never again!!

"Unfortunately, ladies, this item is a one-off" Stacey held up what looked like a sailor suit dress. The item featured a smart white top half with blue sailor style stripes and piping. The bottom half featured a short rah-rah skirt. To Shauna, it looked like something a seven year old girl would wear and, judging by the size, she wasn't too far off.

However, the sailor dress proved very popular. The lady to Shauna's right was clearly very impressed. Shauna was going to ask if it was for her granddaughter until the lady declared that it was just the sort of thing her husband would love to see her in. She rocked backwards and forwards on the sofa until she had gained enough momentum to release herself from the cramped conditions.

At the same time, Daisy had also expressed a real interest in the sailor suit dress. To be fair, Daisy had the figure for the dress and was more appropriate in age. Daisy said it was too good for the bedroom and that she would team it with a pair of heels and wear it to go clubbing.

For a while, the atmosphere turned a bit ugly. Shauna's sofa neighbour clearly thought she had seen it first. She was the one who had made the first verbal appreciation and therefore felt entitled to own the dress. Daisy, being closer to the clothes rail, had been able to reach the item first. Both ladies put their arguments forward to Stacey who was now being expected to make a judgement.

Shauna, ever the peacemaker suggested each lady submitted her paper penis to an independent picker who would select the winner of the dress.

Daisy and Shauna's sofa neighbour were hesitant and seemed reluctant but, as the remainder of the group deemed this to be the fair option, they submitted to the suggestion.

Two impartial judges were required. Cue Lisa's father and brother. Lisa's brother refused to hold the penisis, despite the fact his big sister pointed out they were only made of paper. Lisa's Dad was quite happy to join in the fun and used the opportunity to make jokes about how he wished women were as keen to fight over his own penis. Lisa groaned with embarrassment. Lisa's mother scoffed and told him he should be so lucky. Laughter restored. The paper penises were folded into small packages (no more innuendo please) and held out for Lisa's brother to pick. Once selected, the paper penis was unravelled to reveal the winner…….. Daisy.

Daisy was triumphant and a bit of a gloating winner. Not a very attractive trait. Shauna tried to console her sofa neighbour but the poor loser was clearly not happy and continued to mumble under her breath at every opportunity. Daisy was aware of this and was also heard to mumble that she dreaded the thought of the older lady trying to squeeze her fat arms into the tiny sailor dress, and how would she ever be able to slip it off in the heat of passion without a pair of scissors!

Fortunately it was time to change the scene. This time moving on to the sale of creams and lubricants. Tubes and tubs of soft, slimy, moisturising, scented love goodies were passed around the room. Blobs of lotion were applied to the backs of hands, sniffed and appreciated. Stacey, again, used the opportunity to provide an insight into her own bedroom exploits……. Hmmmm, best not to try to imagine too much of that!

"And, of course ladies" Stacey's breathy soft voice returned "Don't forget every item you purchase this evening goes towards earning gifts for your host, Lisa"

Lisa looked uncomfortable "Yeah, but don't worry about that" She added, causing Stacey's smile to freeze into a grimace "It's only a bit of fun so you don't have to buy anything if you don't want to".

A chorus of ladies voices thanked Lisa and gave platitudes indicating they would at least buy a little something for a bit of fun. You know how it is.

Stacey physically appeared to collect her thoughts and enthusiasm "And now for the peassss de resistance" came her fumbled attempt at French "The toys".

"Now ladies" Stacey scanned around the room, making sure everyone was listening "Some of these are my own personal items for display only. They will therefore need to be ordered. However, some are brand new and available for purchase this evening"

The toys and vibrators were passed round the room in a clockwise direction. Stacey provided a summary of the benefits of each product. It was suggested that the power of the vibrators was best tried on the tip of the nose. Far better and less embarrassing than another area with the potential to indicate the effectiveness of these artificially throbbing and pulsing beasts.

Each to their own. Some women showed no real interest whilst others nodded and agreed that certain features would appeal to them.

Stacey made a grand announcement about the final product.

"Now ladies" She straightened her back and treated

the room to full barrels of bosom "This is the Turgid Torpedo. It has been in research for many years and has had input, excuse the pun, from many leading gynaecologists and sex experts across the world. Shame they didn't include me in that category" Stacey laughed heartily.

"As you can see, the item still has a plastic wrapper on the shaft" She held the item aloft with two hands, causing it to resemble a light sabre from Star Wars "This means the item is available for purchase this evening. Please do not remove the wrapper but you are free to try the many functions the product has to offer.

The Turgid Torpedo slowly made its way round the room. Each lady in turn trying the many functions available, pressing buttons and struggling to contain the power of the plastic penis.

Eventually the item reached Shauna's right hand sofa neighbour who appeared particularly fascinated. She studied the Torpedo, pressed its many buttons, held it against her nose, sneezed, and tried again. She frowned. She smiled. Shauna sat squashed beside her, trying to release her arms from the restricted space in order to receive the vibrator once the close inspection had finished.

"Come on Mrs" This remark came from Shauna's left hand sofa neighbour "You've had that bloody thing for ages. Give someone else a chance".

Her arm reached across Shauna and she grabbed the still vibrating multi-function toy from her friends grasp. Now in possession of the Turgid Torpedo and holding it in her hands, the left-hand sofa neighbour seemed a little disappointed.

"It's not that good. What is all the fuss about?"

Right-hand sofa neighbour seemed amazed.

"What's *not* to like about it? It does everything. Up, down, sideway, round and round. And feel the power"

Left-hand sofa neighbour held the product closer to allow better vision, she selected another button. The vibrator commenced a rapid thrusting motion, causing the plastic wrapper to crackle loudly.

Throughout the evening, the family cat had been sitting quietly in the room, despite the guffaws and general excitement of the crowd. However, the friendly feline was suddenly spooked by the plastic bag being loudly assaulted by the Turgid Torpedo and emitted a loud cat shriek. The sound was deafening and unexpected. The cat, in terror, obviously became disorientated and, instead of making straight for the door, headed into the empty fireplace, still shrieking and meowing furiously. He almost ran up the chimney before spinning round and heading back out of the fireplace in search of the exit. On his frantic escape from the room, he clawed at the tights of an innocent party goer propped on the arm of the sofa, ripping a hole in her hosiery and causing a nasty scratch which almost immediately began to weep and trickle blood down the shins of the startled lady.

Shauna made a mental note to remember every aspect of this evening. She wasn't sure what she would do with the memory but she felt it needed preserving in some way. She had mainly been a silent observer of the events and felt as if she were watching a play. However, the acting was not amateur dramatics in the local village hall, it was the real thing. Priceless!

Once calm had been restored, Stacey commenced with the ordering process. Once again she re-iterated the benefit to Lisa of everyone spending lots of money. Again Lisa looked embarrassed and fussed about clearing plates, including the sausage rolls, which nobody seemed to have touched.

Shauna didn't really feel in the mood to order anything so she selected an apron featuring a full-size image of ladies underwear on the front. It would make a fun stocking filler for her Dad at Christmas.

Whilst the ladies sat quietly chatting amongst themselves at the end of the evening, Shauna overheard Meera telling Daisy she was waiting for her son to pick her up. Ah, this must be the one Lisa fancies. Daisy told Meera she fancied the brother of one of her friends. Apparently he had dropped them off at the airport recently. Daisy explained her disappointment that the brother didn't seem to be interested in her. She said it in a way that implied she normally expected members of the opposite sex to find her irresistible.

A knock on the door. It was Rav, Meera's son. He was dragged into the hallway and introduced loudly for the benefit of all in doubt as to who is was. Poor Lisa. Shauna felt she needed to break the tension.

"Hello Rav, nice to meet you. I work with your lovely

Mum" Shauna didn't always have the most intelligent things to say but she knew how to make small talk. What made her say the next thing, however, was a mystery.

"I won this jigsaw puzzle in a game earlier" She held out the box, displaying a picture of the naked man to be re-assembled "It's only got twenty pieces and I've finished it already, would you like it?"

Rav looked amused. He had a cheeky face. Thank God he took it well. Why did she say such a stupid thing?

"Only twenty pieces?" He grinned "My ……." He hesitated and looked across at his mother before continuing "My head would take up more than twenty pieces" He winked and everyone laughed. We all knew what he meant but, out of respect for his mother, he had recovered the rude remark and turned it into something palatable. What a shame some of Stacey's stories were harder to swallow – excuse the pun!

(37) George

Dee had left one of her ladies magazines on the kitchen table. She's a sucker for a tempting front cover promising details of a celebrity bust-up or a feature about someone who has lost six stone in twenty minutes and they'll tell you how inside. I never read them but I know they keep Dee topped up with current soap and celebrity gossip so I'm quite happy to drop a copy in the basket when I'm the one doing the supermarket shop.

Well, I say I never read the magazines. I occasionally treat myself to a look at the problem page. It started out in my youth when I thought reading other peoples problems may help me understand women. Unfortunately, reading their dilemmas has only served to prove just how complicated women are and that most men will never understand them.

I must say, the Agony Aunt in Dee's favourite magazine seems to have upped her game. Some of the responses are quite hard hitting. I suspect the original problem solver has been replaced with someone a bit more gritty and suitable for the diverse problems experienced by the millennium readership.

A quick flick to the page and immediately my eyes are drawn to a problem entitled "Rollercoaster Ride Ruined". The titles often belie the story below so I felt obliged to read the contributor's predicament:

"My husband is very good at using his own personal power tool (if you know what I mean) but, for some reason, foreplay is a bit like riding a rollercoaster. When he's stimulating me manually he can be quite clumsy and it's not always a comfortable ride. I try to make oooh and aaahhh noises if he hits the right spot to encourage him to do more of the same but, no, for some reason he suddenly moves away from that bit and starts to do something else somewhere else. I fall silent. Eventually he may return to the perfect spot. More appreciative noises from me. He gets the speed right. The pressure right. Perfect. Oh yes. I'm climbing to the top of the rollercoaster and approaching the point of no return. Waiting to tip over and enjoy the rush of excitement and pleasure. Oh yes…..Oh YES!... Oh NO! He's slowed down again. He's moved somewhere else. Arrrrgghhh! I almost scream out loud but he may mistake it for an outburst of pleasure so I grit my teeth and prepare to ride the roller coaster round the entire track again until we get back to the peak point in the hope I'll tip over into nirvana this time.

And the Agony Aunt's reply?

"You sound like a very humorous and articulate lady. I would use your skills to SHOW AND TELL HIM! You don't have to be rude or critical and I know, with your expressive gifts, you will be able to make it a gentle and sensitive lesson. Add some humour to the information but make sure you laugh *with* him and not *at* him! Take his hand and ride along together. Just don't leave it too long or you'll get motion sickness on that rollercoaster!"

Well put, I thought. I hope it works out for them and they are soon enjoying the theme park of sexual pleasure in harmony. They will be climbing the rollercoaster loops, peaking at the top and preparing for the inevitable rush. Maybe they'll even be raising their arms above their heads as they speed down the other side, hair blowing in the breeze and smiling for the hidden camera. Oh, I'm getting a bit carried away now. A slurp of tea and I scan the headings for the next problem. My eyes alight upon "Lady Love?" which reads:

"I'm not sure if this is unique to me. I know we all feel we are different to the rest of the world. We always feel like the odd-one-out but we don't always openly admit it. Well, I'm not sure if I am the only woman who feels like this but, let me explain. After having my children, raising a family and negotiating the sweaty maze of the menopause, I'm finding I crave the soft, gentle, knowing affection of women rather than the hard hairy love making of a man. Is this normal? Is my dip in libido part of human nature? Once the child rearing is complete and I start to form a downy moustache on my top lip, do my hormones trigger something that tells my body not to bother any longer? You're not going to have anymore babies so you don't need to find the male of the species attractive or even be attractive yourself?"

I couldn't wait to read the response of the Agony Aunt and here it is:

"You need to get together with the lady stuck on the rollercoaster! You obviously both know your way round the female body. I know that's not necessarily the answer you're looking for but, before we go any further, can I just say I'm sure you are a very attractive lady. Maybe get that 'tash sorted but the fact you know it's there is a start. I have elderly relatives who sport the most vigorous facial hair and they appear totally unaware of it. I'm talking female relatives here. The males have their own problems – trouser waistbands pulled almost up to the armpits, hairy ears, and uncontrollable flatulence! Anyway, you don't want to be worrying about that and I've probably put you off men altogether with that portrayal! In my opinion……"

I didn't manage to read the opinion. My secret foray into other people's lives was brought to a noisy end. Ruby suddenly crashed into the kitchen and commenced her usual angry search for something to eat, slamming cupboard doors, sighing at the contents of the fridge and exuding the familiar predicable wail of "Why is there never anything in this house I like?"

I tried suggesting she may like to buy her own food as her mother and I were providing as much as we could, free of charge, by the way!

"There's literally NOTHING for me to eat" Oh dear. Ruby was building up for a toddler tantrum. I had a choice. I could choose to ignore Ruby's childish behaviour or embrace the opportunity to smooth her ruffled feathers. Not sure Ruby has feathers. Maybe something more like porcupine spines?!

"Beans on toast?" I suggested.

Ruby's pouty bottom lip retreated as she mumbled a barely audible reluctant agreement. The smile returned to her face when I offered to make them. An opportunity for a father and daughter baked bean bonding moment. Ruby lowered herself into a kitchen chair, pulling the magazine towards her. The magazine was still opened on the Agony Aunt page but Ruby was now the one reading it. Shame, I was really looking forward to reading the problem entitled "Is My Son A Bit Of A Plonker?"

(38) Email Beth to Shauna

Oh God Shauna, I miss those parties. In the UK, whenever I was invited to a jewellery or make-up party I would groan. I'd always feel obliged to buy something to help my friend with her party hostess commission. I hardly ever went to one where I actually wanted anything... Except the ladies toy parties. I should have given you a shopping list. Only kidding, but I do quite like the odd battery powered plaything. And, strangely, I now miss those parties where all the girls get together in someone's tiny living room to buy things they'd never consider otherwise. We don't seem to have things like that here. Maybe I should be the first to host one.

Anyway, you're not the only one who's had an encounter with an unexpected willy. Juan and I were out delivering a car to a customer a couple of days ago. He was in the 'runner' car so his job was to follow me as I drove the car to be delivered to the customer and to drive me back to the rental office afterwards. When I say his job was to follow me, that's what happened in the UK. Here in Spain, I haven't got a clue where I'm going so I normally end up following Juan.

It was the usual heart-in-mouth experience. Juan driving erratically at various speeds and often in the middle of the road, displaying no spatial awareness or ability to read the road ahead. On occasion, he would round a blind bend whilst being well over the central white line. The car coming the other way would normally be doing the same. Furious screeching of brakes and lots of hand gestures would follow. I'd be sitting (well back) in the car behind, thinking how easily it could all have been avoided. Juan seemed impervious to the lessons learned from each encounter and would repeat the near miss experience over and over again.

Anyway, we finally reached our destination. For once we were delivering a car to a customer's home address as his firm has an account with us. His house was in a narrow old town street in the pueblo, one of my favourite parts, with all the back-to-back houses and tapas bars. Unfortunately it is very difficult reaching these houses by car so Juan parked at the end of the road whilst I squeezed the rental car down the small lane.

I knocked on the door of the house and shortly after a man's voice called "Hola?"

"Hola, CostaCoches" I said in my best Spanish accent. That was about the limit but, as he was an account customer, I didn't really need to get too involved with the paperwork. All I had to do was ask him to sign on the dotted line, give him the keys and go.

"Hola" came the voice again, as the front door slowly opened.

The customer stood there smiling, holding the door open and gesturing for me to come in.

Completely naked!

I could see everything

Everything!!

Clipboard in hand, I'd prepared myself to hand over a pen and ask him, in my rehearsed Spanish, to sign here and here. I didn't know the words for "hang on a minute, mate, do you think you should put some clothes on. I mean, where are you going to put the car keys?"

"Erm….. urrrrrmmm, un momento por favor" Came out of my mouth. Not sure it made sense but I was surprised at myself for even managing that.

I leaned back to catch Juan's eye. I needed him here with me. I could see him sitting in the runner car, window open, sunglasses on, listening to music and drumming his hands on the steering wheel.

"Juan" I shouted "Juan" Oh Godddddd!! "JUAN" Why was it every time I needed him to be on the ball he wasn't? I started to wave. I jumped up and down – not a good look. "JUAN"

Eventually my energetic movements caught Juan's eye and he looked in my direction. I gestured for him to come over. He looked puzzled. I repeated my mime.

Juan waved back in a friendly manner.

I tried to mime the fact that the customer in front of me was in the nude and that I was not in the mood for Juan's stupidity. He continued to wave.

I stamped my foot like a frustrated child. Why did he

not understand my gesture for a swinging, naked penis and testicles?

Juan could obviously see I was becoming upset. Slowly, frustratingly slowly, he released himself from his mobile disco on wheels and walked over in my direction.

During my party guessing game enactment, I hadn't noticed that the naked customer had walked away from the door. Juan finally reached my side. The customer returned to the door – in jeans and a t-shirt. Rapid Spanish followed, as the two men seemed to be sharing a joke. How dare they. I thrust the paperwork in Juan's hands and left him to deal with the signatures whilst I escaped to the runner car. I marched towards the passenger door and yanked angrily at the handle. Annoyingly, for once, Juan had locked the car so all I gained was a broken fingernail and even more humiliation.

Juan returned to the car, cocky as ever, and eventually explained that the customer's girlfriend is a sculptor and was using him as her life model in order to create a work of art. He had explained to Juan that he'd forgotten he was naked (yeah right!) and didn't think anything of it when he went to open the door. I wonder if I'll ever see the final sculpture on display? To be honest, it would be a striking and impressive item, based on what I saw!!

(39) Email Redhead to Isla

Isla. Thanks for last night. It was great to catch up over a drink and you looked amazing, by the way. Great to know you're having fun at work. Congratulations on the record-breaking sales of sex toys on the Triptees promotion stand. I can't believe your bonus is paid in vouchers for the company though but remember I'm happy to help you spend them if you run out of ideas! The variety of your work certainly seems to suit you and that new bra company promotion is right up your big boobie street!

I forgot to tell you, the agency I work for has given me a new assignment too. Makes a change from the on-line tarot card-reading job. I'm currently playing the part of an agony aunt for a woman's magazine. I've done this sort of work in the past and I've been given all sorts of pseudonyms, both male and female. At the moment, I'm playing a sassy, strong and sensible woman in her forties who dispenses wise words to the readership. Some of the cases drive you absolutely crazy and you wonder why these women are staying with such a bunch of arseholes. It's often quite clear their blokes are having affairs but I'm not supposed to be too harsh. My brief is to guide them and be firm but fair… and sensitive.

I quite like the character I've created though. She's the sort of woman I'd like to be if I were a woman in my mid forties, working in the world of woman's magazines with a wealth of experience behind me. I imagine myself being a buxom brunette with a throaty laugh, piercing eyes, which look knowingly at you over expensive designer glasses. My created character has a penchant for expensive champagne, expensive perfume and expensive men. I did wonder if I should dress up and behave like her to get into the part but the advice I give may be influenced by my appearance so best not, eh?!?

(40) Email Isla to Redhead

Dear Agony Auntie…

Only kidding. I don't have to contact your problem page for help. In fact, you give me your opinion whether I ask for it or not. You know I love you though!

Your agony aunt assignment sounds great fun. I hope you're being sympathetic and gentle with your replies. I've often read heartfelt letters and been surprised by the brutal and honest responses they receive.

Actually, you may be able to give me an answer to this one.

Work sent me on a promotional event for a restaurant launch yesterday. Unfortunately, instead of strolling around looking glamorous and handing out leaflets, as I'd imagined, they pretty much wanted me as a waitress.

It's not that I'm not capable. I've done it before, as you know. But I've come to realise I'm better propped provocatively on a stool at the other side of the bar rather than pouring the pints or mixing the cocktails. Equally, I'm better sitting at the table eating the food rather than delivering it.

Admittedly, when I did the waitressing job before, I received more tips than all the other girls in the family restaurant put together. I think it's down to the fact I shortened the knee length skirt they supplied as part of our wholesome uniform. And, when they asked why mine appeared to have shrunk, I told them I'd burnt it with the iron and that I'd had to cut a couple of inches off. I remember the manager questioning my interpretation of a couple of inches before issuing me with another unflattering knee length number. Clumsy me. I burnt that one with the iron too!!

And the tips kept flowing. Even when I dropped that customer's chicken kiev on the floor right in front of him. I popped it back on the plate and put it down on the table in front of him with a smile. Can you imagine the cheek of me? I apologized with a cheeky giggle and a flash of cleavage and he said it wasn't a problem as he liked a bit of carpet fluff in his kiev! I couldn't believe it when he topped it off with a £5 tip!

Unfortunately yesterday's customers weren't so easy. Why is it that a group of adults, who have been sitting waiting to be served in an establishment selling drinks, haven't decided in advance what they'd like. I turn up with my pad.

"Yes please…." I look around, waiting to hear their orders.

A couple of the group (men) immediately ordered beers. Easy, no problem.

The three girls on this particular table all look at each other. Why? Is one of them the spokesperson? Do they have to ask for permission from someone before opening their mouths?

"I don't know, what do they have?" asks one of the girls to her tablemates.

What the hell does she mean, what do they have? It's a restaurant with a bar. I'm guessing we'll have most things you're likely to ask for.

The young ladies then pick up the cocktail menu and start to slowly run through the choices. Why oh why had they not done this before? I was gritting my teeth so hard, a headache started to form at my temples. I had to go. I smiled at the decisive men and told them I would get their pints and return to take the drink order from the ladies. Hopefully peer pressure would work and the menfolk would speed up the ladies to prevent dehydration and a very long night.

You won't be surprised to hear the same table had to be visited three times before they had decided what they wanted to eat, despite the fact that the menu had been placed in front of them at the point they sat down. Did they want me to choose for them? I would have chosen the door!

I always remember, in my early waitressing days, you would come across a works Christmas party or hen night where one long-suffering woman would have arranged the event, paid the deposit and taken advanced orders from everyone.

Inevitably, some people would not show up, leaving the event arranger with the dilemma of reclaiming the deposit she had paid out of her own pocket. And, unbelievably, even though the menu had been sent to all participants in advance and choices had been made, the guests would look at the food being placed in front of them and claim it was not what they ordered.

The poor organiser would retrieve a battered sheet from her handbag with a list of everyone's choices. This would be shown around the table as proof. Some people would reluctantly agree whilst others would claim this was not what they had interpreted from the wording of the menu and that they expected it to look like something else. What, chicken curry to look like fish and chips or tomato soup to look like melon and ham?

The restaurant launch was really manic. Great for business but not so great for my empty stomach and full bladder. I'd been on my feet for several hours and only been able to drink complimentary water and nibble a few peanuts. I felt in need of a comfort break so I excused myself with the management, picked up my personal belongings from the staff room/cupboard, and slipped off to the ladies.

The restaurant was newly refurbished and obviously some snagging jobs had been overlooked. For a start, the toilet cubicle I selected didn't have a functioning lock. Secondly, it didn't have any hooks to hang up bags and coats. I was forced to put my handbag and mobile phone on the floor. Ewwwww!!!! There must be a statistic somewhere that tells us how many germs are on the average lady's handbag and, even worse, on the front screen of a mobile phone. I don't want to think about what I'm putting up against my face when I'm chatting to you, Red!!!

At least there was toilet paper. I won't go into that one but you can appreciate the familiar frustration of completing a function only to find the toilet paper drum is empty. If there's someone in the cubicle next door you can carry out the much repeated ritual of pushing supplies under the partition but, if you're on your own, it normally involves a frantic look through your handbag for bits of crumpled tissue….. I'll stop here, shall I?

Anyway, I sat down and tried to lean forward to hold the door closed. This didn't work. The door was too far away. I tried to sit with one leg outstretched to keep the door closed. No, too far, even for my long legs. So I resigned myself to being prepared to whistle. As I sat on the toilet seat for a bit of piece and quiet and to carry out the obvious function of the toilet, I became aware that someone had entered the ladies. I assumed they would head for one of the open cubicles, rather than my closed-but-not-locked one. Nevertheless I started whistling.

Suddenly I became aware of a hand appearing from underneath the door. The hand moved left and right until it alighted on my phone. I wanted to stand up and stamp on the stranger's hand but, unfortunately, I was still performing (if you get what I mean) and I couldn't stand up right at that moment without risking an embarrassing incident. I shouted to the person to get off my phone but it was too late. The hand swiftly retreated, taking my phone with it.

I wondered why they hadn't gone for my handbag. I don't think it would have fitted under the gap in the door anyway but it just goes to show how much we depend on technology. I was more concerned about losing my phone than losing my handbag.

Anyway, long story short. The restaurant got really busy. It took me ages to let the phone company know what had happened and to start the claim process. I've now got a replacement on the way but, in the meantime, I've only got a laptop to send long boring emails.

Even worse, it seems my Instatweet and Faceplant accounts have been accessed by the phone thief. Sorry, Red, some of the pictures include you and some are of people you and I have never met before. People who obviously can't afford much in the way of clothing! Somehow they've changed my password and now my user name doesn't exist anymore. I feel totally violated.

(41) Shauna

Shauna and Lewis were meeting Lewis's parents, Bob and Carole, for lunch. Sitting opposite one another in the lovely country pub, Shauna struggled for something to say to Lewis which would not fuel his quick temper. These days, it seemed every discussion topic resulted in a loud, passionate response from him. Even the most ordinary, banal conversations would cause Lewis to physically bounce with the force of expressing himself and his opinions whilst his voice would rise louder and louder to drown Shauna out. His views were always definitive – nobody else was allowed to have a say. He would often start his response to any discussion with the opening words "No, you're wrong". Wow, that's very open-minded, Shauna would think to herself.

Even an innocent question could turn into a pointless argument. Shauna would ask Lewis if he wanted a coffee. His reply would be mumbled. Shauna would ask again. More mumbling. Shauna would try again "Sorry babe, still can't hear you"

"For the third time, I SAID NO!!!!!!"

Wow, Shauna always wondered why it was necessary for Lewis to be so rude? Did he mumble on purpose to create these situations? Did he think he was so important he didn't need to speak properly? Did he love the attention and the fact that Shauna would have to try so hard to get a simple answer out of him?

It was easier to remain silent rather than start a

conversation, which would inevitably exhaust her, and further fuel Shauna's inner knowledge that her future could not be allowed contain this controlling force much longer.

Despite that fact, Shauna still felt the need to be seen chatting casually to her husband for the sake of the other people in the pub and for the impending arrival of his parents.

Scanning the pub for a safe conversation topic, Shauna's eyes rested on the specials board. A selection of tasty home cooked meals were written in chalk on a blackboard.

"Hmmmm, the specials look good"

No response from Lewis. He didn't even look round.

"Hmmmm, the specials look good" Shauna tried again. "Think I might go for the goats cheese salad. I always pick out buzz words like goats cheese, chorizo, avocado......" Her voice trailed off.

Still nothing from Lewis

"What do you fancy?" (Even if it's not me, she thought in her radiohead)

Nothing

"Babe, did you hear me"? Shauna feigned concern, rather than going in on the sarcastic route

"What"?

"Did you hear what I was saying about the specials board?"

"Yes but it was just too boring to reply"

What? Was he the conversation police now? Was he so important he could choose which direct questions he wanted to respond to, become involved in or just plain ignore?

"Wow, you're even more of an arsehole than I thought you were" Shauna's response was reactive. She had no control over what came out of her mouth but, from his response, she could see it had an impact.

"What?" He glared back

"Oh, you heard me that time" Shauna knew she was heading towards a severe verbal stripping down by Lewis but she was so incensed by his dismissal of her attempt at conversation she didn't care.

Lewis threw back his pint and glanced towards the bar. Oh yes, he's going to get drunk and deal with this subject in the car on the way home. Shauna was familiar with this tactic.

Without asking Shauna if she would like another drink, Lewis rose to make his way towards the bar. As he did so, his parents walked through the door, beaming and making a bee-line for their son who it appeared had stood to welcome them.

Bob and Carole hugged their son before turning to Shauna with genuine affection. "Darling" how are you "Hello Shauna, you look wonderful" "How was your journey?" Hugging and kissing "Sorry we're late, we had problems with the Houdini dog again"

Lewis didn't seem to have any difficulty listening to their trivia. So it's just me, thought Shauna to herself. Never mind, Bob and Carole are here and they will neutralise the toxic air with their good-natured presence. They are like my Mum and Dad, Shauna mused. I always feel safe in the presence of these solid, established married couples. I wonder if they've had their trials and tribulations over the years? Have they ever got to the point of giving up but carried on for the sake of friends and family and not wishing to disappoint or let people down? Have they held back from ending their marriage for fear of receiving criticism for the money spent on the wedding day when the marriage only lasted a few years?

As usual, the first half hour of their visit was taken up by news of Lewis's sister, Amadia, and how well she was doing as an Art Gallery Manager in Frankfurt. How her gallery, Blas, was attracting rave reviews from the rich and famous. The thing is, Shauna thought to herself, Amadia is one of the most unassuming, self-effacing people you could hope to meet. Shauna knew Amadia would not be seeking this glowing assessment of her success. Amadia would laugh it off and say it was just a job she loved doing and therefore it made her good at it. She would admit she was very well paid for doing something she thoroughly enjoyed. She would say the rich and famous are just people too. Most of them chose to visit Amadia because of her honest, down-to-earth approach and the fact she didn't 'blow smoke up their arses' her words of course!

The atmosphere in the country pub was relaxed and cosy. The goat's cheese salad was delicious. Lewis even went through the pretense of asking Shauna how her salad was. What an arse. His parents looked on in admiration – what a lovely caring, attentive son they had raised. If only they knew how rude and sarcastic he was going to be to Shauna in the car on the way home.

The chat continued in a relaxed way. Lewis obviously thought he was on form and continued to crack jokes and make witty remarks.

Bob was talking, shot-by-shot, through a recent round of golf where he had struggled to reach the putting green in his usual three. His ball had ditched in the bunker and Bob described, with his usual flair, the frustrated attempts to launch it out of the sand.

"There I was, sand wedge in hand, desperately trying in earnest to......"

"I thought you said you were at your usual club, Dad"

"Pardon, son?"

"I thought you said you were playing at your own club but you just said you were in Earnest. Where's Earnest?"

"Very funny darling" came Carole's gentle retort "Now let your father finish his story."

The hole-by-hole verbal replay of Bob's game was, indeed, boring to anyone who hadn't been there at the time but Shauna felt he deserved the respect of their attention. Lewis did as he was told by his mother and remained silent whilst Bob verbally completed all eighteen holes. Lewis did not declare this conversation too boring to listen to but he was clearly anxious to get it over with. Shauna suspected Lewis was waiting for his father get to the part where he recounted the chat and drinks in the clubhouse bar afterwards. At which point, talking about booze, Lewis would use this as an opportunity to get another round in.

Bob duly reached the eighteenth hole. As expected, and much to his son's delight, Bob moved on to describing the post-game drinks and conversation. Being an easy raconteur, Bob sashayed straight on to describe his and Carole's renewed interest in salsa dancing, something they had stopped doing after Bob twisted his knee during 'an over enthusiastic move one evening'. From the bashful looks on their faces, Shauna often wondered if the over enthusiastic move was on the dance floor or the bedroom floor!

Ballroom blushes spared, Bob and Carole launched into a joint story about the dog. Their black Labrador had a habit of bolting through the front door as soon as it was opened and the opportunity for escape presented itself. He was seemingly a happy, well-treated pooch, but could not resist the thrill of freedom. Somehow he'd pushed through the legs of whoever was standing on the doorstep that morning. Carole had continued chatting to their visitor whilst Bob dashed up the road in pursuit of their four-legged friend.

Ordinarily the dog, affectionately nicknamed Harry after Harry Houdini, would restrict his escape plan to a few metres from home. However, on days where he sensed he was about to be left alone for a protracted period of time, he would extend his distance to several miles. Bob feared this was one of those occasions so he returned to the house, collected his car keys and set off on a canine finding quest.

He eventually found Harry, galloping around a park almost a mile from home.

"Cheeky monkey was taunting me. Every time I got anywhere near him he ran away, but only just far enough for me not to be able to reach him"

Bob was telling a great story with all the mannerisms – both his and Harry's actions being reenacted.

"Eventually I grabbed his collar and put him in my boot"

"Blimey Dad, you must have big feet" Lewis again

"Same size as yours, son"

"No, you said you put Harry in your boot so you must have big feet to accommodate a Labrador in……. oh, forget it"

"The boot of the car, son" Bob seemed to be tiring of the constant interruptions but he bravely plodded on with a further story of another one of Harry's escape attempts.

Throughout all this small talk, Shauna couldn't help feeling there was something waiting to be said. She could sense, from Bob and Carole's body language that they may be waiting to say something difficult. Either that or they both had trapped wind from the rather rich and heavily potato based meals they had both chosen. Now that *would* be funny, she thought to herself. Shauna still possessed a very childish amusement towards bodily function noises. It wasn't very ladylike, of course, but the sound of an accidental fart, trump, pump or whatever you wanted to call it, would always make her throw her head back with laughter.

Bob shuffled in his seat, twizzled the stem of his wine glass between his thumb and forefinger and leaned forward slightly "We'd like to discuss a little offer we'd like to make to you both"

"Oh god, you're going to ask if you can come and live with us" joked Lewis

Privately Shauna thought that might be preferable. At least Lewis would be more tolerable with his parents around to impress.

"Don't be silly darling" laughed Carole "You wouldn't cope for five minutes before showing us the door"

"*Ten* minutes mother, what sort of heartless bum do you take me for?" Lewis's witty reply struck an element of truth in Shauna's heart.

"No, it's not about increasing your household by two but maybe by *one*" Bob pursued

"Dad, we don't want a puppy, thanks" Lewis again. "I have enough trouble clearing up after Shauna, I don't need anyone else tiddling on the kitchen floor"

Shauna was now screaming inside for someone to get to the bloody point. She'd had enough of this conversation being railroaded by her annoying husband. Ordinarily that comment would have made her laugh but not today.

"What we're saying darlings" Carole battled on "Is that we're aware you may have trouble conceiving and, knowing how difficult and traumatic it can be, we'd like to help if we can"

"Dad, are you offering to get my wife pregnant?" Lewis was on a roll and he wasn't going to stop "Cos if you are, thanks very much, but that's my job and I'm man enough to do it"

Bob shuffled in his seat again and opened his mouth to speak

"Or Mum, are you offering to be a surrogate? Cos if you are then….." Cringe "Oh wait, no that won't work because I would be the father of my own brother or sister" Double double cringe

"That's enough now Lewis, I think the drink has gone to your head and…." Bob tried to diffuse the combined embarrassment of the table.

"What are you saying, old man?" Oh God, was Lewis going to front up to his father "Not only am I man enough to get my wife pregnant but I'm also man enough to hold my drink"

"Yes, darling, we know that" soothed Carole. "We were just going to say, if you need any financial help with conceiving then we're here to help. We'd love to have grandchildren and, if IVF is the only option, then we would like to help you with the cost"

Shauna felt obliged to step in and help her well-meaning in-laws. She was seriously wondering whether she would ever long for another baby with their abominable son but she felt a genuine respect and affection for his parents.

"Thank you very much" Shauna smiled back at Bob and Carole "We really appreciate your offer and we will bear it in mind, thank you" All of this was said without Shauna making any eye contact with Lewis. At that very moment, she couldn't bare to acknowledge his presence, let alone contemplate coming into contact with his baby making equipment again!

Lewis obviously had a different idea.

"Come on Mrs Studmuffin, let's get home and make some babies" Lewis lifted his pint glass and drained the remaining contents "Parents, thank you for your hospitality. I too will be a parent shortly and, of course, you will become Granny and Granddad. I'll let you know when"

Lewis walked, or should that be weaved towards the door, turned to make sure Shauna was also standing to leave, and continued his attempted confident swagger towards the car park.

"I'm so sorry" Shauna found herself apologising to Bob and Carole for their son's behavior.

"Don't be darling" Carole's blind love was annoying at best, sickening at worst "He's just a bit emotional after losing the baby"

Shauna had never bitten her tongue so hard. He's emotional after losing the baby? Lewis? What about me? ME ME ME? Why is everything about Lewis? Yes, it's hard for him, of course, but I was the one carrying the baby. The baby was inside me and I lost the baby too. I'm not behaving like a spoiled brat or turning to drink. Lewis was guilty of both of those things before we lost the baby so what's the difference?

No point saying anything, she thought. Leaning in to kiss Bob and Carole farewell she thanked them for the lunch (even though it was a disaster).

"Shauna. SHAUNA!"

Lewis had returned to the door of the pub. Shauna was used to him calling her like a dog and often made fake woof noises when he demanded her obedience.

"Shauna. Come on!" Lewis gestured and pointed to where he wanted his wife to be – standing right next to him.

Shauna was incensed by her husband's public attempt to control her but fought to conceal her anger, as usual. What didn't help was Carole's embarrassed giggle.

"Better get going" Shauna faked a happy-go-lucky attitude as she faced her in-laws "We need to stop off and get something on the way home"

As she made her way from the table, Shauna clumsily

tipped her chair into the back of the chair behind. She turned to apologise to the occupant. Her heart stopped. The blood drained from her face. She felt faint. She felt safe in the comfortable warmth of his eyes. She wanted to laugh, she wanted to cry.......

"Shauna, are you coming or should I get another pint?" Lewis was now drawing attention from nearby drinkers and diners. Pairs of anonymous eyes were looking from him to Shauna. Lewis didn't seem to care. In fact, believing he was in the right, he would enjoy the attention "And you know I hate shopping. What do we need that's so important?"

"Yes, I'm coming" Shauna tried to look nonchalant in an attempt to disguise her rapidly beating heart "We need batteries for your remote control"

Lewis nodded initially, as if he understood and then cocked his head to one side, looking puzzled.

Shauna wished she had the courage to speak out loud but instead she spoke to her radiohead "Batteries for the remote control you use to control me"

Lewis shook his head and turned in frustration at his wife's vague nature. As he strolled towards the car, he turned repeatedly to ensure she was following like a good dog. Shauna deliberately held back. At this moment in time, she really didn't feel like being close to Lewis any longer than she needed to.

As she watched him make his way to the passenger door, Shauna recounted a memory from earlier that day. Lewis had been particularly bossy that morning, ordering her about and tutting at her accident-prone nature. Shauna had taken smug pleasure when placing a plate of buttered toast in front of her grumpy husband. One of the pieces resembled a coffin. Shauna imagined the bread manufacturers were trying to tell her something. No, not to kill her husband!............ She saw it as a symbol of the end of their relationship.

(42) Isla to Redhead

Yes, Red, I did see that documentary on annoying and obvious things people do. God yes, I agree. Why is it that people who are prone to headaches never carry headache tablets? They are always bumming off others. And, when you offer ibuprofen they say "haven't you got any paracetamol?" as if you're a chemist!!!

I did have to laugh at the bit which referred those people who tell you they say what they think. Basically they are just warning you, in advance, that they're going to be rude to you. They're gonna give you their unsolicited opinion, advice and criticism. Hmmm, yes please. I can't wait to hear what you think!!! Mind you, some old ladies get like that too so you'd better watch out Red – for both of our sakes. I may turn into one of those old ladies who embarrass their family with the unspoken truth.

Oh God, talking of people saying things they should probably keep to themselves…..

I took my brother out for lunch the other day. It was his treat for taking me and Daisy to the airport recently and for putting up with Daisy's flirting.

The pub was really busy when we arrived so I told Sean to grab a table whilst I went to the bar. Whilst I was at the bar waiting to be served, I got a text from Daisy asking for my brothers number. Oh yeah! She said she wanted to thank him personally for giving us a lift. Oh yeah, I bet she did. I sent one back with a little bit of a white lie. I told her his phone had broken so he was changing it and going with another provider. Just to delay her a bit more, I told her the new provider insisted he change his number...... I know, quite unlikely these days but, hey ho, I needed to play for time. Hopefully she'll forget and focus on someone else instead.

By the time I got to the table with the drinks, my brother had been sitting alone for about ten minutes. The people on the table behind us were leaving. Well, one of them had obviously already gone and one of the others was saying goodbye. As she stood to leave, she clonked the back of her chair into my brothers. He turned towards her to move his chair out of the way. It was really weird. Time seemed to stand still. They both stood there staring at each other, not in an angry annoyed way, but in a sad, heartbreaking way. I swear she had tears in her eyes.

My phone started to ring. It was Daisy. Oh bum. I didn't want Sean overhearing my conversation so I mimed an apology and walked way from our table in order to deal with Daisy's libido in private. I ended up walking into the ladies where I stood, watching myself in the mirror as I fabricated stories of the nightmare Sean was having with his phone. God, I'm good. In fact, I was so convincing, I heard a flush at one point and a lady appeared from one of the cubicles, gesturing to her phone and mouthing that she was having the same problem.

Daisy postponed, I returned to Sean. As I approached our table, I could see the lady from the table behind was now walking out through the door. I had a flashback to seeing her before but I couldn't remember where. You know how small this town can be. I've probably tried to sell her a box of chocolates or some cellulite cream somewhere sometime.

Obviously I asked Sean about what I'd just seen. He dismissed it. I said something had clearly happened there but he said it was nothing.

The atmosphere needed cheering up a bit so I decided to tell him about Daisy.

"No thank you" was his instant reply to being told Daisy was after his phone number.

"Really?" I was secretly glad but also surprised to hear he wasn't interested in an attractive young lady who was making herself clearly available to him. Maybe that was the problem. A girl can be too obvious. I should know, I've made that mistake more than one time too many.

"Really" his certainty was clear.

"I thought you might like to be seen with a pretty little thing like Daisy on your arm. She'd look good in your car".

"I've already met the woman I'm going to spend the rest of my life with" OMG Red! It was like something from a film.

I couldn't believe it. I found myself bouncing up and down in my chair and clapping like a performing seal. He's never opened up like that before and I've never behaved like a performing circus animal before….. No comment from you, thank you Red!!

"Yes, but she doesn't know it yet" came his wistful response to my excitable behaviour. At least he didn't try to throw a plastic hoopla ring round my neck or throw a fish in my mouth. I stopped bouncing and clapping. This was heavy stuff. My brother was showing a gentle, romantic side I'd never seen before. Whoever this woman was, she was missing one hell of a show!

(43) George

I watched a great program on TV the other night. It was about all the stupid and annoying things people do. They had the usual batch of celebrities telling us about the things that annoy them, mixed in with ordinary folk on the street. Dee was laughing all the way through. She kept saying I should be on it. Well, to be honest, I should. I could fill an entire series with my observations and suggestions to improve the world.

I was delighted to see that one of my own personal gripes was featured. Several of the celebrities and two of the more frantic members of the public being interviewed moaned about people hovering at the till in a supermarket. They bunch all their stuff up, totally unfazed and disorganized, making very little attempt to pack. When the cashier gives them the total they slowly rummage around in their bag or pocket for money. Did they not expect to pay? Could they not have their purse or wallet handy? They finally pay, often in small change, whilst their shopping sits untouched in a small mountain at the end of the conveyor belt. Then, without consideration or probably in an effort to meet their productivity target, the cashier starts to scan your stuff and push it down towards the pile of purchases belonging to the previous customer who, of course, is still slowly packing their goodies.

And then, when they finally leave the shop they stop right in the doorway, blocking everyone's way. It's like people who get off a busy train and just stand there on the platform with everyone else behind them still trying to get off the train squeezing round them before the doors close and they end up stuck on the train and going onto the next stop.

Last week, Dee and I got so tangled up with the previous customer in the supermarket that we ended up inadvertently bringing home a tube of cream for intimate feminine itching and a pack of abrasive cleaning pads. Those two kind of contradict each other, don't they! The customer who followed us must have gone home with my Chockywocky Crunchjack biscuits. Either that or Dee is trying to put me on a diet again and watched with a smug smile as the other customer dropped my favourite teacup dippers in their bag.

Oh, and I'll tell you something else that annoys me. When you're looking for something in a shop and you find an empty shelf where the thing you're looking for should be. You ask one of the shop assistants for assistance (hence the job title) and they say in a slow, bored drawl "if it's not on the shelf, we haven't got it". This happened the other day so I asked the shop assistant to check in the warehouse. I watched the young lad disappear into the warehouse. Dee carried on shopping whilst I waited nearby. I couldn't believe it. About five minutes later, I saw the same lad sneak out of the warehouse and walk off in the other direction. I was just about to chase after him but Dee caught up with me and mimicked "if it's not on the shelf, we haven't got it'.

Dee was having a go at playing the 'how come' game the other day. Shauna was round and we were all standing in the kitchen chatting. You know what it's like. Shauna was leaning against a run of units and I was standing by the fridge. Dee was pottering around making tea and putting biscuits on a plate. Fig rolls and Garibaldi biscuits. Disappointing. I think Dee buys them because she knows I'm not keen. Another subtle way of putting me on a diet. Fortunately Dee also put a couple of mini Battenberg cakes on the plate. Now I *do* love them. Unfortunately, so does Shauna so there's always an unspoken war over the delicious marzipan coated cakes.

"How come you're always where I need to be?" says Dee with her hands on her hips. I move sideways to allow her access to the fridge. This puts me in front of the back door.

Dee continues to fuss about and I start to wonder how quickly I can tuck into a mini Battenberg. Is it rude to take one off the plate before we've officially started? Shauna pretends to be casually chatting but I know she's thinking the same thing.

"How come" Dee again "When you move out of the way, you move to somewhere else I need to be and get in my way again?" She has the empty cake box in her hand and obviously needs to get to the recycling bin outside the back door. I quickly take the packaging from her, open the back door, drop the box in the recycling and rapidly return to the kitchen to keep an eye on the previous occupants of the cake box. I notice there are only four perfect miniature Battenberg cakes on the plate but the box contains 5. I ask Dee about the missing fancy.

"I'm saving a piece for Alex" she informs me.

Ah, mummy's little boy has to have his cake. Shauna and I share a knowing look. Dee has never been very good at hiding her obvious over-protective side where Alex is concerned. He doesn't seek the special attention but he doesn't decline it when it's offered either. Clever boy!

I often think about how difficult it must be to live in a blended family. In the past, Dee and I have disagreed about our different views on parenting Shauna, Alex and Ruby. All three of the children are ours biologically but we still have times when arguments about our differing opinions have threatened the happiness and harmony of our marriage. It must be a real strain when the children you argue over are not yours. You may not even like them. I have mates at work who really struggle to bond with their stepchildren and Dee has a colleague who was reduced to tears when his girlfriend couldn't accept his young daughters from a previous relationship.

Dee's brother has a great relationship with his stepson, Martin, though. This brother was a bit of a wayward child. He was obviously very clever but used his intelligence to buck the system. Nana Buckle was a very open-minded, giving mother who encouraged her children to be adventurous and different. This brother took it a bit far at times.

On one occasion, he told Nana Buckle he was going away for a Scout camp weekend. Bags were packed, large amounts of food squirrelled away and pocket money safely stored. Nana Buckle offered to take Dee's brother to the Scout hut but he was more than happy to make his own way. Nana Buckle was proud of him for his independent streak and waved him off.

Her next encounter would involve a large bag of dirty washing so she set about making sure the mud-free laundry was all done and cleared in his absence before the machine was required to handle a post Scout camp load.

Two days later, Nana Buckle received a call from the father of another Scout enquiring as to the location of the camp. The boy's mother had gone into labour and the father wanted to make sure he was doing everything correctly whilst his wife was busy giving birth to another child. Nana Buckle admitted she didn't actually know where the camp was. As she said it, she realised how bad it must sound. This was all prior to mobile phones so there was no opportunity to contact the Scout leaders directly at the camp.

Nana Buckle offered to find out the location for the expectant father. She hung up and looked through the phone book. She would call the wife of the Scout leader. Number located, Nana Buckle dialed and was surprised when the Scout leader himself answered the phone. The Scout leader was also surprised to hear there was a camp taking place this weekend. In fact, no, given the circumstances he wasn't at all surprised. This brother and his two amigos were a trio of terror. He could quite believe they had fabricated a camp in order to spend some time alone in a field somewhere.

Sure enough, that is what they had done. Each of the three boys returned home with exaggerated stories of what a great camp it had been. Nana Buckle managed to draw out all sorts of elaborate tales from her son before he cracked under the scrutiny and admitted the truth. One of his companions returned to find a baby sister in the house.

At the time, the antics of this brother were frowned upon by the senior members of the family and applauded by his siblings and younger cousins who thought this brother was really brave. They didn't consider the risks and stupidity of being alone in a field at such a young age.

This brother continued to get himself into trouble. Never really harming anyone else, other than almost worrying Nana Buckle to death. Some of his teenage activities involved self-harm and drug abuse. Nana Buckle had instilled an open house approach to people in trouble but never thought one of her own children would become a person in need.

This brother turned to others for support. It hurt Nana Buckle but she understood his need to heal away from the family. He found Christianity and formed a youth group for youngsters in trouble. Through the group he met a fellow helper who had found Christianity following the break up of a violent marriage. She had a young baby, Martin, who she was trying to protect from his cruel background.

Baby Martin was the saving of Dee's brother. He fell in love with Martin and luckily fell in love with Martin's mother too. He subsequently married her and went on to have three children with her. Martin was never made to feel any different from the other children in the family. He was loved and grew up to be a really nice lad.

I know it's not fashionable to marry your cousin these days but I've often thought Shauna could have done a lot worse than marry Martin. He is a balanced, stable young man. Nothing like the sneaky secretive Lewis my lovely Shauna had unfortunately married.

Talk about Marriage, we received an invitation to Martin and Jackie's engagement party today. It's been a while since we had a family get together so it should be a great night. Dee's family are great fun. Quite outrageous at times but their hearts are all in the right place.

(44) Shauna

You know when you don't want to face up to the truth, you hide things from yourself. You try to protect yourself from hurt. At the end of the day, the only person you can truly rely on is yourself. You are the only person who will always be kind to you and always take your side. The only one who will see life exactly the way you see it. Nobody else has access to your un-edited private thoughts and fears.

As a child, Shauna once cut her toe and it bled quite a lot. She covered up the injury because it had been sustained whilst she ran around bare foot, despite the warnings from her mother that a glass had been smashed on the kitchen floor and that everyone should wear slippers until it was deemed safe again. Unable to tell anyone, Shauna sat at the dining room table, heart thumping with fear, not saying a word but looking around her family thinking "this is the last time I will see you all. I'm going to bleed to death in a minute"

Fortunately Shauna didn't die but she continued to keep many of her fears hidden from others. More and more she suspected Lewis was being unfaithful. His behavior was even more erratic than normal. On occasion he would be charming and entertaining. At those times, despite herself, Shauna found Lewis very attractive. She would look at him with appreciative eyes and look forward to time alone with him in bed.

As easily as it had come, Lewis's good mood could cloud over and he would become secretive and argumentative, particularly if Shauna tried to talk to him whilst he played with his phone. That bloody phone never left his side. He took it everywhere with him. On those occasions, Shauna found Lewis very unattractive.

Lewis was treating Shauna to one of his playful moods. He had just emerged from the shower and was looking pretty gorgeous with a towel wrapped around his waste. The radio was on and Lewis opened and closed his towel to the beat. Shauna laughed. Lewis jumped on the bed, opened the towel and thrust his hips in time to the music, causing his penis to flap up and down. Shauna giggled. Encouraged by her appreciation, Lewis twisted his torso rapidly left to right, causing his penis to slap loudly on his thighs.

The couple were now laughing together and sharing a private and very amusing moment.

A mobile phone ringtone broke through the happy moment.

Shauna turned to pick up Lewis's phone from the dresser behind her.

"LEAVE IT" Lewis shouted as he jumped off the bed. The towel fell to the floor, leaving him naked. Lewis glanced at the phone and then pressed what he referred to as the 'eff off button' to silence it's ring.

Shauna did not want to hear his excuses. She suspected it would be a lie anyway.

"I'm putting on a wash" She returned to domestic

normality "Can you let me have anything you need me to put in the machine please".

"Errrrm, yeah" Lewis scanned around for dirty laundry and moved to collect some from the bedroom floor. As he bent over, Shauna was exposed to the rear view of his bare bottom and dangling testicles.

She marveled at how animal like his genitals looked when viewed from this angle. Evolution had seen many changes to the human form but these vulnerable plum shaped items were still as comical as ever! As if aware of her scrutiny, Lewis straightened up and handed Shauna a collected bundle of clothing.

"There you go, wench" Lewis teased "Have my breaches boiled and starched by banquet time"

"Hmmmm, looks like you've been entertaining an auburn haired maiden in your royal turret" Shauna faked good humour as she pulled a long red hair from Lewis's washing bundle and held it out for inspection. She didn't want to directly accuse him. There was probably a totally innocent explanation.

"For fu………." Lewis was so quick to reach anger point. No effort to calmly deny any knowledge of the source of the long red hair. No quick and easy response to quash her suspicions. Shauna tuned Lewis out and turned on her radiohead to avoid hearing his ranting fury.

Shauna needed to turn to someone who made her feel happy and safe. She really wanted to get out of the house and drive to Nana Buckle's but she didn't want to give Lewis another opportunity to rack up more talk-time on his best friend, the mobile phone.

Instead, she lifted the lid of her laptop and began a humorous email to Beth. She described Nana Buckle's gentleman friend and how Nana tries to play it cool by saying he only wants her for her coconut tarts.

Before she knew it, Shauna had painted a happy vibrant picture for Beth and de-stressed herself in the process.

(45) Beth to Shauna

Shauna, sorry I haven't been in touch for ages. I can't believe the photos you sent in your last email. Alex is certainly growing up. He's what your Nan would call a handsome young man. I love the one with Ruby and the cat. Do they like each other now? I could never work it out but they both look like they're about to strike. Great photo – sums up your sister perfectly!

(46) Text Shauna to Beth

Just a quickie, forgot to say, I've noticed Barbara at work is wearing a silver bracelet with a 'B' entwined in the design. It's exactly the same as the one I had made for you as a memento when you left for Spain. I asked where she got it from and she said her sister Val gave it to her…. LuvUxx

(47) Text Beth to Shauna

WTF!!!! That's my bracelet. Leave it with me. LuvU2xx

By the way, just before I got your text I was looking for my hairbrush. Haven't seen it for ages. Opened a drawer in the spare room. Thought a hedgehog had decided to hibernate in there. Turns out it was my hairbrush – completely full of Val's hair. Enough to knit a jumper for a guinea pig. LuvUxx

(48) George

Why is it that, when you've taken the rotating tray out of the microwave, you can never get it to fit back in properly?

This morning I was disgusted to find the microwave in a filthy state. The kids use it as if it has secret self-cleaning properties. Someone must have heated up a chicken tikka masala in there last night and the entire thing was splattered with orange dots. I shouldn't have cleaned it. I should have left it for the curry consuming culprit to scrub off their sauce splashes but I wanted to make scrambled eggs for breakfast and I didn't want my fluffy yellow toast topper to taste of the east. My anger at finding the microwave in such a state was made worse when I tried to re-house the rotating glass turntable. I couldn't get the lugs to sit properly, resulting in loud clunks and clatters.

I looked up to see Ruby, hands on hips, glaring at my efforts.

"Oh, it's you. I thought it was Alex making all that racket" She mumbled

I guessed I was being let off the hook from an angry display of her disgust at being woken up by my loud and desperate attempts to return the microwave to a useable condition.

Without saying a word, Ruby gently pushed me to one side and, with the palm of one hand placed in the centre of the turntable, eased it into submission. How did she do that?

Unfortunately my suggestion that, as she was so good at it, she should clean the microwave in future did not go down well.

"Rubes, could you keep the noise down pl...." Alex entered the kitchen but discontinued his plea for silence when he realised the source of the noise could potentially have been me.

"Yeah, Stinky Boy, you thought it was me" Ruby loves an argument with her little brother and was shaping up for an early morning attack.

In an effort to prevent things escalating further, I offered to make them both scrambled eggs on toast for breakfast. Both accepted, of course, and Alex even offered to help. He opened the fridge to bring out the milk and eggs but also brought out a pungent aroma.

"God Alex" Ruby, as ever accusing her brother first before being proven guilty "Have you dropped one?"
Ah no, I realised the smell was not down to flatulence, it was down to another natural fermentation process. Dee and I had a bit of a craving for some fancy cheeses the other day and, as usual, instead of just buying one or two pieces, Dee had purchased enough cheese to feed the entire population of the Isle of Wight. Unfortunately, some of the cheese was becoming rather fruity in the fridge.

"Brie smells of wee" This was Ruby. My beautiful, cocky, scary, opinionated daughter who, when she let her guard down, reverted to the fun loving little girl she had once been.

"And you smell of poo" Alex this time.

Luckily this went down well with Ruby and her resulting peels of laugher caused Alex and me to join in too. What a great start to the day. Pity Shauna was missing it.

(49) Shauna

Shauna sat at her desk, tentatively sipping a hot chocolate from the office vending machine. Why was it so hot? I know it's called 'hot' chocolate but it was almost melting the plastic cup.

The phone on Shauna's desk rang. The unexpected trill made her jump and splash hot chocolate over the rim of the cup and onto the desk and keyboard in front of her. Oh bum! Why does a small amount of liquid travel so far? Whilst lifting the receiver of the phone, Shauna scanned around for something with which to mop up the sweet brown liquid that she now noticed had also splattered across some very important documents. Oh no, and all over the computer screen and, urgh, in her lap, forming an embarrassing stain on the front of her dress.

"Shauna Robertson" she answered the trilling device. All she could find to mop up with was a blank sheet of A4 paper, not known for its sponge-like absorbency. In fact, all it seemed to do was take on the watery brown hue of the hot chocolate without soaking any of it up at all.

"Hello Shauna, it's Barbara"

What else could she use? Shauna distractedly scanned around, opening drawers, lifting folders, picking up pens and other useless items of stationery. No, nothing. She made a mental note to buy a box of tissues.

"There's a courier here with that urgent parcel you mentioned"

Shauna reluctantly lifted her waterfall cardigan from the back of the chair and began mopping up the sugary drink with it.

"Shauna?"

"Oh, sorry, Barbara. Yes, I'll be straight down"

How annoying. Shauna knew the delivery was very urgent. A Marketing Department meeting was taking place in the conference room and a table full of creative brains were waiting for the contents of the package. Grrrr, Shauna would have to deal with the rest of the mess on her return.

"Hello love" Barbara lifted up her beautifully made-up face to Shauna as she approached. Her eyes then travelled down Shauna's dress to rest on the suspect brown stain at her crotch.

"Hot chocolate" Shauna explained with a shrug, before taking the package from Barbara. Why is it that, even though she knew what it contained and to whom it was addressed, Shauna found herself turning the parcel over in her hands and examining it. Was she playing for time? Luckily Barbara saved the day.

"I've had a call from my sister, Val. She's a naughty girl, isn't she" Barbara laughed, dispersing any potential awkwardness. "She doesn't mean to do it, you know, she just has a very open attitude towards other peoples possessions. She is a very generous lady and would give you the moon if you asked for it.

The trouble is, if the moon was yours for one night, she would borrow it, take it out to light her way and leave it in a taxi on the way home"

Barbara paused, glanced sideways in thought, before continuing.

"I've lost so many possessions over the years, having Val as my sister, but I've gained in many other ways. I know Beth is like a sister to you too. She was telling Val about your friendship and how much she misses you" Barbara paused and smiled softly "She told Val that you will definitely be Godmother to her first baby"

"Oh, that's lovely" Shauna grinned "Don't know when that will be but I'll buy a hat just in case"

"Well, she's fourteen weeks now so the time will fly by" Barbara's response hung in the air for a while. Shauna wasn't sure she'd heard correctly.

"Pardon?"

"Oh, maybe it's fifteen weeks. Not sure. I think Sean's mother told Val it was fourteen but that was a few days......... Shauna?"

Shauna didn't hear anymore. She was heading for the door. For some fresh air and the chance to compute what she had just discovered. Beth is pregnant. Beth is having a baby. I didn't know.

Three o'clock in the afternoon. The car park contained a few precious empty spaces. Visitors had been and gone. The prime spots were now free. Shauna walked aimlessly up and down the tarmacked space. Not being a smoker, she felt the need to do something to explain her presence in the car park. Suddenly she found something to do.

Cry!

The tears, which had initially been painfully held back, trickled down her face but, when Shauna finally let go and allowed the tears to flow freely, her entire face became soaked with salty fluid. Some of it must have been snot. For the second time in as many minutes, Shauna wished she had a tissue handy. She didn't even have her waterfall cardigan. It was draped over her desk, soaked in hot chocolate.

Shauna started to gasp and swallow lungful's of air as she struggled to control and let go of her emotions at the same time. It hurt. Her temples ached. Her throat hurt. Her heart hurt.

Traffic must have been passing the building during her emotional outburst but Shauna hadn't noticed. Suddenly her ears detected the sound of a vehicle slowing down nearby, followed by the sound of a handbrake being applied. The engine fell silent. A door slammed.

"Shauna" The concern in his voice broke her heart further.

"Oh God, Sean" she laughed and cried at the same time "Every time you see me I'm crying. I'm not like this all the time. Honest. It's just that I've found out that Beth is pregnant and she didn't tell me. I think she was trying to protect me because I lost my baby but I wish......."

Sean was holding her tight. Oh, she needed this. She allowed him to comfort her. Yet again, she found herself melting into his strength whilst covering his shoulder in snot and tears.

Shauna loved the fact that he didn't say a word. Lewis would have given her a token hard and uncomfortable hug before commencing a lecture on what she was doing wrong and what she should do now. Sean allowed her to cry it out. His arms around her made her feel safe and removed from reality.

"Shauna?" She lifted her head and turned to the shiny glass front doors of the building. Lisa had tentatively leaned halfway through the door in the way people do when they don't want to interrupt. Shauna had a momentary comedy thought. Would the automatic doors try to close on Lisa? Would she have to choose whether to jump back into the building or jump outside into the car park? The doors remained open allowing Lisa to step outside and begin a slow, almost crouching, walk towards Sean and Shauna as if they were frightened animals that may dart away any moment.

"Sorry to interrupt but the conference room guys have asked me to come out and get the package from you" Lisa nodded towards the building.

Oh dear! In her distress, Shauna had paid no attention to her exact location. She had inadvertently chosen to have her meltdown right outside the large expanse of windows which formed an entire wall of the conference room. She must have put on quite a show.

Shauna turned to the face the windows, mouthed and exaggerated "sorry" and handed the package to Lisa who had now reached Shauna and the good-looking man. She must remember to ask Shauna who he was and if he was available. Bit of a dish. If Meera's son, Rav wasn't picking up on her flirting she could do worse than flutter her eyelashes at this young man.

Taking the package, Lisa smiled winningly at Sean. Shauna felt a pang of possessiveness. Sean was *hers*. Well, not in that way but he was still *her* hero. Lisa would have to find her own knight in shining armor. What about that Rav bloke? He was obviously more in love with himself than he could ever be with another human being but Lisa had already declared Rav her goal. Lisa now appeared to be playing a different game on a different pitch. Shauna needed to send her off. Her mounting feelings of jealousy were immediately dissolved when Lisa reached out and handed Shauna a tissue. One tissue wouldn't be enough to clear up all her face fluid and nasal build-up but it was a start and a very thoughtful gesture.

More than anything, Shauna wished she could turn to Sean and bury herself in his arms again. Unfortunately she was now in control of her faculties and bodily fluids as well as her spatial awareness. She was due for her annual appraisal in two weeks and her boss was one of the audience members in the conference room who, annoyingly, still seemed to be focusing on the car park capers. Didn't they have work to do? Why were they still staring? Didn't anyone have any privacy round here?

What Shauna didn't know was that the subsequent TV commercial being discussed for one of the company's top clients would be based on the scene the conference room occupants had just witnessed. Through the glass, Shauna was unable to see the tears in the eyes of some of her female colleagues and, truth be told, some of the men's too!

"Maybe next time we meet I'll have a dry face" Shauna laughed as she dabbed at her cheeks. She would have to wait until she had safely entered the ladies before she blew her nose. She knew it would be a horrendous, bubbly noise and really didn't want to put Sean through that particular ordeal.

Sean laughed and studied her face with kind eyes. His gaze then travelled down her body to rest on the brown patch at her groin.

"Oh no, that didn't just happen" Shauna cringed. Was there no end to the way she could embarrass herself? "It's hot chocolate. Honestly. It's all over my desk and my cardigan"

Why? Why did she keep talking?

"Sorry Sean, I'd better get back to my desk" Shauna turned and pointed to the building, as if he didn't know where she worked "Some very important paperwork is now decorated with brown polka dot spots"

"No problem" Sean nodded before continuing "You know where to find me if you need me"

Shauna planted a quick, shy kiss on his cheek and hurried towards the office doors. Still being watched by Sean, she held her head up high and turned to smile one final time. Shauna put on her best brave face, gave Sean a little wave and promptly crashed into the automatic doors. The doors hadn't quite finished their automatic opening procedure and the shiny glass now sported a streak of snot, perfectly traced as the doors dragged Shauna's nose to the left and slid across her damp cheek.

Oh, that hurt! Turbo charged brave face required here. Shauna turned and gave a thumbs up gesture to Sean as she accurately entered the foyer this time. As soon as her back was turned, she cupped her hand to her throbbing nose and rushed into the ladies to salvage what was left of her appearance.

....

As Shauna walked back to her desk she could hear a constant beeping noise. At first she blamed the photocopier. She could see the top was up and one of the access doors to the paper trays had also been flung open. Oh dear, someone must be in the middle of trying to clear an annoying paper jam. Shauna guessed they had walked away before they resorted to childish behavior and adult language in the face of the invisible and irretrievable piece of paper.

As she walked beyond the filing cabinets that defined the various work spaces, Shauna realized the beeping noise was emanating from her desk. Daisy was bent over the desk with a cloth, obviously trying to do her best with the hot chocolate explosion. One of the endlessly patient IT technicians was standing beside her, opening a box which, to Shauna's embarrassment, seemed to contain a brand new keyboard.

"The old keyboard obviously didn't drink hot

chocolate. It only types Zs and beeps now" The IT guy said with a wink "Don't tell my boss about this or he'll ban you all from drinking at your desks….. again!"

Shauna was humbled by the kindness of others. She wanted to cry again but couldn't risk it – the new keyboard probably didn't drink saline!

(50) Ruby

I know it sounds odd but I love those days where it's wet and dark outside and comfy and warm inside. It got really dark at about 3 o'clock this afternoon. The heavens opened and the rain was smacking hard on the pavement outside the salon.

Normally we don't allow dogs inside but I was doing Mrs Galbraith, a lovely old regular. She reminds me of Nana Buckle but not so scary! Anyway, Mrs Galbraith had Dougal, her Cairn Terrier, with her, as usual. We normally turn a blind eye to Dougal 's presence in the salon. He's so well behaved and unassuming – a bit like Mrs Galbraith!

Fabio was working on another client in the chair next to us. She was a pretty, little over-the-top posh girl with a ridiculously loud voice. Every time pretty little over-the-top posh girl (let's call her PLOP!) laughed, Dougal lifted his head in a disgusted 'you've disturbed my doze' way.

Mrs Galbraith and I were enjoying a little bit of banter, although I don't think she would refer to it that way. Mrs Galbraith would probably call it a chinwag. She tells me about one of her granddaughters who is about my age and I tell her about my friends and my occasional boyfriend troubles. The troubles aren't the occasional bit, the boyfriends are, but I'm not bothered. I quite like being single and having flirty fun. Once you've got what you want, it's not so much fun anymore. That can be said for lots of things in life. My wardrobe can testify to that!!

Anyway, the rain was pouring down and the windows steamed up. The sound of hairdryers and the feeling of warmth created by them made the salon a cosy haven. It reminds me of the time Mum sent me to the launderette against my will. I have to say I wasn't impressed. Alex had come home uncharacteristically drunk one night and thrown up all over his bed in the night. I woke up to find him sitting on a bench by the back door with his head between his knees. Mum was fussing all around him and treating him like a baby. She wouldn't have done that for me!

Mum bagged up Alex's duvet in a black bin liner and asked me to take it to the laundrette. Yuk!! What a cheek. I mumbled and moaned but changed my mind when Mum gave me a £20 note and told me I could keep the change.

The launderette was full of regulars who knew exactly how much money to put in each machine and how long it would take. There was obviously some sort of laundry etiquette I didn't know about. A couple of customers took pity on me and showed me which machine to use, where to put the money and the best program for my needs.

I popped next door to the petrol station, picked up a self-service coffee and a packet of biscuits (thanks Mum) and returned to the launderette. I was reading a cheesy bonk-buster at the time and pulled it out of my bag. I was a bit embarrassed by the front cover so I folded it over, opened the book at the page with the turned down corner and started to pick up the story where I had left it.

It was then I began to become aware of my surroundings. The cosy warmth, the steamy windows, the smell of washing powder and fabric conditioner, the gentle hum of the machines. It was great. I loved it. The industrial machines worked faster than Mum's washer at home. Far too soon, the wash was over. I tried to string out the tumble drying as much as possible but the duvet was starting to cook and become too hot to handle. Eventually my time in there was over. I'm not saying I encouraged Alex to vomit on his bedding on a more regular basis but I did ask Mum if there were any other large items of bedding due for a spring-clean in the near future. Who'd have thought it? Rock and Roll Ruby loves the rumble of a tumble…… dryer – tee hee!!

It was difficult to hear Mrs Galbraith. The appliances were drowning her out but PLOP could clearly be heard trilling above the hot blast of a chorus of dryers.

PLOP was recounting a story of a recent holiday to Greece where she had apparently saved her nervous friend from a pack of wild dogs. Ruby suspected Fabio was able to smell a small pile of bullshit here and was clearly bored of being patronised with this tall tale. He strategically headed her off the verbal pass with a question Ruby suspected was designed to bring an end to her boasting.

"So, is there a special man in your life at the moment? A hero to fend of packs of slathering wild animals?"

"No, I'm between boyfriends at the moment." She announced, as if being interviewed on a TV chat show "But I have a couple of options. A friend of mine has an absolutely gorgeous brother. He's recently become single. I mean, he's not the sort of man you would dump. I don't know why his previous girlfriend let him go but I'm hoping he's ready to get over her and get over me instead"

A piercing laugh emitted from PLOPS pretty plump lips. Poor Dougal lifted his head in disdainful response.

"They had a little starter home together. I'd like to start a home with him"

Giggle

It's never cool to laugh at your own jokes. Not only did PLOP laugh at her own joke, she rocked backwards and forwards in the chair, forcing Fabio to pause his styling task and glance around in mock fear.

"Get it. I'd like to start a home with him. Starter home. Start a home"

Another piercing laugh emitted from PLOP's lips, followed by a loud blast emitting from her pert bottom on the ergonomically designed coiffure chair.

Why is that, when general chatter is taking place, the atmosphere is filled with sound but, when something awkward or embarrassing is said or done, the area is suddenly silent?

The loud reverberation of PLOP's fart was heard by the entire salon. Stylists stared at the reflected faces of their clients in the mirrors. Faces contorted with the effort of holding back stifled laughter. Dougal did not possess the same degree of decorum. He lifted his

255

head and whimpered before looking pleadingly up at the divine Mrs Galbraith. The poor lady was forced to remain in her seat due to the trappings of hairdressing paraphernalia and a freshly delivered cup of tea poised midway to her lips.

Dougal decided to fend for himself. He trotted towards the front door and began scratching on the bristle doormat in an attempt to dig his way out of the now stinky salon. His day was saved by the arrival of a representative from a regular supplier. The van driver, desperate to get out of the rain, pushed open the door, tripped over Dougal as he raced though his legs and stood on the mat in the sanctuary of the warm, dry salon. His face changed almost immediately.

"Blimey girls. I know peroxide can have an eggy aroma but I think you've overdone the mix this time"

He turned to open the door and let in some welcome fresh air "You can sign for the parcel next time. Looks like I've got a dog to catch"

(51) Shauna

Shauna felt the need to make contact with Beth. Part of her dreaded the inevitable conversation but the other part just needed to get it out of the way and move on.

She chose to make the call at her parent's home. Somewhere she felt safe and where she could turn for support when it was over. Shauna sat on Ruby's bed. She felt comforted by the pretty, girly chaos of it all. In fact, the entire room was a bit of a mess. Unbelievable when you considered how groomed and beautiful Ruby would be every time she walked out of there.

The family had invited Shauna round for lunch. Well, Shauna and Lewis were invited but nobody was surprised to hear Lewis had work to do and wouldn't be joining them. Secretly they were all relieved. They were surprised, however, to hear Shauna say she had an important phone call to make before she joined them all downstairs. They looked from one to another as Shauna made her way up to Ruby's bedroom and closed the door.

Shauna dialed……

"Shaunaaaaaaaaaa" Beth sounded delighted to receive a call from her best friend

"Beth" Shauna tried to sound upbeat "Or should I say Hola Beth, how are you?"

"Good. Good, thanks. So great to hear from you. I was

going to call you today actually"

"Really?"

"Yes, honestly, I was"

"To tell me about a certain person's arrival?"

"What!? Oh you know. It was supposed to be a surprise"

The front doorbell rang

"I knew you'd be pleased but I wanted to reveal the surprise myself"

Shauna felt hurt. She knew Beth understood how upset she was when she lost her baby. Surely she would treat this with a little bit more sensitivity.

The doorbell rang again, a longer trill this time. Obviously nobody else in the house had bothered to answer it.

"Hold on a minute, Beth. Suddenly everyone in this house is deaf"

Still holding the phone up to her ear, Shauna made her way downstairs to the front door.

"Give me a minute. There's someone at the door" Shauna held the phone to her side as she opened the door with her other hand.

"It's ME!"

"Beth!" Shauna couldn't compute. But Beth was on the phone. For some strange reason, Shauna held her phone up to her ear. She felt obliged to properly end the call.

Beth didn't wait. She dived towards Shauna and gave her a powerful hug, followed by their customary play kissing where they would repeatedly kiss each other's cheeks and blow raspberries at the same time. Shauna wanted to stand defiant. She wanted to be stern but ten kisses later she was giggling and snorting with laughter. She returned the raspberry kisses with ones of her own.

Another hug and the girls stood apart.

"Well, I must say you look fantastic" Shauna looked her best friend up and down, like an approving Grandmother "You've got a tiny little bump but it's cute, nothing too matronly yet"

"Yeah, I know" Beth looked down and rubbed her belly "It's all that good Spanish food. I need to cut down on combining it with English puddings though"

"Well, the baby won't complain about the odd egg custard tart, I'm sure" Shauna was pleased to discover any jealousy she may have felt had turned to pride in her blooming friend.

"Who's baby?"

"Yours"

"I'm not having a baby" Beth raised her eyebrows

"I heard you were pregnant. Steve's mum told Val who told Barbara…."

"Bloody woman. I'm not pregnant. Steve's sister-in-law is pregnant" Beth shook her head "Not only can she not remember which underarm deodorant is hers, she can't remember which woman belongs to which brother!"

"I hope you can remember which brother you belong to though Beth"

"Hey and what's this about me having a pot belly. Did you seriously think I look pregnant?" Beth cocked her head to one side. I'm not ready to be a brood mare yet".

Shauna patted Beth on the bum

"Let's get you in the kitchen and make you a pint of English tea and a slice of cake. May not have any of your favourite egg custard tarts but I'm sure we can find a bit of Battenberg hidden somewhere"

(52) Email Redhead to Isla

Gorgeous girl! Good to see your new phone is working well and your Instatweet and Faceplant accounts are now showing pictures of YOU and not those scantily clad lovelies. I have to say I miss the variety but at least you can hold your head up high now. Can't believe some of your work mates didn't realise you'd been hacked. Do they really think your preference is buxom blondes and brunettes? I notice there were no postings of redheads. We like to keep our clothes on. Don't worry about trying to prove me wrong. I know you have photos of my bare bum, topped by my gorgeous red locks on that hot day in Brighton. I looked hot too – oh yeah!!

I have to say, I'm really getting into the swing of this agony aunt assignment. Unfortunately it seems the original aunt is coming back from her sabbatical soon. The management have told me the feedback from my page is good. They like my "refreshing brutal honesty" but I think they're just wallpapering over the words "harsh and nasty" to quote a direct message I received on TwitTwit yesterday.

Sometimes I think people write into the magazine, hoping the person they are digging at is a regular reader and will recognise their own traits and failings in the letter. I read one this morning which I'll have to edit to fit on the page. We can't include the entire letter but I feel this girl needs my help so I'm going to put as much of it in as I can. I'm going to cut and paste her letter here for you to have a sneaky peek. I've removed any names and specific details, so you won't see anything you shouldn't – unlike that day in Brighton!!

"Dear Agony

My boyfriend and I have moved to Spain. Our relationship is strong but obviously it's a challenge being away from friends, family and familiarity (try saying that after a pint of wine!) and, at times, there is a strain on our relationship.

Sometimes I think of this place as a beautiful prison. Everyone keeps telling us we're "living the dream" and asking "are you still happy here?" What do they expect us to say? The pressure to be living the idyllic lifestyle is too much at times. It's like everyone has invested their hopes and dreams in us. Would they ask us the same question if we'd moved to Birmingham or Carlisle? (Don't ask me why I picked those places, it's just an example). Can we ask them if they are happy? Maybe best not to open up that can of worms!!

The biggest strain seems to arise when we have visitors staying in our villa. Unfortunately, most of the visitors are from my boyfriend's family. My best friend hasn't been able to come out to see me yet and I really miss having her around.

My boyfriend's mum brings a friend with her; let's call her The Borrower. The Borrower is such a lovely lady, so full of fun and really kind hearted. The problem is, and you can probably tell by the nickname, she borrows everything – normally without asking. There is no boundary to our private space or possessions. I feel as though we're permanently living in a glass bowl and we're being examined as some kind of social experiment whilst being pushed to the end of our patience.

Recently, The Borrower misinterpreted some good news. Via a route I won't bore you with, she sent news to my best friend who recently miscarried, that I was pregnant. She was so upset. Partly because she is still getting over the loss of her baby, struggling with an arsehole of a husband (I said that, not her, but he really is an arsehole) but mostly because I hadn't told her. The truth is, if I ever did fall pregnant, my best friend would be one of the first people I would tell. In fact, she would probably know before I did!!!

Luckily, I'd planned a secret weekend visit to the UK to see her so I was able to explain. In fact, I didn't even know I was supposedly pregnant. She did remark on my baby bump, which was a bit disconcerting as it's actually my sister-in-law who is pregnant – not me!!

This is proving very cathartic for me. I'm sorry it's a long letter but I'm finding it very therapeutic to write. I hope you're still awake!

Whilst I was visiting the UK, I noticed my best friend's husband was even more anti social than usual. He seemed to spend most of the time on his phone or was just not there at all. My friend said he has a lot of extra work to do at home but I have my suspicions that the extra work may involve a bit of human relations, if you get my drift.

At one point, I heard him on the phone in the garden. Don't know who he was talking to but he started giggling. Never heard him giggle before – it was horrible! I was walking down the side of the house and into the back garden, trying to send a message to my boyfriend in Spain but my phone was playing up. I started to call it some rude names and I must have jolted the arsehole into reality because, when he realised I was there, he suddenly became all serious and said to the mystery caller "Yes, that's great. I'll book that up and let you know". He hung up and started mumbling about an important work conference. A conference for two, I suspect!!"

Anyway, the letter goes on a bit more but you've probably got the gist. I haven't composed my response yet but, in my usual gritty way, I will tell her that her best friend's husband is clearly having an affair and that she should tell her. I know that's hypocritical of me, based on my current liaison with a married man, who by the way frequently cuts me off the phone in the same way. It's always different when you're viewing other people's lives. You forget about your own shortcomings. Suddenly I develop morals.

(53) Shauna

Lewis was feeling playful. He was privately enjoying his own smug thoughts and trying not to make it too obvious. A major source of his self-satisfied state was not derived from Shauna. She was innocent and totally unaware of his infidelity. The excitement of his dual life and the fact that he was managing to live on the edge and get away with it was creating a heady rush of adrenaline. Lewis kept telling himself to stay grounded. Don't be too buoyant or self-assured. Shauna would become suspicious and pop the duplicitous bubble of exhilaration and sexual tension he inhabited.

In an effort to fill their lives with fun and frivolity, Lewis had suggested a weekend away in a spa retreat. To be fair, the idea wasn't completely his own. In fact, the truth was, the weekend was a complimentary promotional gift from a health and leisure consortium who were pitching for a collaboration with the company Lewis worked for. Shauna would never know that though. She believed the suggestion was a romantic, spontaneous gesture. Lewis had been particularly amorous recently and could barely contain his libido. She assumed the weekend would involve face packs, toweling bathrobes and lots of vigorous sex on white sheets someone else would have to wash at the end of it all.

Lewis was basking in his cat-with-the-cream lifestyle and smiled to himself as he remembered an event a few years before. He and Shauna were invited to friend's new home for a dinner party. Neither of them particularly fancied the idea of show-off cuisine and small talk in the new build dining room. However, as often happens, when you dread an event, it turns out to be so much better than expected. All four friends were in good spirits and, indeed, large quantities of spirits were taken. For once, Shauna accepted the offer of a bed for the night so she could relax and enjoy a few above the drink-drive limit. Lewis had been surprised but he was pleased to see Shauna relaxing and enjoying an extra drink or two.

The following morning, Shauna was suffering. Lewis, despite his excessive alcohol consumption, was feeling full of life and, as usual first thing in the morning, he was also feeling quite horny. He tried what he thought was subtle kissing and caressing but Shauna was having none of it. She seemed to be playing dead but, rather than showing any sympathy, Lewis was becoming more aroused by the challenge and showing no regard for Shauna's throbbing head. His only concern now was his throbbing penis.

Lewis continued to stroke and squeeze various parts of Shauna's body, his hands prizing her clamped legs apart to enable further probing of areas she was hoping would remain dormant this particular hung-over morning. Shauna yawned loudly and turned onto her side. Lewis chose to disregard her groans. He preferred to assume she was now turned on and raring to go and proceeded to adopt the missionary manouvre he had perfected over the years – a technique that Shauna had become accustomed to but one that would always leave her amazed at the speed with which Lewis could flip her onto her back and mount her like an animal in the wild.

Shauna obviously didn't feel up to being bounced on and somehow managed to swiftly slip out from under Lewis's arms as he prepared to pin her down. She almost kicked him onto his back. As soon as Lewis realised what was about to happen, he moaned with pleasure, closed his eyes and allowed the lovely lips of his wife to relieve his pent-up pressure. Lewis was aware that, at times, Shauna was struggling with her gag reflex and was not only relieving his build up but was fighting her own bile up. Fortunately she managed to contain her stomach contents and Lewis eventually released his boy bits contents across Shauna's chest and face.

Act complete, Shauna did not hang about for any possible cuddling or further rummaging around her body parts. She folded her arms across her breasts and scuttled into the bathroom to clean up.

Their hosts were waiting downstairs in the kitchen and gave knowing smiles when Shauna and Lewis appeared for breakfast. Shauna gratefully accepted their offer of coffee and toast in the hope it would quell her rising nausea. Whilst they waited for the toaster to produce some alcohol absorbing goodness, Lewis chatted casually to their friends before suddenly faltering and looking concerned. Three pairs of eyes turned to Shauna.

"What?"

"Babe, you've got some sort of rash on your face" Lewis leaned in and started rubbing Shauna's left cheek.

"Is it red?"

"Well, it is now I'm rubbing it. It's gone all flaky"

Shauna blushed "No, Lewis. It's fine, honestly"

"Seriously, babe, it's not good. You need to see a doctor about this"

"Lewis, it's fine" Shauna pleaded with her eyes but Lewis seemed oblivious

The toaster popped

Shauna took Lewis by the wrist in an effort to pull his hand away from her cheek

"I know what it is"

Nothing from Lewis. Except a frown.

"I know what it is. It's from….."

Ah, the penny dropped. The morning's bedroom activity and the subsequent clean up had been frantic and rushed. Shauna, without her trusty baby wipes, had obviously failed to fully clean up the evidence. The penny had not only dropped, it had clattered noisily, rolled across the floor and crashed into someone's ego and that someone was now gloating. Oh yes, he was clearly proud of himself and delighted to note that his friends were sharing knowing looks. They must be thinking what an insatiable stud he was!

Back to the present time, Lewis reflected that Shauna was now a skilled lover, under his tutelage of course! The Redhead already possessed the most amazing oral skills. It would be difficult to pick a winner there. Lewis allowed himself a little fantasy involving the two of them competing to satisfy his pleasure. He shifted in the drivers seat and coughed. Need to focus Lewis. This car won't drive itself.

As a distraction, Lewis attempted to tune into to the local radio station. The result was a bit hit-and-miss. The in-car entertainment system didn't appear entirely convinced as to the stability of the frequency. It seemed to be hovering on a band somewhere between two competing stations. An advert would appear "Have you ever wondered how to get rid of your….. unsightly joints. We have the answer. Our qualified technicians will ……….. tailor to your personal requirements in a choice of soft or hard……….surfaces. We offer many creams and oils to discreetly treat all types of……. exhaust or big end problems.

This went on for some time, Lewis, uncharacteristically giggling as each clipped sentence rolled into another. Catching himself being a little bit too happy, as opposed to his normal cool silent brooding demeanor, Lewis leaned over to try another station.

"Just going to fiddle with my knob to see if I can satisfy you" he looked sideways towards Shauna and winked.

Shauna wasn't entirely comfortable with this strange frisky Lewis but she found herself laughing. Emboldened by her response, and whilst approaching a pedestrian crossing, Lewis started on a little lighthearted car banter.

"Come on you two, get on with it" Lewis gripped the steering wheel and hunkered down as if he was about to take part in a dragster race "Look at them ambling across, not making eye contact with us, as if they have all the time in the world. Do they think *we've* got all the time in the world too?"

"Mmmmmm" Shauna felt obliged to make some kind of affirmation sound

"I mean, who do they think they are? Are they so important they feel everyone else has to wait for them? Or are they lacking in confidence and feel this is the only way to get people to do things for them? What are they like when *they* are the ones behind the wheel? Do they wish pedestrians would GET A MOVE ON?"

"Babe, that was a bit loud. I think you've frightened them" Shauna, feeling embarrassed on behalf of her husband, mouthed the word "sorry" to the nervous pedestrians.

"Probably the most exciting thing that's happened to them today" Lewis put the car into gear and moved on, once the couple had moved off the zebra crossing, of course!!

"Have you been listening to my Dad again?" Shauna teased "You're coming out with the kind of things he says"

Part of Shauna wished she wasn't enjoying the company of Lewis so much. It didn't feel natural to be laughing and joking with him these days but, she thought to herself, it's got to be better than arguing. She knew, whenever Lewis was trying to win her round, he only had to mention her Dad in a positive way and she would brighten up. She didn't like the feeling of being worked on in such an obvious way but she had to admit Lewis was good company today....... so far anyway!

The results of a phone-in quiz helped to further cement the amicable atmosphere in the car. Lewis and Shauna agreed on the answers to all three questions and, it turns out, they were right.

"Yesssssss" Lewis punched the air in an exaggerated celebration.

Unfortunately for the phone-in contestant, he had failed to achieve the same hat-trick and had come away with a score of two out of three. He was, however, allowed to give a 'shout out' to friends and family. He began an endless list of names, which seemed destined to take up the remainder of the show.

The DJ attempted to interrupt and cut him off several times but the caller continued to reel off what now appeared to be the local phone book – so many names!

"I think I'm going to change my name to Anyoneelsewhoknowsme" Lewis nodded "That way, I will be mentioned pretty much every day on the radio".

"And anyone else who knows me" the caller chimed on cue.

"Oh yessssssss, back of the net" more air punching from Lewis. He turned to smile at his wife who returned the gesture.

Shauna studied her husband. Isn't it funny, she thought? If someone is being mean and horrible you find them unattractive, even if they are technically good looking, but if they're happy and fun you find them attractive. Lewis, aware of her scrutiny, took his eyes off the road to glance towards his wife. He was clearly enjoying the look of approval on her face.

In order to avoid too much adoring eye contact, Shauna reached round to locate her bag on the back seat. She tugged at the handle and pulled the overstuffed bag clumsily towards the footwell. En-route the bag became caught between the two front seats. Shauna tugged at it furiously causing Lewis to frown, roll his eyes and shake his head disapprovingly. She hated it when he did that. What an arse!! What an unattractive arse at that!

"Water?"

"Yes please" Lewis lifted the bottle to his lips and slugged greedily before handing the bottle back to Shauna "Don't worry, I didn't backwash!"

Shauna pulled a family bag of crisps from her bag. Crisps were her greatest weakness and something she would usually try to hide from her husband, even resorting to standing with her head in the cupboard whilst secretly stuffing fistfuls of ready salted into her cheeks like a hamster. Unfortunately, in the limited confines of the car, Shauna was forced to openly indulge in her passion for potato crisps under the scrutiny of her husband.

Shauna scooped out a handful and pushed them towards her mouth. She was aware that several crisps had broken off and fallen into her lap. She also suspected there were shards of crisp on her cheeks and probably up her nose too.

She offered the bag to Lewis who reached in and withdrew a man-sized portion, lifted them to his mouth and hit a clean bulls eye. What no crumbs?

Shauna then worked on dispensing a one for you two for me ratio of portions.

"Alright there Little Miss Piggy?" Shauna hated it when Lewis created nicknames that befitted her penchant for certain types of food. She wasn't a greedy overeater but when she liked something she *really* liked it. She feigned ignorance.

"What do you mean?"

"You're stuffing those things into your mouth as if a giant hand is going to reach into the car and pull the bag away from you any minute"

"Who are you?" Shauna was angry and upset at his critical but accurate observation "the food police or something?" He barely took any notice of her these days so why was he so concerned about a bag of sliced, deep fried potatoes sprinkled with salt?

Shauna childishly screwed up the bag and threw it on the back seat, immediately hating and regretting her behavior. She wanted to enjoy the crisps without observation. Now she had been forced to sacrifice that pleasure.

"Don't be such a baby" Suddenly his face clouded over. A familiar sight. "You've got no self control. It's disgusting to watch"

"You're a fine one to talk. What about all the beer and wine you drink? No self control there" Shauna turned to stare angrily out of the window before turning back to face Lewis "Not to mention all the cigarettes and whisky chasers. *That's* disgusting to watch"

"I have to be drunk to fancy you" His barb was intended to hurt Shauna but she found herself feeling numb.

On queue, the next track on the radio began "You've Lost That Loving Feeling"

How ironic!

"Oh and, by the way, you've got a piece of crisp stuck to your ear. You look ridiculous"

Oh God, how did it get there, Shauna wondered, whilst attempting to nonchalantly sweep the debris from her ear lobe. She was sure that, when she exited the car, there would be a Shauna bum shaped stencil on the car seat depicted in crumbs. She lifted her head in mock defiance and tried to ride out the shameful exposure of her uncontrollable appetite for family bags of loveliness!

Like a mobile phone, Shauna had discovered she could turn off her personal settings. After being the victim of Lewis and his sharp tongue and cold love for so long, Shauna found she could isolate her emotions. Turn on neutral mode. Turn on prostitute mode! Shauna hovered between two options before rejecting brave face mode and selecting self-preservation mode. Self-preservation mode meant becoming numb and void of all emotion. In this mode, she would block all hurtful feelings. She often pretended she was an actor playing a part when reverting to this mode. This was a part in a movie. This wasn't Shauna, it was someone else. Doing this made it easy for Shauna to protect herself from further harm.

Lewis never smoked in his precious car. Shauna tried not to look or show any expression of surprise when she saw him lift a pack of cigarettes to his mouth, clench one with his lips and pull the remainder of the pack away before lighting and taking a long, deep drag.

"That was the harmonious Righteous Brothers" crooned the radio DJ "And now, who can resist a little Careless Whisper by the late, great George Michael"

Shauna picked up her phone. She had dreams of writing a book one day. She had ideas and themes in her head and would often put them down on paper, only to lose them. Eventually, Shauna decided to harness modern technology and put her thoughts down in her phone for safe-keeping. When an idea struck, Shauna would pick up her phone and commit her thoughts to the continuous notes page. Most of the emotional outpourings were fuelled by Lewis. Shauna worried the book would be too full of bile to ever publish. However, she found the act of venting her feelings in private to the inanimate phone very therapeutic, whether her book ever made the best sellers list or not!

Lewis looked across. Shauna was used to seeing him tapping away furtively on his phone but he rarely caught her using hers. Shauna secretly loved the fact that he appeared concerned by her rapid and frantic activity.

"And now for a very angry young lady" The upbeat DJ was getting on Shauna's nerves "Taylor Swift and We Are Never Getting Back Together"

(54) Ruby

I wish my sister would grow a pair. But if she did, she would be my brother!

I know I shouldn't have done it. It's almost as bad as reading someone's diary. But I'm glad I did it. I think I can help. What am I talking about you ask?

Shauna and arse-face (I'm talking about Lewis, if you haven't guessed) came round to Mum and Dad's for lunch at the weekend. Lewis was meant to be helping Dad lay new lino on the bathroom floor but he spent so much time in the garden on his phone Dad gave up and said they could do it another day. This was the second time Lewis had let him down. Poor Dad. I'm going to help him do it instead. It can't be that difficult, can it? I've heard washing up liquid helps.

Shauna and Lewis were due to be away at a spa resort for the weekend but they only managed one night. Lewis said he had too much work to do but, judging by the stony looks between them, I suspect they couldn't get through an entire weekend alone and even the idea of lunch at Mum and Dads was more inviting than a weekend of fresh air, healthy food and those complimentary miniature shampoo and shower gel bottles. Ooooh, I just made it sound like they drink the shower gel. You know what I mean though, don't you!

Anyway, back to what I was saying. We were all sitting in the lounge with plates of sandwiches on our laps. I'm sure Lewis thinks we're common but it was cosy and great to have everyone together. Nana Buckle was with us too which meant we had to have her soap omnibus on the TV because she didn't want to miss the cliff-hanger bits. Correct me if I'm wrong, but isn't the omnibus a collection of all the episodes shown during the week? Unless she's been out clubbing this week instead of staying in and watching TV as usual, that must mean Nana has already seen all five episodes separately but we're happy if she's happy. We even get sucked into the storylines.

Nana has the TV on so loud it's difficult to have a conversation so we usually end up mouthing things to each other or using hand gestures and body language to converse. Nana also has a habit of providing a running commentary of what's happening on the screen, even though we are all watching the same thing and can see perfectly well for ourselves. She sits there laughing "Oh, look, he doesn't realise she's already in the car" or "Well, he's hiding in the bushes because she's a real chatterbox and he doesn't want to get caught in a conversation but she's seen him and she's going to stop and chat to him in the bushes" Sometimes she gets angry with them "Oh, you stupid woman. He's obviously having an affair. Don't be such a doormat"

Lewis was making it quite obvious he didn't want to be with us. Apart from the constant phone calls and text messages, he spent the rest of the time checking his watch. Then, without any warning, he suddenly announced to Shauna that it was time to go. How bloody rude! He made no effort to apologise or to thank Mum and Dad for their hospitality. Nana Buckle, being as direct as ever, turned from the TV screen and said "Going already? Well we've hardly seen anything of you, young man. You have been giving all your attention to that telephone of yours. Did your parents not teach you any manners?"

Go Nana, Go Nana, Go Nana. I was cheering inside. I could hardly contain myself.

Alex was caught unawares by Nanas remarks and actually spat back the mouthful of tea he had just taken in.

Lewis completely ignored Nana and everyone else for that matter. He pulled the car keys out of his pocket and left the room. Shauna mumbled an apology although I don't know why. She's got nothing to apologise for. Other than marrying that berk.

It wasn't until they had left that we found Shauna's mobile. It must have fallen out of her jeans pocket and become wedged down the sofa cushions. Being the trusting soul she is, the phone doesn't have a lock or password. Like I said, I shouldn't have done it, but I found myself flicking through her phone, checking out her music downloads (hmm, not bad taste) and browsing through the apps she had downloaded. The photos were what I'd expected. Some great ones of Shauna and Beth which made me smile. Loads of me – yaaaay! Some other family ones. A few of Alex the pain – only kidding and a photo of a cute little bag she once owned that has now found its way into my wardrobe. Oh dear, she must be trying to replace it. Better give it back!

All pretty standard stuff and nothing to write home about until I stumbled across her notes pages. One of them was entitled 'Radiohead'. I thought it referred to the band until I opened it. I almost gasped out loud. I had to leave the room and take the phone upstairs to my room to read it in private. I didn't want the rest of the family seeing my reaction. Having said that, I don't think any of them noticed I was playing with Shauna's phone in the first place. Only Alex would know it wasn't my phone and he didn't seem to be paying me any attention. As often happens, he was cuddling up to mum whilst teasing the cat with a smelly sock he'd found stuffed down the side of the other sofa. Amazing what we lose in there. Must remember to check out for loose change. There's probably a fortune in our furniture!

Rather than risk Shauna coming back straight away to collect her phone, I cut and pasted the notes and emailed them to myself. I then deleted the sent item on Shauna's phone. I know, I'm sneaky, crafty, cheeky, bold, creative, nosey, interfering. Don't tell me. But my heart is in the right place. I want to know more so I can try to help. Shauna obviously hasn't confided in me, I don't know why, but the notes on her phone have given me an insight into a world she hides behind her brave face.

The email looked like this:

Notes on Shauna's Phone:

Bad Points:

Evil eyes, Sneering smile
Taste smoke/cigarettes from deep in lungs
Impatient
Poser
Ignores me when he chooses

Sends impersonal texts – if he even bothers to reply
Shows me up in front of others

Feelings:

Right now I feel shit
I feel unloved
I feel lonely
I want to leave and go HOME
I want things to be how they used to be
Things have changed
I am not happy
I am treated like a dog
I have no independence
I have no say
I am undermined
I am contradicted
I am not happy

That was Sunday – now it's Monday

I am ever more alone than ever
I have been corrected and controlled and now I'm being shouted at
This can't last

He agrees with everyone else and always takes their side, never mine. He taunts me and encourages them. So they do the same and gang up against me.
He's a bully.
What's the point of having an opinion?

I'm not with the man I first knew

Being kind is free
Being polite is free
Calmly responding to someone's question is free
Being too rude to acknowledge that your partner has just said something is free but IT'S NOT RIGHT, IT'S NOT KIND, IT'S NOT POLITE

I'm hurt
But I'm also dead inside
How can I cry when I've stopped caring?
Maybe I'm just crying at the injustice of it
Maybe I'm crying because it's cruel
Maybe I'm crying for the girl I used to be
The carefree, happy, independent girl
The girl who made the same mistake twice
The girl who is being controlled again
The girl who is disappearing
The girl who is strong inside
The girl who will break free and heal

Do what you're told!

ARSE!!!!!

Anniversary. What is there to celebrate?
Another year of CAPTURE & CONTROL
It won't last
It can't last
Yes, I can put on a happy face
Yes I can put on a brave face
But underneath the mask is a sad face

*I'm talking .... I'm interrupted ..... I'm contradicted ......
I'm shown up*

Bloody Hell. That's powerful stuff. Shauna is a very deep thinker. She was always the calm one who kept her feelings to herself. I was always the loud high maintenance one. At least I air my grievances and issues and get them off my chest. I know it's a big chest but I've got a lot of things to get off it – Tee Hee! Shauna obviously bottles her emotions up, puts on a plucky face, and makes out everything is rosy. The way the notes appear, it looks like she's been adding to the list over quite a period of time. That's a long time to keep up a brave face!

This isn't the first time she's been stuck in a controlling relationship. They say women often repeat their mistakes and go for the same type of man over and over again. Her last boyfriend was a bit of a tool. At least they didn't get married. They were only together for a year but, in that time, he sucked the life out of her, refused to socialise with her friends and work colleagues, persuaded her to move in and share a house with his mother (eeeek!) and to sell her lovely little car, her only form of independence, so they could share his and save money. When they split, Shauna became a 3D person again. She stood out bold, strong and independent. She was out and about having so much fun. And then she found Lewis. I hate to say it but history is repeating itself.

(55) Email: The Redhead to Isla

You know sometimes, when you think you've had enough of a person and you finally realise you don't need them as much as you thought you did, they come running to you? There were times when I craved the married man. I used to torture myself with thoughts of him and his wife having amazing times together. Sharing relaxed weekends together, going to the theatre in London, seeing a show and staying in fabulous hotels where they'd make fabulous love. Yuk. Barf!

Well, recently I've been very proud of myself. I don't know why but I've had a light bulb moment and realised I deserve more than waiting around for his limited time and attention. Waiting for him to reply to my text messages, changing my plans to fit around his and being disappointed when he cancels at the last minute, always feeling like a dirty little secret. Which, to be fair, I am! I'd decided to tell him it was over.

We were due to meet in one of those corporate business hotels just off the motorway. Not very exclusive or romantic but easy to blend in and be anonymous. Plus, if anyone sees you in a place like that, you can say you are just popping in for a coffee whilst you visit the shopping centre next door or checking out their special gym membership offers. It doesn't mean you're meeting a married man for a hurried furtive few hours in the middle of the day before you both scuttle off to your respective public lives.

I know you don't approve of what I've been doing and I don't expect you to feel sorry for me. I never set out to have an affair with a married man. The initial casual frisson soon wears off and you end up turning into a needy, jittery wreck who is always looking over their shoulder or searching in a crowd in the hope they'll catch the eye of their secret lover. Oooh, now I sound like the Bee Gees!

My plan was to tell him immediately but it was like one of those times when you are about to have your hair cut. You look at yourself in the mirror and suddenly your hair looks amazing. You find yourself questioning whether you actually need to have it cut at all. Just like that, Mr Married Man arrived looking gorgeous, immediately causing my resolve to wobble and my knees to go weak.

Oh well, I may as well have one last hearty meal before starving myself. One more exciting escapade under the sheets to send me off with a bang, as it were. Sorry, that was crude but it helps to explain my feelings at the time. I wanted it to be good so he would remember me and miss me forever.

It was very nice actually but, to be honest, nothing spectacular. Obviously Mr Married Man (or MMM as I have him saved in my phone) didn't know it was going to be our last encounter so he didn't put in as much effort as I did to make it memorable.

Later, the bit I hate, we dressed to leave. Both of us involved in our own preparations to walk out of the hotel room door and blend into the foyer as if nothing had happened. As if we hadn't just rented the room by the hour. I'm sure we were not the only couple in that particular hotel doing the same thing that day. I'm sure the staff in these establishments have seen and heard all sorts of things. Do they ever spot regular clients with their betrayed husbands or wives away from the hotel, in bars and restaurants and find their professional discretion being tested by the knowledge that a particular customer was seen showering a different lady with flowers only the night before.

And talking of gifts, MMM reached into his bag and produced a wrapped gift for me. We had agreed early on not to exchange gifts. Or *he* had told me we wouldn't be giving each other anything to link us or cause suspicion. This announcement had been firmly made to me after I had spent a great deal of time recording a cheesy mix tape for him. Yes, I know it wasn't a mix tape as such, it was a digital version, but everyone loves the romance and nostalgia of the idea of the old cassette tapes our parents or grandparents would have used.

What's wrong with me? I keep waffling on as if I'm writing a novel here. Anyway, back to the gift. It was beautifully wrapped in expensive paper and ribbon. I felt like a film star as I looked at him questioningly. What a treat. A present for me? You shouldn't have!

As I carefully unwrapped the gift, MMM explained he had picked it up from a gallery which specialises in sculptures from across the world. This particular piece was apparently by a contemporary Spanish artist whose style was to create the same figure in various sizes and mediums. She often used the naked form of her husband as her muse. This particular piece was a study, approximately thirty centimetres tall, with a wire frame coated in layers of papier-mâché made up of strips of the local Spanish newspaper. Some of the words and pictures could clearly be seen although I don't know what they mean.

It was amazing. I loved it. And the husband must be a real hottie, judging by the reproduction of him that I held in my hands.

"I thought you could think of me when you look at it" said MMM. What a big head!! For a second I thought Rav was in the room with me. That's just the sort of thing he would say. In fact, Rav would make a remark about just how many newspapers it would take to reproduce his penis in papier-mâché.

Honestly, babe, you would have been so proud of me. I took the time to compose myself, holding the sculpture and loving it. Then I told him I couldn't keep it. I told him I didn't want anything from him and that he should take it home and give it to his wife. He looked surprised. I opened my mouth and took a deep breath, preparing to drop the "it's over" bomb when his phone rang.
Normally he silences his phone or presses the "go away" button when it rings but not now. He'd had a good time. He'd got what he wanted so now he was free to up and leave me again. As I started to form the words, he raised his finger to shush me then turned away to take the call.

"Hello darling"…… OMG! It was his wife. He was actually talking to his wife with me in the same room "Yes……. Oh yes…… What time does it start? …….Yes, I don't see why not……"

I was gone. I took the opportunity to leave the room. I

couldn't get out of there quick enough. I was aware that he would probably try to follow me, whilst presumably still making plans with his wife on the phone. I couldn't risk him catching me up and seeing just how upset I was.

As soon as I was in the hotel foyer I scanned around for somewhere to hide to avoid him seeing me dash for the car park. Would the comedy effect be too great for me to hide behind one of the large palm plants? Could I sit next to a lone gentleman and pull him towards me in an embrace to adopt the persona of a loved-up couple? No, I'd already got myself into enough trouble with messing around with a married man, I couldn't risk attracting another one.

I heard the ping of one of the many lifts descending and opening its doors behind me. Perfect! I dived into the lift and selected the fifth floor – the highest this particular building would allow. I would have liked to go higher but that would have meant orbiting the earth like Roald Dahl's Charlie in the Great Glass Elevator but my life isn't quite that fantastical….

(56) Shauna

Lewis sat behind the leather steering wheel, skilfully negotiating the twists and turns of the country lanes. Yes, he was master of this moving marvel of German engineering and revelled in his role of virtuoso of the vehicles roar and horsepower. The Oxfordshire countryside flashed passed, light, shade, light, shade as they passed each tree, field, overhanging branch, cottage, shrub, barn, shade, light, shade, light. Shauna felt the warmth of the sun through the windscreen as she closed her eyes to reflect on the calm and tranquil atmosphere that existed between her and her husband on this glorious day.

Life is rather like this journey, Shauna thought to herself. Light and shade. No one person is living a perfect life. We each have jubilant days, sad days, nostalgic, traumatic, happy, joyous days. One hopes that we feel more of the suns warmth, more of the light days but nature dictates that there will always be the darker days. Shauna was an optimist and an expert in the art of putting on a brave face. Her exterior persona often belied the pain and struggles that were going on inside but she tried her hardest to protect those around her from those feelings.

As they'd been driving, Shauna had found herself singing along to the tracks being played by the radio DJ. Fair enough, she didn't know all the lyrics but that didn't stop her having a good stab at it. And those lyrics she didn't know, she'd just invent her own. Her father had done the same when they were younger. A chorus of "Oh Dad, that's not the words" would go up from the back seat but George didn't care. He loved music and he loved singing. The fact that the words were more than a little inaccurate didn't matter to him. Later in life Shauna had often found herself disappointed to discover the true meanings of the songs her father had adapted in his own unique style.

A small petrol station appeared on the horizon. Lewis announced that he needed to stop for petrol. Shauna also knew he was running low on cigarettes and would need a large supply to get through the ordeal of socialising with her family. Shauna was tempted to suggest he bought a pint of vodka to ease the pain of mingling with her relatives but she knew that sort of accurate humour would not go down well and would, more than likely, be used against her later.

Instead, Shauna sat patiently in the car whilst Lewis filled the tank with the small amount of petrol it actually needed before making his way to the kiosk to pay.

Lewis had left his keys in the ignition and his phone still attached to the fancy satnav music system. The car was silent. Shauna fancied something cheesy and uplifting to listen to. Normally Lewis chose the tracks they would play but, whilst he was occupied, Shauna hoped he wouldn't notice if she slipped on something to remind her of her happy childhood days. Days travelling in the back seat of her fathers car, squashed between her younger brother and sister, singing along to their fathers country and western greatest hits tapes.

Shauna reached across from the passenger seat to

turn on the ignition. Her boobs pressed into the gear stick. It didn't hurt. It was just a bit uncomfortable. The angle was awkward, but Shauna managed to turn the key the one click required to light up the dashboard. Now to find the cheesiest track. The satnav started working through it's start-up welcome routine. Shauna was expecting to be presented with some kind of in-flight safety demonstration but fortunately the car was engineered for speed and efficiency and it swiftly moved onto the next screen featuring the menu.

Being a touch screen device, accuracy was required in order to select the function desired. Shauna was not known for her dexterity and, instead of hitting the musical note icon full-on, she missed slightly and pressed the telephone icon in error. No worries. Shauna was familiar with her own clumsiness and resolved to reverse away from this option and try again.

Unbelievably Shauna's finger missed its target again. What was wrong with her? Was this screen inaccurately calibrated? Were her fingers the size of sausages? This screen presented a list of recently used numbers. At the top of the list was an out-going call to someone named "Redhead". The call was made thirty minutes ago. Just before Shauna and Lewis had left the house.

Shauna stared at the screen, her heart beginning to thump, her energy levels rising. She recognised the fight or flight mechanism and the effect it was having on her body. Not necessarily useful in this situation but arming her for battle or escape, whether she needed it or not.

Shauna thought back to the long red hair she had once found in this very car. The owner of the long red hair she had discovered in his aptly named dirty laundry. This must be the owner of that hair, a lover with flowing locks of bright red beauty? The owner of the long red hair she had once found on the shoulder of Lewis's jacket. The one he had tried to blame on someone he had collided with in the rush to board a train. So did that very same person ask for a lift home? Is that why the same hair made it's way to the back seat of the car?

Shauna had the ideal opportunity to answer that question. The number was there in front of her. All she had to do was touch it and it would ring. Presumably. She wasn't sure actually. She wasn't sure how the phone worked but she had a feeling it would be that simple.

Only one way to find out. Before she had time to think and before Lewis had time to return to the car to stop her, Shauna pressed the "Redhead" entry.

As she listened to the ring tone being projected by the car speakers, Shauna became aware that her mouth was dry, despite the sudden perspiration forming all over her body. Would she be able to speak if the call was answered? Would her voice come out as a squeak? Did she really want to do this? Should she hang up?

"Hello" A woman's voice

Shauna froze, suddenly cold all over

"Gina?" Shauna frowned "Gina Baxter?"

"Oh God, Shauna, I'm so sorry" Gina sounded anxious and almost breathless. "Honestly I wanted to tell you. I even tried once but Ruby arrived at your house"

What? Shauna didn't understand. What has Ruby got to do with this?

"But Terrence wouldn't let me"

"Ah, I *knew* his real name was Terrence"! Shauna almost fist pumped the air but then checked herself. What was she doing? She should be verbally scratching the eyes out of the gorgeous redhead.

"What's Terrence or Trey, or whatever his name is, got to do with it?"

"He tried to stop me"

"What? He tried to stop you sleeping with my husband or he tried to stop you telling me about it"?

"No, no" Gina sounded hesitant "It's not *me* who's been sleeping with your husband, it's……"

But Shauna didn't hear Gina's final words. Something had distracted her. She looked up to see that Lewis had returned to the car. He was standing, frozen by the open door. She met is gaze. The look in his eyes was the only confirmation she needed.

Time stood still. Everything seemed to slide into slow motion as Shauna struggled to compute what she had just heard. Yes, she had her suspicions but to have them finally confirmed was something she wasn't ready for. Not like this. Not now. It was inconvenient.

In the background, still on speaker-phone but now muffled by the blood throbbing in her ears, the sound of raised voices.

"Gina, What are you doing on my bloody phone? Who are you talking to?" Some kind of sibling tussle was taking place and eventually the line went dead, leaving Shauna and Lewis alone.

For some reason, when disaster occurs, human nature often directs us to focus on something routine or banal. Shauna found herself turning to the dashboard of the car in an attempt to continue her search for some light-hearted music.

"How do I get the music playlist up on this thing"?

Shauna was aware that her voice was trembling slightly and had become much higher than normal but she couldn't give in to emotion. She couldn't break down now. Something in her told her that, to preserve her immediate sanity, she had to get to their destination emotionally intact. Shauna and Lewis had taken a key role in organising a surprise birthday party for one of Lewis's old school friends. She and Lewis must keep up their obligation to attend, regardless of what had just happened. Shauna would never let her friends or family down. Lewis was not her real family and he had let her down but she would deal with that later.

Time to put on the Happy Face mask. Why was it so

easy? So many times over the years, Shauna had put this familiar fake face on. It was an old friend and she could hide behind it. Nobody would know the turmoil inside her.

(57) Email Beth to Shauna

Shauna, I miss you. I must make more of an effort to come over again but, of course, I'd love you to come here too. I've sent you a few photos of the villa here. Can you spot Val's knickers drying on the naya table? Despite their size, I didn't spot them until I'd taken the pic. I've also sent one of my new haircut. Hmmmmmmm - no comment.

Yesterday, Steve returned to a barber he'd previously used in the town. There was a young girl in there last time who said she cuts ladies hair too. Great, I thought I'll have mine done at the same time. When we walked in this time, the young girl I'd seen before wasn't there but a funky looking lady with blue and green hair agreed to do mine whilst Steve had his trimmed. In my limited Spanish I told her I'd like it quite short so she showed me some images on Google and we both agreed on a Charleze Theron style. She's a good-looking woman and, with her choppy haircut, she looked fabulous and I wanted to look fabulous too.

"Look Steve" I said "I'm going to look like Charleze Theron in a minute" I pointed to the page on the computer as Steve sat in the other chair having his hair expertly styled.

Steve nodded and looked pleased with my choice. I smiled and did a thumbs up to the stylist before taking my place in the chair and waiting to look like a stunning Hollywood star.

Well, it was a bit like that scene in Friends where Phoebe mistakes Demi Moore for Dudley Moore when she cuts Monica's hair. The thing is, that scene was for a successful hit TV show. Mine was for real. It was too late to stop her shaving off huge swathes of hair with a razor and, as they fell onto the floor, I realised that, more than ever, I looked like my Dad!!!!

At the end of it, I kept saying "muy bien" and "gracias" - why!!!????? And, even worse, all the premature grey at the side was now fully on show. As soon as we got out and I'd paid her to make me look like a transvestite version of my father, we went to a nearby supermarket where I struggled to read the Spanish on the hair colour products. I had to cover the grey and give some definition to the side of my almost bald head. Steve has a very short attention span and was rushing me. To take the pressure off me and give him something to do, I told him to choose a hair colour for me. He went for a honey blonde. So why, after putting it on, is my hair dark red?!?!

Until my hair grows longer than the bristles on my toothbrush, I will need to make sure every time we go out I put earrings in and wear plenty of mascara and blusher. I wore a dress today so people wouldn't think Steve was dating David Hasselhoff. Tomorrow at work, in the androgynous uniform, I will get called mate or señor more than once!

(58) Conversation between Shauna & Ruby

Shauna: I need you to step up to the plate like I have for you.

Ruby: What?

Shauna: All the times I hid your cigarettes from Mum and Dad. And the times I had to light one up and have a drag just to prove they were mine.
And not telling them about your tattoo. And not telling Mum and Dad about the time you tried to pierce your own belly button

Ruby: Ewww, that still makes me squeamish

Shauna: Me too. Not to mention the time you smuggled Trey Baxter into the house. I still think his real name is Terrence, by the way. Anyway, I kept him in my room all night because Mum and Dad locked up the house and the squeaky floorboards made it impossible for me to organise a midnight escape plan.

Ruby: Yes, but you didn't have to kiss him goodbye in the morning.

Shauna: I had to make it look convincing for Mum and Dad, didn't I? Whilst also lighting up yet another one of your stinky cigarettes.

	By the way, what happened to Trey Baxter?
Ruby:	He's still around, and his sisters, Gina, Jade and Jasmine. Bet their parents get them mixed up. Luckily Gina has gorgeous auburn hair to help her stand out from her more mousey sisters. And I've heard Trey is gay. That rhymes!
Shauna:	He was so gorgeous. Maybe Alex could get together with him. Then all of us will have kissed him!
Ruby:	I'm telling you, Alex is not gay! Anyway, what's this favour? What's the plate I need to step up to?
Shauna:	It's a plate that may smash your reputation for a while.
Ruby:	Oh God! Not another......
Shauna:	No, stop. Not that sort of reputation. I mean your professional integrity.
Ruby:	Shauna. I love you. You've never said I have integrity before. Thanks sis.
Shauna:	You may not thank me for long. Your integrity may be shattered like the plate I'm asking you to step up to.
Ruby:	Oh God Shauna. You've tied me up in word riddles again. Just get on with it and tell me what you want me to do..........

(59) Ruby

I had an interesting conversation with Shauna earlier. She was round visiting Mum and Dad and suggested we go into the kitchen to make a cup of tea. Well, I was a bit slow on the uptake. Why did it take two of us to put the kettle on? Shauna repeated her suggestion and started nodding her head towards the door. Then she started rolling her eyes and gritting her teeth. The cat, which was nestled in Alex's lap as usual, became a bit un-nerved and dug his claws into his thighs. Oww! That must have hurt. We have to watch him because he has a habit of piddling in our shoes by the front door when he's agitated. The cat, not Alex!!

Shauna must have cricked her neck with her over-the-top gestures but I finally got the message and followed her into the kitchen, mumbling about her amateur dramatics and why didn't she just *tell* me what she wanted. Mum and Dad must have realised something was up but they probably think we're planning some kind of surprise party for their wedding anniversary. Which we'll probably have to do now, after all the mystery!

Shauna carried on being furtive and secretive but finally got to the point. I think she may be losing the plot but I'm happy to help. Not to help her lose the plot but to carry out the plot!!

When Shauna left, I raced upstairs to my bedroom to get ready for a night out with the girls. Lots to do. The salon chicks all make a really big effort so I had some serious personal foliage to attend to – hair removal, hair plumping, spot squeezing (don't judge me!) eyelash extending, curling, coating, toenail painting...... So much to do.

As I rushed about, pulling things out of my wardrobe in frustration at the fact that I have absolutely nothing to wear, I noticed Shauna was still sitting in her car outside the house. She seemed to be rummaging through her handbag. I thought she'd lost her keys but then, being slow off the mark again, I realised she wouldn't be sitting inside the car if she hadn't used her keys to unlock it. What's wrong with me today? Does it have anything to do with the hangover I'm still suffering with from last night? Why am I going out again tonight? Don't answer that!!

Shauna's car is a heap of junk. Lewis is a bum-hole for letting her drive it when he has such a flash car himself. He only lets her drive his car when he's drunk or he wants to impress someone. To be fair, in his case, both of those things are quite frequent occurrences but it's not the point. Poor Shauna has to put up with breaking down at all times of the day and night or not even being able to start the car in the first place.

Being selfish, I needed to keep moving to get ready. I assumed Shauna would eventually start the car and move off so I carried on with my beautification routine.

I kept glancing out of the window and realised that Shauna was de-cluttering her handbag. There's nothing better than a good clear out of all those receipts, vouchers, broken leaky pens and used tissues (yuk!) that accumulate in your bag. When you turn the bag upside down, there's always a shower of crumbs (not just me, I hope!) and, if you're lucky, a few coins you didn't know were lurking in there.

Oh well, I had enough to do to make some kind of work of art out of my slightly tarnished canvas of a body so I left Shauna to her handbag de-fluff and continued with my own personal de-fluffing.

As I left the house, looking amazing, several hours later, I flicked up the lid of the wheelie bin to deposit the wrapper of my chewing gum, designed to make my teeth glow in the dark and invite gorgeous young men to kiss my minty fresh mouth! As the lid was coming down again, my eye caught a few interesting words, written on a piece of paper in Shauna's handwriting.

Hmmmm, what to do? I walked away. It's her rubbish. It's her private rubbish. But her life is a bit rubbish at the moment too and I may be able to help further. Just not now. I don't have time. I'll do it later. After my fantastic night out. If I have time, that is, after responding to all the messages I'm gonna get from admirers. Tee Hee – that's me. Smiley face!

But what if Mum and Dad open the bin? What if they see those words? OK, I'll take it out to save them the shock. Shauna has saved me often enough. I need to return the favour. I also need to lower my standards by lifting up the lid of a wheelie bin and standing on tiptoes to reach inside for that piece of paper.

As I leaned into the bin, the hard edge rubbed against my ribs. It really hurt. My eyes bulged as I leaned down to stretch towards the paper. My fingers couldn't quite reach but if I leaned over any further I would fall into the bin, head first, with my legs up in the air, revealing the accuracy of my earlier get-ready personal grooming preparations, if you get what I mean!!!

"Can I help?" I heard the voice of my neighbour. You know the cool Dad next door whose children I babysit for. Well, I couldn't see him because my head was deep inside the bin, I could just hear his voice. The bin was almost empty. The paper was right down at the bottom. My bottom was in the air. I'm not very good at physics but I suppose inevitably, something heavy on top of something relatively light is going to win. As I tried to lift my head out of the bin to reply to cool-Dad-next-door, the laws of physics took over and the bin tipped towards me, my tummy pressed into the hard plastic edge of the bin, and my kicking legs, rather than returning to the ground to secure my dignity, propelled me inside the bin which continued to lean and finally fall to the ground with me in it.

Oh bugger!!!! All that hard work. All that washing, polishing, plucking and preening and now I was laying inside a dusty wheelie bin on my parents lawn, head buried under damp tea bags and rotting banana skins and with my knickers on display for the cool-Dad-next-door to see.

"No, I'm fine thanks" I replied. My voice was echoing inside the plastic bin. I was tempted to just lay there, inside the bin, as if it was my intention but I knew Mr Cool wouldn't believe that. Swallowing what was left of my pride and a small amount of what I hoped was discarded mayonnaise, I reversed out of the bin, bum first, on hands and knees to see the highly amused face of cool-Dad-next-door smiling down at me.

Wow, he really is cool and really rather gorgeous too. And very married. And very clean. Whereas I was now very dirty. And not dirty in the way the boys at school would sneer and snigger. No, I was literally dirty. I became aware that something was stuck to my cheek but I didn't dare touch it. I didn't want to think about what it could be.

Cool Dad lowered his hand to help me up. I was just about to take it when I remembered the reason I was in this predicament. I was already in such a state, nothing else could be worse. I asked Cool Dad to hold on a minute as I returned to my black plastic hell on wheels. By now, Shauna's note had been stirred into the mixed mess. I could have left if there. Nobody would find it. Nobody would read it. But my interest was peeked and my make-up was ruined so I shamefully rummaged about in the rubbish until the note was located and retrieved.

Cool Dad was still there when I reversed out for the second time. Unfortunately so was Alex. He stood there with his arms folded, shaking his head like a wise old man. Who did he think he was to judge me? I demand respect. I am the fearsome child in this family. I am the foot-stamper, the one who always gets their own way. The one who makes other people look stupid. I am not supposed to *be* the stupid one!

The sight of Alex in that pose awoke something in me. Something from childhood. I threw down Shauna's note, rose to my feet and charged towards him. With both hands outstretched I rushed into his chest to barge him over as I had done so many times before. Unfortunately for me, Alex was now bigger and stronger than me. As a child, he'd been easy to push over. As a young man, he stood solid whilst he casually observed my embarrassing attempt to recreate one of our many childhood scenes.

I was fuming. Absolutely furious. I could feel red mist rising. I know what I'm like. I still have the same 'volume and attitude' temper Alex has identified. The only thing that has changed is my ability to recognise when I'm becoming hysterical. I walked away. Yes, you'd have been proud of me.

I can't say I left with dignity, bearing in mind what had just happened, but I did save myself from deteriorating scenes of my bad behaviour.

Heading to the bathroom for some much needed decontamination I glanced at myself in the mirror. My hair was decorated with strips of that red rubber coating from individual cheeses, my carefully applied false eyelashes were dusted with…. dust, actually, and the suspected mayonnaise on my cheek? I still don't know. I'm really really hoping it was mayonnaise. I've never wished to have an egg based product smeared on my right cheek before but, in preference to what it could be, bring on the Hellmans any time!

(60) George

It was one of those days where you think the main event has happened. You assume the most interesting, challenging, difficult part of the day has happened and that you will talk about it as the main focus of *that* particular day if you're ever called upon to comment.

Shauna popped round for a visit today. As usual, it was great to see her. There was an unusual exchange between her and Ruby at one point. Shauna was obviously trying to get Ruby into the kitchen so they could have a private conversation. Ruby was a bit slow on the up-take. I even felt like saying "Ruby, Shauna would like to have a private conversation with you in the kitchen" but eventually Ruby clicked and they disappeared for a hushed conversation. I'm not saying anything to Dee but I'm wondering if they are planning some kind of surprise for our wedding anniversary. Dee's not stupid either, and I'm sure she was pretending not to know what was going on but I'm guessing she has the same idea as me. How lovely of them.

Several hours after Shauna left, Ruby set off for a night out. Yes, it was several hours because that's how long it takes Ruby to get ready. She is a beautiful young woman who could easily get away with going out without a scrap of make-up on. Try suggesting that to her? Oh, I have in the past and been rewarded by a tirade of abuse and insults. Try saying something nice to someone and look what happens!

Ruby popped her head round the door to announce her departure. We dispensed the usual wise words about not drinking too much. Staying together with friends. Don't let any girl go home alone and, my favourite "no kissing". It was a family tradition. I would always send them off with a "no kissing" tease or, the following morning, I would enquire "was there any kissing?". Shauna always took it with good nature. Ruby would accuse me of being old-fashioned or derelict or something like that. Alex would always be very private about his response. We never really know what's going on with his matters of the heart, if there are any at the moment.

Anyway, not long after Ruby left, Alex went out through the front door without saying goodbye. Dee and I looked at each other, thought it was a bit rude, but Alex is prone to moments of sulky silence so we let it go.

A few minutes later we heard a scuffle taking place outside and the familiar high-pitched sound of Ruby losing her temper. Dee and I, for the second time in as many minutes, glanced at each other and then made our way to the window where we could see Ruby, covered in what appeared to be rotting food, seemingly trying to push Alex over. The wheelie bin was laying on its side and, to our horror, the next door neighbour was surveying the entire scene in amused amazement.

Alex was surprisingly impervious to Ruby's attempts to push him to the ground as she had been able to do so many times throughout their childhood. Ruby became more and more frustrated until she eventually gave up and stormed into the house and straight upstairs with such force that I feared for the tread and integrity of the stairs. One day she'll put her foot straight through.

Alex strolled back inside the house, victorious and as cool as a cucumber. Cool until he looked down and surveyed his brand new, apparently very expensive, trainers at the front door. One of them was filled with a familiar yellow liquid. Oh dear. The cat had demonstrated its distress again.

"Ruby….. Ruby…….ROOOOOOOBY" Alex bellowed up the stairs. "You owe me a new pair of trainers. Your volume and attitude has made the cat piss in my hundred quid trainers"

Silence

"Ruby…..Ruby….."

The bathroom door opened and something came flying out. We all ducked. The item, which turned out to be one of Ruby's shoes, bounced on one of the top stairs before ricocheting off the carpet and into a wooden heart, carved by Alex as part of his school woodwork project. Proud mother Dee had hung the heart on the wall so that every time she walked up or down the stairs, she could survey the creative talents of her youngest child. Why hadn't the shoe hit the peculiar artwork on display higher up the wall? The one Ruby had made as a reluctant student of textiles. The decoupage creation which featured a large papier-mâché head, covered with swathes of fabric and wool would give anyone of a nervous disposition severe, bedwetting nightmares. I secretly longed for the day it would spontaneously and mysteriously combust without damaging the other artwork or wallpaper surrounding it. They say be careful what you wish for. Ruby must have been 'going through a phase' when she created it. Having said that, Ruby has been 'going through a phase' for most of her life.

We watched the heart bounce its way down the remaining stairs before catching the edge of the penultimate step, causing it to gain renewed height and dive headfirst into the telephone table at the bottom. Why we still have this telephone table I don't know. It was a wedding present to us from my mother who thought such things were the height of elegance and sophistication. Now, talking about being careful what you wish for. Another secret dream of mine was directed towards a heavy object landing in the middle of the glass-topped telephone table, rendering its depiction of a bullfighter in tight trousers taunting a large black bull with a red rag basically buggered.

Well, that particular wish *had* come true. The glass table shattered. The bullfighters tight little bottom was now confetti, sprinkled in tiny pieces amongst the shattered bull. Rough justice, I'm sure which has ended the permanent fear and anticipation for the bull but now we had to deal with the carnage of millions of pieces of glass embedded in the patterned carpet. The kids keep telling us we need to become more modern and 'contemporary'. They keep telling us to ditch the ancient patterned carpet and go with solid floors. We've fought against them, happy to have the high quality, hard wearing paisley carpet which hides a multitude of stains but, on this occasion, I really wish I could get out a dustpan and brush and sweep it all away in one safe affiair. As it is, I fear we will be finding tiny pieces of the bullfighters sombrero for months to come.

Surely that was enough drama for one day? Ruby calmed down and even mumbled an apology. She offered to pay for the table to be repaired.

"NO" her mother and I both almost shouted. What we meant, in a more gentle way was, no thank you Ruby. The table has served us well over the years but now it's time to move on and modernise. We may even consider solid flooring. Perhaps you kids can help us decide?

Ruby and Alex went into tidy-up mode, insisting Dee and I sit down and relax and to leave it to them. Something about the joint effort must have brought them together again because we could hear the sound of them chatting and eventually laughing together. Something we don't always hear from those two so it was a rare and happy treat.

(61) Email: The Redhead to Isla

You'll never guess what. I've had another text from Rav. It was so long it was almost a book so I'll summarise:

He said he wanted me to know something about him, something to help me get to know him better. I could tell him something about *me*....... I'M NOT INTERESTED!

Anyway, Rav reckons that, when he was travelling during his gap year, he visited a remote tribe in New Guinea. Apparently the menfolk deemed him to be a perfect human specimen and begged him to impregnate their women in order to pass down his amazing genes. Can you actually believe that? Does he expect me to actually believe it?

He declined, for obvious reasons. Probably because it isn't true and he's just made it up in his own self-loving world!!!!

Oh, and talk about strange and random events. My sister, Gina, went to the hairdressers the other day. She went to the salon she's been using for years. Apparently, on arrival, she was told that her stylist Fabio was unable to do her hair but that Ruby was free.

Gina and Ruby put their collective heads together, looked at some magazines and chose a really soft, feminine style for Gina's gorgeous, long, auburn hair. Gina was chatting and engaging with other clients, as she does. She was looking down at her phone at one point and looked up too late. Too late to stop Ruby grabbing Gina's ponytail in one hand and cutting the entire thing off with her scissors in the other.

(62) Ruby

I can't believe I got away with it. Shauna's brief was confusing and quite out of character for her. She's never normally spiteful but I loved seeing the spark in her. Unbelievably Gina said she loved her new hair cut. It seems I'd given her the push she needed. So the mistaken identity has ended up giving Gina a new identity!!

Anyway, Fabio now thinks I'm amazing and brave and a stylist who isn't afraid to express their individual creative talent. Wonder what I can get away with now!! Maybe the lovely Mrs Galbraith would suit a Mohican?

And just to make my days brighter, Fabio's cousin, Juan, is over visiting from Spain. Hubba Hubba! He's absolutely gorgeous.

Can you imagine, my cute Italian boss laughing and chatting with his gorgeous Spanish cousin in Latin tongues. I can't understand a word they're saying but it sounds beautiful. They could be discussing the local sewerage system or a festering boil on one of their bums but it still sounds poetic. Wouldn't mind being on the end of one of those tongues, if you get my meaning. Tee Hee!!

Never mind Brexit, whether you were an innie or an outie, I'm into this European Union!

I must remember to ask Juan if he knows Beth. Mind

you, Spain is a huge country so it's very unlikely. He goes home tomorrow so I may need to make noises about visiting Beth and then finding a way to track Juan down. I'm sure Beth won't mind me making the most of her hospitality. Plus she's got great taste in clothes so I could wow Juan in some of her great little fashion finds.

(63) Shauna

The venue was Greenways Golf Club, a municipal club which proved to be very popular in the local area due to it's large conference and wedding reception facilities. The venue was also used for antiques fairs, salsa dancing lessons and, on this occasion, engagement parties.

Shauna's cousin, Martin, had proposed to Jackie who, luckily for him, had said yes. This was their engagement party. No date had been set for the wedding and the pair had declared they were in no rush to get married but they wanted to have a big bash to share their happiness.

Shauna and Lewis arrived well after all the other direct members of the family but, fortunately, space had been left for them at the table. George stood up and gave his daughter a strong and comforting hug. Shauna wanted to cry. She loved her Dad so much and missed his constant care. She had given herself over to a complete and utter arse in place of this respectable, decent man.

After saying hello to Shauna, George, ever the gentleman, shook hands with Lewis as Shauna bent down to hug her mother. Dee appeared to have already taken on board a couple of drinks and was looking slightly flushed.

"Darling" she breathed heavily into Shauna's ear "Why don't you let Lewis drive tonight and have a little drink with your Nana and me"

Shauna straightened up. Amused by the giggly appearance of her mother and saddened by the fact she couldn't confide in her mother that she (Shauna, not Dee!) had married a selfish, cheating sexist pig. How could she tell her mother that this was the greatest challenge of her ability to put on a brave face ever? Her husband had been cheating on her. It was too much to take in. How could she find the words to tell her parents when she hadn't been able to make sense of it herself.

"Darling" Nana Buckle lifted her face for a welcoming kiss. She looked radiant and so happy to be surrounded by her young family.

"Why don't you join me in a Tequilla Sunrise" Nana held up her glass. It looked so inviting. Nana loved the occasional treat of this tipple and would always repeat the same information to accompany it. Nana raised the glass higher in a cheers gesture and took a sip.

"Tequilla Sunrise is made of unmixed tequila, orange juice and granadine syrup" Nana took another sip and looked around to ensure the immediate group was listening "It's called Tequilla Sunrise because the gradations of colour make it look like a…… sunrise darlings" Nana held up her glass again. Unfortunately, it was almost empty and the remaining liquid looked like a Tequilla tornado!

"Nana, thanks very much for our engagement present" It was Martin "We can start adding to that dinner service as we go along" Jackie stood beside her fiancé, smiling.

Pleasantries were exchanged before Jackie hooked her arm in Martin's and ushered him away to say hello to other guests.

"She'll certainly make use of the large dinner plates" was Nana's first remark. Ruby and Alex glanced at each other in shared enjoyment of their grandmother's witty but often harsh observations. "And she'll need to lose a few pounds before the big day or her father will break the bank paying for all the fabric needed to make the dress".

"OK mother, that's enough now" cautioned Dee. Her brother was not far away and was in danger of overhearing his mother's remarks relating to his future daughter-in-law. Not that he hadn't heard similar things before, directed at other members of the family and found it amusing at the time.

Shauna was heartened to see Ruby and Alex clearly enjoying each other's company. Only the week before she had walked into the family home to find Ruby screaming from the bathroom upstairs "Mum, can you tell Alex to stop wiping his smelly bum juice on the towels please". Hmmm, what a lovely welcome Shauna had thought at the time. At least Ruby had said please. Tonight the siblings seemed to be locked into some kind of shared secret. Shauna felt a bit like the odd-one-out.

Lewis had installed himself at the bar. What a surprise. He hadn't offered Shauna or any member of her family a drink. Lewis had a tendency to latch onto a fellow hardened drinker and to spend a family social event locked into bawdy conversation with that one person. At the end of the night, he would drunkenly repeat over and over what a great laugh that person had been. Tonight, Lewis appeared to be paired up with the brother-in-law of one of Dee's cousins. An ex-London cabbie who had entertained the family many a time with his stories of famous and infamous passengers of the past.

Shauna was so happy to be surrounded by her family. She considered them to be 'normal' but most people believe their family are the normal ones and that everyone else's is slightly odd. She buzzed around, catching up with relations she hadn't seen for ages, chatting with aunts and uncles, gossiping with cousins and dancing with little toddlers.

Shauna used the opportunity to process her thoughts, to focus on other people, ask about their lives and give herself time to think about what to do next. As usual, Shauna was somehow managing to park her real emotions until the end of the evening. She would take them out and re-visit them then but, in the meantime, there was a family party to be enjoyed. Her duty was to be the ever steady, reliable and happy Shauna.

She returned to the table, making an excuse to rest her feet, but feeling the need to be close to the people she was closest to. Shortly after Lewis returned too. With a pint in his hand, of course, but nothing for anyone else. Shauna wondered why he'd left his place at the bar? Lewis sulkily explained the ex-London cabbie had been summoned to sit and spend some time with his wife.

Alex stood to leave the table. Jokes were made about him going to the bar and requests for unacceptable amounts of alcohol were made. Alex shook his head and laughed as he made his way to a door at the back of the room.

"Nana, what's happened to your gentleman friend?" Shauna enquired of her flushed face grandmother.

"Darling, I realised he was just looking for someone to look after him" Nana attempted a sip from her glass but realised it was empty. "Let's put it this way, I won't be experiencing any Tequilla Sunrises with him. I hear he's got his knees under Mrs Galbraith's table now. Lovely lady but not a very good pastry chef. Cold hands make good pastry. Her hands are obviously too warm but maybe that's what he sees in her"

The supressed laughter around the group was interrupted by the crackle of a microphone and some unfortunate heavy breathing. A high-pitched screech followed and everyone winced.

The DJ turned down the volume and announced that the next performance would be from The Rotting Romantics, a local band made up of Alex, another family cousin and two former school mates.

The door at the back of the room opened. Alex and his three band-mates took their places on the small black stage in the corner by the dance floor.

No hellos. No thank you for coming. Just a mumbled

"This song is dedicated to my brother-in-law" from Alex

Shauna's heart stopped beating. She looked at Lewis

who seemed to be displaying a cocky grin. What was going on? Too late, the boys were playing the opening bars.

Then from Alex "This song is entitled Little Dick"

Laughter around the room. But not from Lewis.

Alex leaned towards the microphone once more and, in a surprisingly clear, tuneful voice sang:

Little Dick, you are a prick
You always come far too quick
Little Dick, you come too quick
You sweat so much it makes me sick
Little Dick, you go soft so quick
I get no fun, you're no big hit
Little Dick, you think you're it
But you are just a deluded twit

Oh, one day I'll get over You
One day I won't be so blue
But one thing that I know is true
You can never escape from You
You have to live with the things you do
The bull you sprout to make people like you
Your cocky ways can be seen right through
I know it's not me who's lacking – it's you

You need to hear how wonderful you are
You need to hear that you're a star
I used to worship you from afar
Not knowing what a lying jerk you are
You tell me what you think I need to hear
Not the truth – now there's a good idea!
I should never have got mixed up with you

But now I know what I'm gonna do

I'll keep my distance and avoid your gaze
Go back to my happy, carefree ways
I don't know what will happen in the end
But I'm gonna find a loyal and true friend
Never be taken in by flattery
By someone who loves himself more than me
Who throws his net of compliments to catch
A heart which will double that praise, not match

Why should I waste more of my life
With one whose indifference cuts like a knife
Little dick, you no longer interest me
Why stick with someone who's not what I need
You built me up and then brought me down
But I'm gonna turn my life around
Yes that is what I'm gonna do
But Little Dick, YOU are stuck with YOU!

Shauna felt totally exposed. Nobody else could know these were her words. Or could they? She had written this angry poem during a bad time with Lewis, although that could be any time recently. She had been afraid he would find it so she had…… oh, wait a minute…… she had thrown it in the bin at her parents house.

Shauna looked round to her little sister. Ruby looked at her with sad eyes. Shauna turned to see what Lewis's reaction had been. He'd gone. She hadn't even noticed. Ruby stood up and moved to take Lewis's place at Shauna's side. She explained that, after discovering the poem in the bin, there had been a humiliating incident with a pint of mayonnaise and the next-door neighbour (what was she talking about?) and it was, in fact, Alex who had retrieved the words from the front garden and put them to music.

The Rotting Romantics had received a raucous response to their performance. The majority of the audience would have thought it was all tongue-in-cheek. Nobody would have guessed it was genuinely written about Lewis…. by his wife! Shauna caught Nana Buckle's eye. Without being given the facts, Nana somehow seemed to know.

The Rotting Romantics ploughed on with their next brutal number, "He's In Love With The Boy Next Door". Oh My God! Shauna looked at Nana Buckle for help. Could she explain how Alex seemed to have the words for her every thought? Apparently not this time.

Nana seemed very confused by the lyrics of this song. This one explained how the married man was in love with the boy with long red hair. How he was in love with the boy who had been a trusted friend of them all and had once been loved by the little sister. How the married man was in love with the boy who was often taken for being a girl on account of his flowing auburn locks. A boy who was taken for the girlfriend of the boy singing this song. "Oh no, not me. I'm not that boy. I'm in love with the sister of the boy with the long red hair"

Shauna turned to Ruby.

"Alex is in love with Gina?" Her voice was so high with amazement she could hardly hear it herself. She expected packs of dogs to run into the room in response to it's high pitch. "Gina Baxter?" Shauna couldn't bring her voice down any lower "The girl the boys called Ginger Gina?"

"The girl who now has an amazing foxy short hair cut, thanks to me and a bit of mistaken identity from you" Ruby reminded her big sister.

Oh God, yes, Shauna was responsible for that copper coiffure crime via the scissors of her sister or Ruby Scissorhands as she called herself on Faceplant. If that was her only crime it wasn't the end of the world though. And it sounded like Gina now had a fabulous new look. And a new boyfriend too……

Shauna looked at Alex and then turned to Ruby

"But I thought Alex was gay"

Ruby said she hated to tell her so but she had never believed he was. She knew Alex was deep and caring and very private about his love life but she never thought he was gay. His friendship with Trey/Terrence Baxter was just that. A friendship. Shauna was amazed at Ruby's understanding of Alex and his feelings.

"What are Alex and his Rotting Whatevers going to sing next?" Shauna asked the question in jest, but no sooner had she said it than the band struck up the next song

"I have a secret. My secret to me……
I've dumped you and soon you will see
I'm no longer your lover – you don't know it but you will one day

One day soon
The power of holding this secret inside
Is the energy that keeps me going, keeps me alive
I distance myself. Self-preservation
You think everything is OK, well it's not, it's a living Hell
I'm playing the dutiful lover and serving you well
You get your kicks and licks but you don't ring my bell
I'm dead inside. It's all an act
I can do it, I can get through it if I pretend
Fake it, make it just don't drop my guard
The mask is on, don't let it slip
Sad face, happy face, brave face
One day someone else will take your place"

Shauna couldn't understand how the cumulative angry notes from her phone had come into the hands of her little brother but she suspected Ruby's hand was in this one too. Ruby certainly seemed to know a large percentage of the lyrics, judging by the way she was singing along…..

Oh My God, Alex gave them real passion with the melody. His band mates seemed to revel in the gutsy, raw honesty of the words they were singing and gave a powerful performance. Did they know these sentiments were from the heart of Alex's big sister? The sensible, easy-going girl with an almost permanent smile on her face?

Shauna scanned the room. Her friends and relations were transfixed. The group of men at the bar had turned away from the wait to be served to marvel at the brutality of this song. Only one man could be seen lifting a glass to his lips. Lewis! Shauna thought he would have had the good manners to leave but no, the cocky little shit was still knocking back the pints, mistakenly thinking his wife would drive him home at the end of the evening.

> "I am a robot. Your robot. I'm hollow inside
> The girl I was has disappeared
> The robot looks like me, talks like me
> But look into my eyes – they are dead
> Listen to the voice – the voice is dead"

God, I write great lyrics, Shauna thought to herself. I should do this as a career!

Shauna looked towards Nana Buckle who would normally wince in the presence of the 'F' word but she looked enthused and empowered by the use of all this bad language

> "This isn't working
> It's not going to last
> This relationship has turned toxic
> You tell me you'll help me
> You tell me you're there for me but all you do is talk
> Control and talk, control and talk
> Actions speak louder than words, they say
>
> Well, *my* actions speak louder than words so I'm shouting through
> You never listen but I want you to
> You never listen but I want you to
> Oh, what the Hell
> ….. I'M LEAVING YOU!!!"

(64) Email - Redhead to Isla

Isla,

Hello there lovely friend. I hope your OK. I haven't heard from you for a while.

The original Agony Aunt returns from her sabbatical tomorrow. Through office gossip, I've heard she could probably have done to take some of her own advice but nobody's perfect. I know that only too well.

I'm pretty much finished for the day but fate must have dealt me a cruel blow. My final letter…..

"Dear Agony,

I've written to you before. I know you didn't publish my whole letter but you did publish the problem I was having with visitors to our villa in Spain borrowing things and breaking or losing them. I know the worst culprit is a regular reader of your magazine so I knew she would see it.

A very special bracelet of mine has been returned. The Borrower has also had a similar one made for her sister. I won't explain why – it would take too long!

You didn't publish the concerns I had about my best friend's husband. Sadly it turns out I was right about him. He was having an affair with a guy who once went out with my best friends sister. Yes, it sounds like a soap opera but unfortunately it was true.

The hurt and upset this has caused across two families is obvious. My best friend is putting on her usual brave face but I know she is devastated, despite the fact she knew the marriage was turning sour. She is such a lovely, easy-going good-natured girl and I know she would have tried anything to return to the early happy years of their relationship. Unfortunately her ignorant, aggressive (and sexually confused) husband was being his usual spoilt selfish self and only thinking of (and pleasing) himself ...... and probably the guy he was seeing!!

Hopefully something and someone better is not too far away for her. A gorgeous guy is waiting patiently for her. Unfortunately, it seems his sister knows the guy my friend's husband was having an affair with. Apparently she did try to talk her friend out of the affair but the damage is done and you can't blame other people for the libido of others.

My friend is coming out to see me in Spain tomorrow. Can't wait. She can borrow, break or lose anything she wants – tee hee! (Her little sister is coming too but her motives for visiting seem to be focussed on a male colleague of mine – another story!) Hopefully when my friend returns home she can slowly start to build a new life and forget the betrayal. I really hope her sad face and brave face will be replaced with a happy face.

Thanks again for your help and I wish you all the best, whoever you are!!"

The best friend's sister she mentions is Ruby. She had a misplaced school-girl crush on me. I even ended up kissing Shauna, once to save Ruby from her parent's anger. They found me sneaking across their landing in the middle of the night. I'm not explaining very well and I don't think we were very convincing at the time either. Ruby's mum and dad correctly assumed I was sleeping in Ruby's room but, when the shouting and pointing fingers started, Shauna stepped in and took the flack. She claimed I was *her* boyfriend and, as if to prove the point, grabbed both my cheeks (on my face, not my bum!) and gave me a longer than necessary kiss. What a great girl. She didn't deserve to be hurt.

Isla, not sure if you're even reading this. Are you getting my Faceplant private messages and my text messages? I've tried calling several times. Your brother picked up your phone yesterday. He said you couldn't talk at the moment. I'm guessing he's waiting patiently in the wings for her to get back from Spain and recover from the betrayal. Hopefully soon he will look after her and treat her well.

Please don't hate me, Isla. I know you warned me but I never meant to be part of something so destructive. I'm trying to put on a happy brave face but it keeps failing and revealing the sad face behind.

Thank You for reading this book
And well done, dear reader, you got to the finish line
Unless you came here first to see how it ends!!

If you've enjoyed the book and you'd like to leave a review, that would be very lovely of you ☺ and thank you very much,
Catherine xx

ACKNOWLEDGEMENTS

When I was approaching my 18th birthday, my parents asked what I'd like as my milestone gift. I asked them for a typewriter and confidently told them I was going to write a book.

Since that date, millions of people have written books but I wasn't one of them. My electric typewriter was superseded by a streamlined laptop upon which, until recently, I still hadn't written the book.

I have now written it, as you know because hopefully you've just read and enjoyed it. If you're happy to read on a bit more, I'd just like to thank a few people…..

My Dad. The biggest influence on my reading and music taste. Colin, my amazing father, is an avid reader. On family holidays, when he had ploughed thorough his own paperbacks, he would read my Enid Blyton adventure stories rather than face the remainder of the holiday without some pages to turn.

My Dad has always passed on his good reads to me so I have him to thank for instilling in me the love of the written word. I'm just sorry the book I've produced isn't exactly a literary classic but hopefully he will be proud of me none-the-less!

My Mum, Patricia. The most gentle, calm, ladylike, nurturing lady ever. At my age, and a mother myself, I still seek approval from both my parents. At times, when I have worried about telling them something, they have surprised me by being open-minded and fully supportive. I'm obviously concerned that my Mum will find some of the language in this book inappropriate but I'm just as likely to catch her laughing out loud at the bits I've worried about!

Adam, my partner. Adam has the ability to bring out the best in people. To encourage them to do things they don't always want to do, to push them out of their comfort zone and, most of the time, it results in a positive experience! He also seems to be a bit psychic and a mind reader - scary at times! I don't know how he knew about the dream, gathering dust on the shelves of my mind but, very early on in our relationship, he told me I should write a book. When I told him I'd wanted to do just that since I was 18 he said "well, why haven't you?" as if it was the most simple thing in the world.

Adam has proudly supported my book writing and, in his inimitable style, told everyone who will listen that I'm writing a book. I end up making excuses for it and telling people not to be too excited or expect too much. However, Adam's actions and support have been a huge drive behind my frantic typing. He is dyslexic and struggles to read and understand fiction. He has therefore told me he will probably never read the book himself but I owe him a big thank you. Please tell him I said that if you read this bit and bump into him one day!

Penny, my amazing friend. Penny and I worked together for many years. What a joy to do a job you love with a person you love - someone you can confide in, laugh with and cry with. When Adam retired and we moved away for an adventure, I resorted to communicating to my loved ones via email. Penny was a recipient of many a lengthy story from me and would frequently reply to tell me I should write a book. Sometimes her email replies would begin with the words WRITE THE BOOK or WRITE IT NOW. Being able to make someone laugh is an honour. Penny has reduced me to pelvic floor challenging hysterics on many an occasion so I hope to be able to do the same for her with this book. Thank you for the encouragement Penny.

Judy. Oh, the lovely Judy of Horsham. We met in Spain but share a link to the wonderful West Sussex town my amazing brother, Michael, calls home. I could go on mentioning and thanking people for ever so I'd better get on with it...... One evening, whilst being graciously hosted by Judy and her husband Steve, Adam told the entire room that I was writing a book. All eyes on me, oh dear! I did the usual mumbling about how it wasn't quite finished and that I wasn't sure what to do with it, etc. etc. The divine Judy immediately offered to proof-read it for me. I can't think of anyone more grounded, gracious and intuitive than Judy to have been the first person to read my written ramblings. Thank you so much, Judy, for everything. My life is richer for knowing you – I just hope reading my book hasn't scarred you for life!!

And then, the old "anyone else who knows me" bit. So many people in my life and too many to mention individually. I have been blessed with fantastic friends and family, past and present. At the time of writing this, my daughter Kirsty and her partner Darren are expecting my first grandchild, making an Uncle of her brother Mark and Great Grandparents of my previously mentioned perfect parents.

You are all a big part of my life and I love you all – getting mushy!!! Sorry.

Right, that's enough waffle from me. I may write another book one day so ………… good luck everybody!!

Just a reminder, if you have enjoyed this book and you'd like to leave a review, that would be very nice of you. Thank you very much.

Last thing, I promise!! If you've enjoyed my waffle, have a look at my blog page: **www.catsfurball.com** or, if you'd like something to watch rather than read, I have a You Tube channel called catsfurball too.

DISCLAIMER/COPYRIGHT

This is a work of fiction – a creation of the authors rambling and chaotic mind.
All characters and events in this publication, other than those clearly in the public domain, are fictitious and any resemblance to real persons, living or dead, is purely coincidental.
Equally, unless already in the public domain, the places, products and social media sites are fabricated and tongue-in-cheek. Any unfortunate matches with genuine places, products and social media sites are also coincidental.

Printed in Great Britain
by Amazon